THE BURNING

ALSO BY LINDA CASTILLO

Sworn to Silence

Pray for Silence

Breaking Silence

Gone Missing

Her Last Breath

The Dead Will Tell

After the Storm

Among the Wicked

Down a Dark Road

A Gathering of Secrets

Shamed

Outsider

A Simple Murder (A Kate Burkholder Short Story Collection)

Fallen

The Hidden One

An Evil Heart

THE BURNING

A KATE BURKHOLDER NOVEL

Linda Castillo

MINOTAUR
BOOKS
NEW YORK

First published in the United States by Minotaur Books, an imprint of St. Martin's Publishing Group

THE BURNING. Copyright © 2024 by Linda Castillo. All rights reserved. Printed in the United States of America. For information, address St. Martin's Publishing Group, 120 Broadway, New York, NY 10271.

Designed by Omar Chapa

ISBN 9781250781116

This book is dedicated to my sisters, Debbie and Kim.

Love you always.

The Lord trieth the righteous: but the wicked and him that loveth violence his soul hateth.

—PSALMS 11:5

THE BURNING

PROLOGUE

Milan Swanz figured he'd chosen the wrong night to get drunk and walk home. He'd spent the evening at the bar, guzzling drafts and alternating with the occasional shot of Wild Turkey. His drinking buddy had abandoned ship at some point, leaving him without a ride. At the time, Milan hadn't cared. He had his eye on the redhead in the tight jeans and low-cut sweater. The one that had climbed onto the pool table to make a tricky jump shot that won her the game. Unfortunately for Milan, the redhead had disappeared shortly after his ride and now here he was, horny and shit-faced and wading through ankle-deep snow with another mile and a half to go.

"Uppity bitch," he muttered as his boots crunched along the gravel shoulder of Dogleg Road.

It was so dark on this lonely stretch that he could barely see the hit-or-miss asphalt beneath his feet. Frickin' Ohio winters. It had been a comfortable fifty degrees when he'd walked into the bar at six P.M. In

1

the hours since, the temperature had dropped, two inches of snow had fallen, and now he was officially freezing his ass off.

He'd just passed the bridge over Little Paint Creek when headlights flickered against the bare-branched treetops ahead. He turned to look behind him, and sure enough a vehicle was approaching. Milan sidestepped onto the shoulder. The hiss of the tires against pavement sounded and then a car rolled to a stop next to him. The passenger-side window slid down.

"Heck of a night to be out walking," came a friendly voice from the driver's seat.

Stopping, Milan bent and looked into the interior, felt a puff of heated air waft over his face. "You ain't lying."

"Where you headed?"

"Home." Hopeful he'd landed a ride, Milan motioned in the direction of his house. "A mile and a half down the road."

"I'm going that way. Want a lift?"

"Man, that'd be great."

The door locks snicked as they disengaged. "Hop in."

Brushing snow from his shoulders, Milan reached for the door handle and slid inside. A sigh eased out of him at the soft embrace of heat, the smell of warm leather. "Thanks, man."

"No problem." The driver glanced in the side-view mirror and pulled back onto the road. "Hate to see anyone out in this kind of weather."

"Had a ride but he left me."

"Happens."

A pleasant song Milan couldn't name purred from the sound system. He leaned back in the plush seat, soaking in the warmth, a sense of relaxation washing over him. One of these days, he was going to own a vehicle like this. One of these days, he was going to catch a break and—

A shuffle from the back seat startled him. A blur of movement inches from his face. The next thing he knew something slapped against his throat and was yanked tight against his Adam's apple.

"Hey!" The word burst from his mouth in a garbled chirp as his voice box was crushed.

Instinctively, he raised both hands, tried to jam his fingers beneath the strap. But it was impossibly tight. Cutting off his air and the blood to his head. His fingers dug into his flesh, fingernails scratching his skin, but he couldn't get them beneath it.

A rise of panic overtook him. His body bucked, hips coming up. He kicked out his feet, pushed against the seatback. Raised a knee, rammed his foot into the dash. Plastic shattered.

The strap was yanked tighter. He couldn't breathe. Couldn't speak. Arching his back, he twisted left and then right. He lashed out with his feet. Tried to get his leg up to break the windshield. Not enough room to maneuver. He slung out his left arm, tried to punch the driver. His forearm struck the steering wheel.

Mindless panic descended. He plunged his fingers into the flesh at his throat. His right leg came up. He kicked at the glove box. Once. Twice. Heard the vinyl split. His mouth opened, but the scream was quashed. Tongue sticking out between his teeth. No air. *No air.*

The lights flickered and dimmed. The music faded to babel. His hands fell to his lap. His bladder released. By the time the warmth spread across his crotch, he could no longer feel.

•   •   •

Milan Swanz woke to darkness, cold, and a headbanger of a headache. An icy breeze cut through his coat and jeans. Confusion swirled in his brain. He was outside, shivering his ass off. He remembered the car picking him up. A strap looped over his head, someone in the back seat trying to strangle him . . .

He opened his eyes and looked around. A wall of trees surrounded him. Gray night sky above skeletal branches. Snow falling like ash. No one in sight. He tried to get his bearings, but recognized nothing.

Where was he?

What the hell was going on?

He was upright, but not quite standing on his own power. An alarm inside him shrilled when he realized his wrists were bound behind his back. Something solid and rough against his spine, supporting him. He tried to loosen the binds, but his wrists were tightly bound with what felt like wire or stiff cord. He looked down, saw that he was standing on a stack of wood pallets. Someone had also piled what looked like firewood and kindling at his feet.

"What the fuck?" His voice echoed among the trees. The only reply was the tinkle of snow and the hard drum of fear in his chest.

"Hello?" he shouted. "Who's there?"

Footfalls sounded. He squinted into the darkness. Saw the shadowy figure walking toward him, a few yards away. The guy in the car, he realized.

"Dude, I don't know what the fuck you're up to, but you'd better get over here and cut me loose."

The man reached him, his demeanor unhurried and resolute. His expression unperturbed. For the first time, Milan noticed the container in his hand, and a quiver of uneasiness roiled in his gut.

"What the hell are you doing?" Milan snarled.

No response.

"Cut me loose!" he shouted.

A second figure emerged from the shadows. Male. Long winter coat. Hat. Gloves. Similar container in hand. This time, Milan recognized it. Diesel fuel. Despite the chill, sweat broke out on his back.

"Let me go, man." He'd intended the words as a command, but they came out like the squeak of a child. "Come on, dude."

Without acknowledging him, the figure closest to him uncapped the container and began to pour onto the pallets. The stench of diesel fuel rose in a plume. An instant of disbelief descended and then terror lit up every nerve ending in his body. Adrenaline pumped like nitro through his veins. Milan struggled against his binds, jerked his arms hard, felt the wire cut into the flesh at his wrists. He twisted and bucked against whatever he was tied to. He tried to lash out with his feet, but his ankles were tethered.

Dear God in heaven, what was going on?

"What the hell are you doing?" he screamed.

Neither of the men looked at him. They worked in tandem. Thorough. Expressions calm and inscrutable. A methodical team set on completing their task.

The smell of diesel fuel mingled with the cold and filled Milan's nostrils. Terror overwhelmed him. Bile filled his mouth. Afraid he might be sick, he spit.

"Are you nuts!" he screamed. "You can't do this! Let me go!"

Milan strained against the binds, arching his back, twisting his head from side to side. He tried to yank his arms from the constraints, rocked his body left and right, grunting with the effort, putting his weight into it. Again, he tried to kick out his legs. If he could shove some of the wood away, he might have a chance. . . .

"Help me! Help! *Someone!*" His voice was the howl of a dog. Unrecognizable. Filled with the sound of terror.

Finished with their task, the men stopped working. They backed away, set down the containers. Unspeaking, they bowed their heads.

"Crazy fuckers!" Milan screamed. "Why are you doing this?"

The odor of diesel fuel hung heavy in the air. Milan looked down at the pallets, the kindling and wood piled around his feet. Fuel soaking into it. He knew what they were going to do. And for the first time in years, he prayed for God to help him.

"Please!" he shouted. "Someone! Help me! *Help!*"

One of the men started toward him. Milan spotted the lighter in his hand. "Wait! Wait! *Don't!*"

A rush of panic at the click-scratch of the flint. Terror crawled over him as he took in the tiny flame. A thousand pins pricked his spine.

"Are you fucking nuts?" he screamed. "Don't! *Don't!*"

The man tossed the lighter. A faint clink as it struck the pallets. Shock and horror washed over him as it rolled and disappeared into the kindling. An instant of hope that it wasn't going to ignite. An orange flicker. And then a *whoosh!* as the flames leapt.

"Dear God! God! *No!*"

Heat swept against his shins and rolled up his thighs. The smells of burning wood and fabric. The pain came like a branding iron against the front of his legs. Heat climbed up, seared his crotch and belly.

He smelled singed hair, felt fire against his face. In his mouth. His eyes. The horror of knowing what came next. Blind panic exploded inside him. He screamed, sucked in sparks. Lungs on fire. Spit boiling in his mouth. Too much pain to process.

His bowels released.

He howled in agony.

And the flames burned away the night.

CHAPTER 1

Officer Chuck "Skid" Skidmore was no stranger to mistakes. He'd made a few in his time. More than a few if he wanted to be honest about it. Some had cost him. From others he'd emerged unscathed, but walked away a wiser man. Most of his mistakes were of the innocent variety. A lapse of judgment. Poor planning. Or maybe he simply hadn't tried hard enough to do the right thing.

Tonight, as he stood on the span of the covered bridge and watched fellow police officer Mona Kurtz pull up behind his cruiser, he figured the one he was about to make was as far removed from innocence as he could imagine. For the life of him he didn't have the self-discipline to stop.

It was half past two A.M. and snowing like the dickens. He'd been on duty since midnight and hadn't taken a single call. Boredom and lust were a bad combination for a man who'd been obsessing over a woman—a coworker—for almost six months now.

"Fancy meeting you here," Mona said as she slammed her car door and started toward him.

"I was just thinking the same thing." He held his ground, leaning against his cruiser, arms crossed, and for an instant he simply enjoyed the sight of her. Long legs. Hair a little wild. Her coat was open; she was still wearing her police uniform and he could just make out the outline of her figure.

"You off?" he asked.

"Free as a bird."

Without invitation or hesitation, she went to him, fell against him. The contact was like a bomb going off in his chest. His arms encircled her. She smelled of coconut and mint. He breathed in deep and it only made him want more. He didn't intend to kiss her, but the next thing he knew his mouth was on hers.

Then she was flush against him. Her arms flung around his neck. Breasts against his chest. Pelvis grinding into his.

"You know this is not smart, right?" he murmured.

"Totally aware," she panted.

He started to say something about their careers and good judgment, but she took his mouth again. Heart raging, he spun her around, pressed her against the car door. Hands beneath her shirt, fingers seeking the closure of her bra. Blood rushing from his head to just south of his belt.

"Back seat," he ground out, reaching for the door handle.

"Hurry."

He fumbled the handle, got his fingers under it, opened the door. He was so focused on getting her into the back seat, he almost didn't hear the scream.

Mona went still in his arms, turned her head to break the kiss. "Did you hear that?"

"Yeah." Skid straightened, gave himself a hard mental shake. "Sounded like a scream."

Not just a scream, he thought, but the kind of sound that made the hair on your neck stand on end.

"Who's screaming their head off in the woods at this time of night?" she whispered.

He eased away from her and looked around, his cop's instincts slowly returning. Only then did he catch the smell of smoke. "Something burning."

Mona looked around as if to get her bearings. "I smell it."

"We need to check."

"Yep."

Tugging the mini Maglite from his belt, Skid set the beam on the woods. Sure enough, fingers of white smoke hovered among the trees.

"Wind's out of the north," he murmured.

"Skid, there's no farm in that direction," she said.

"Too damn cold for anyone to be camping." Tilting his head, he spoke into his lapel. "Ten-seven-three," he said, letting his dispatcher know there was smoke in the area.

Margaret's voice cracked over his radio. "What's the twenty on that?"

"Dogleg Road," he said. "By the bridge over Little Paint Creek."

"Do you want me to get the fire department out there?"

"Let me take a quick look-see before we get anyone out of bed."

"Roger that."

They crossed the road, traversed the ditch, and climbed over a beat-up wire fence. Darkness closed over them as they entered the woods. The smoke was thicker there. Woodsmoke laced with something vaguely unpleasant. Skid listened as they wound through fifty yards of new-growth forest, pockets of raspberry bramble and winter-dead weeds, but the only sound came from their boots crunching on leaves left over from fall.

"Fire." Mona pointed. "Two o'clock. Through those trees."

"I see it," he said. "Eyes open."

"Yep."

They broke into a jog. Staying as quiet as possible, not quite succeeding at being totally silent. All the while, Skid kept his hand over his sidearm.

"Painters Mill Police Department!" he called out as they neared. "Identify yourself!"

No response.

He heard the crack and pop of the fire moments before they entered the clearing. It looked like some type of bonfire. Wood piled high and burning profusely. Flames leaping fifteen feet into the air. Not a soul in sight.

"Police department!" Twenty feet away, Mona entered the clearing. "Show yourself! Now!"

The only response came from the crackling of the fire.

"Looks like whoever was here flew the coop," Mona muttered.

Skid took in the details of the scene, felt a slow rise of uneasiness. He'd assumed they'd stumbled upon an impromptu party of some type. Young people sitting around a bonfire, drinking beer or smoking dope and freezing their butts off. But there was something off about the scene. No beer bottles. No trash. No place to sit. Not too many footprints.

"What the hell is this?" he muttered.

"Skid."

Something in Mona's voice caught his attention. She stood a few feet from the fire. Hand up to shield her face from the heat. Her head cocked in confusion.

"What is that?" she whispered.

A post jutted from the center of the blaze. Eight or nine feet tall and thick as a telephone pole. Something hanging on it. A shape that was oddly human.

10

"Son of a bitch," he said.

"Is that . . ."

"Go get your fire extinguisher," he said. "Hurry! I'm going to see if I can get him out of there."

Spinning, Mona sprinted toward their vehicles.

Skid started toward the fire, but the heat drove him back. Unable to take his eyes off the humanlike thing secured to the post, he hit his lapel mike. He knew his ten codes just fine, but for the life of him he couldn't figure out which to use for this. "I got a fire out here! A burn victim. Ten-fifty-two," he said, using the code for an ambulance.

"Roger that." A concerned pause and then, "Are you in a structure?"

"Negative. Just . . . the woods. Call the chief, Margaret," he said. "I think we got a homicide here."

CHAPTER 2

The rattle of my cell phone pulls me from a dead sleep. Rolling, I slap my hand down on it, bring it to my face and squint at the display. DISPATCH. 2:47 A.M. I answer with a curt utterance of my name.

"Burkholder."

"Sorry to wake you, Chief," comes my graveyard-shift dispatcher's voice. "I just took a call from Skid. Says he's got a fire and body out on Dogleg Road."

A quick punch of dread sends me bolt upright. My feet hit the floor. "A structure?" I ask, rising and going to the closet for my clothes. "House? Barn?"

"He's in the woods," she tells me. "Out by the covered bridge."

My befuddled brain tries to make sense of it as I yank a uniform shirt off a hanger. "A vehicle accident?"

"He didn't say. Sounded kind of shook up to be honest with you."

"Tell him I'm on my way," I tell her.

I'm vaguely aware of my husband, John Tomasetti, sitting up, rubbing his hands over his face. "Everything all right, Chief?"

"Not sure." I tug my trousers from a dresser drawer and step into them. "There's a fire in the woods off of Dogleg Road. Skid says there's a body."

"Odd combination." He picks up his cell, checks the time. "You want some company?"

Tomasetti is an agent with the Ohio Bureau of Criminal Investigation and a former detective with the Cleveland Division of Police. We've worked together on a dozen cases over the last few years. Not only do we make a good investigative team, but we've gotten pretty good at the whole husband and wife thing, too.

I grab my equipment belt off the chair and buckle up. "Don't you have to be in Columbus at seven?"

"Unfortunately." Groaning, he gets to his feet, rounds the foot of the bed, and puts his arms around me. "I'd rather hang out with you."

"Dead body might be a third wheel."

"Easy to ditch."

We've been married for two months now. A change I still can't quite reconcile. A joy I'm almost afraid to feel. Maybe because for the first time in my life, I'm unabashedly happy and I like the way it fits.

He kisses me.

I kiss him back, pull away an instant before I start to free-fall. "Tomasetti, has anyone ever told you that you have a macabre sense of humor?"

"I get that a lot."

Pulling away, I open the night table drawer, snatch up my .38, and holster it.

"Be careful out there, will you, Chief?" he says.

"See you at dinner," I tell him.

I brush my mouth across his and then I'm out the door.

• • •

Rural Ohio sleeps like the dead this time of night; the back roads are quiet and dark. Snow flutters in the headlights. Behind the wheel of my city-issue Explorer, I hit my emergency strobes, crank up the speedometer, and blow every stop sign that threatens to slow me down. It takes me seventeen minutes to make the usual thirty-minute drive.

Located in the heart of Amish country, Painters Mill is a picturesque village of fifty-three hundred souls, a third of whom are Amish. I was born Amish, but left at the age of eighteen when fate pulled the rug out from under me. I ran as far away from Painters Mill—and my roots—as I could, ending up in Columbus, where I found my way into the unlikely vocation of law enforcement. I attended the school of hard knocks, made a ton of mistakes along the way, and I learned how to *not* be Amish. Once I became a patrol officer and my life settled down, the roots I'd left behind began to call. When the position of chief came open and the town council courted me for the job, I went for it.

There have been plenty of bumps since, but I never looked back and I never regretted my decision. My parents are gone now, but my siblings and their families still live in the area. They're still Amish. We've come a long way since those early days. In terms of getting back the close relationship we once had, we're a work in progress.

By the time I make the turn onto Dogleg Road and head toward the covered bridge, big, wet flakes are coming down in earnest. I spot the emergency lights of Skid's cruiser, which is parked on the shoulder, and pick up my radio mike. "Ten-twenty-three," I say, letting my dispatcher know I've arrived on scene.

A tinge of surprise slips through me at the sight of Mona's personal vehicle parked behind the cruiser. She's the department rookie and the first female officer to grace the ranks of the Painters Mill PD. I happen to know she worked until midnight. She's prone to hanging around after her shift, especially if there's something interesting going on, so I don't think too much about her being here.

I park behind her car and get out. There's no one in sight. No other vehicles. No sign of a fire. But the smell of smoke hangs heavy in the air. I hit my radio. "Skid, what's your twenty?"

"Due north of my vehicle, Chief. A hundred yards."

Discerning the tension in his voice, I grab my Maglite, spot two sets of prints, and follow them through the ditch. I climb the fence, sweeping my beam left and right, and I break into a jog. Twenty yards into the trees, I spot the flicker of flashlights ahead. All the while, I try to imagine a scenario that might've led to a fire and dead body. This is a remote area that's prone to flooding in the spring. There are no farms or houses in the vicinity, and no road or dirt track that would accommodate a vehicle.

So what the hell was someone doing out here and how did they end up dead?

A hundred yards in, I enter a clearing. Ahead, I see the smoldering remnants of a fire, white smoke rising. Skid and Mona are standing about ten feet from the pile of glowing embers. Skid's holding a fire extinguisher at his side. I can tell by the way they're pacing around that they're agitated.

"We got someone in the fire!" Skid calls out.

I break into a run. As I draw closer, I notice the blackened post jutting from the center of the smoldering ash. Foreboding quivers in my gut as I take in the vaguely human form secured to the post.

"Is he alive?" My voice sounds normal as I reach them, but my pulse is racing, the hairs at my neck standing on end.

Linda Castillo

Of all the officers who work for me—all five of them—Skid is the most likely to put forth some smart-ass comment at an ill-timed moment. Tonight, all I see is disbelief and bafflement on his face.

"Can't get close enough to tell," he says. "Too damn hot."

"Was this burning when you arrived?" I ask.

"Fully engulfed." He hefts the extinguisher. "Chief, this dude was alive when we pulled up. Mona and I heard a scream. By the time we found him, he wasn't moving."

"We just now got the fire out," Mona says.

I look at her, notice the smaller extinguisher in her hand. "Hit those embers with foam."

She does.

"We gotta get him out." I glance at Skid. "Ambulance?"

"En route. Fire department, too."

In the years I've been a cop, I've come upon victims with thermal injuries of varying degrees. I've responded to house fires. Vehicle accidents. Chemical burns. Smoke inhalation. I've never seen anything like this. The torso is in an upright position. The clothes have burned away. The exposed flesh is brown and black with hideous rust-colored patches. The neck is rust colored and wet looking. The head is bowed, the lower part of the face brown, the forehead blistered and bloodied.

"We've got to get him out of there," I say.

"I'm game," he says.

The problem is the victim is surrounded by four feet of glowing embers on all sides. No way to reach him without getting burned.

"Mona." I toss her the keys to my Explorer. "Grab my toolbox. Water. Shovel. Hurry!"

She catches the keys with one hand, spins, and sprints toward our vehicles.

I look around for something—a log or flat stone—we can stand on or use to shove away the embers, but there's nothing around.

"Shit." I get as close as I can, reach out, but the heat sends me back. No way to reach the victim. It's an excruciating situation. I speak into my radio. "Expedite ten-fifty-two," I say, requesting a rush on the ambulance. "I got a burn victim."

Skid jogs around the periphery of the clearing, looking for something we can use to protect our feet. There's nothing but scraps of wood and kindling.

I can't stop looking at the victim. There's no movement. The body is affixed to the wood post. His hands are behind his back and held in place with something that didn't burn through.

"Chief!"

I glance toward the woods to see Mona running toward us, my equipment toolbox in one hand, two folding shovels in the other. I rush to her, grab a shovel, snap it to length, and jog to the smoldering ash. Setting the blade to the embers, I scoop away red-hot coals, toss them aside. Skid puts the fire extinguisher to use. Mona yanks a quart-size water bottle from her pocket, squirts it. The embers sizzle when the water hits. In the back of my mind, I'm aware that this is a crime scene. That we're probably contaminating evidence. No way to avoid it, because the preservation of life always comes first.

"Lay some foam on those embers!" I tell Mona.

She raises the smaller extinguisher and throws foam onto the freshly exposed embers.

I shovel for another minute. When there's enough room for me to reach the victim without getting burned, I go for it. Vaguely, I'm aware of Skid digging. Heat presses against my calves, walks up my legs. I smell fabric burning, feel the heat coming through the soles of my boots. I keep going.

The victim is monstrous. I hold my breath against the stench of singed hair and burning clothes. The underlying horror of cooked meat. Dear God.

Craning my neck, I get my first good look at the bindings. Wire. "Give me the bolt cutter!"

Mona thrusts the tool at me. I grab it, set the blades against the wire, and make the cut. The victim's arms swing free, lifeless. A second wire binds the torso to the post. I shift the bolt cutter and snip. The body slumps and begins to fall. Rushing forward, I grasp the victim's biceps with both hands. I feel the flesh slip beneath my duty gloves, and I steel myself against a wave of revulsion. Then Skid is beside me, taking the other arm, and we drag the victim from the embers. Twenty feet. We place him on the ground in a supine position. Arms outstretched at his sides.

"Water!" I say.

Mona knows the protocol and has it at the ready. I pour the entire bottle on the victim's head and throat and upper torso. It's not enough, but I know it doesn't matter. We're too late to make a difference. This victim is gone. The burns are too extensive.

For the span of several seconds, the only sound comes from our labored breaths. The woods are so quiet I can hear the tinkle of snow. The flutter of dry leaves. The low hum of wind through the branches. The sizzle and pop of the embers.

The distant wail of sirens breaks the spell. I look down at the victim, try not to recoil. I recall from my training that any burned clothing, shoes or belts, should be removed or cut away. This person is burned so severely I can't discern fabric from flesh.

Without speaking, Mona jogs to the edge of the clearing and throws up. Skid digs into my equipment box and pulls out a thermal blanket.

"What the hell happened here?" he says as he snaps it open and covers the body, leaving the face exposed.

At first sight of this victim, I'd wondered if it might be the result of someone trying to do away with a dead body. But having seen the wire bindings and knowing Mona and Skid heard a scream upon their arrival, I realize that's not the case.

Mona joins us. She's no shrinking violet, but her face is the color of paste.

"Did either of you see or hear anyone out here when you arrived?" I ask. "Signs that anyone had been here?"

"I didn't see anyone," Mona tells me. "To tell you the truth, Chief, we were so focused on putting out the fire we might've missed something."

"I didn't see a soul." Skid shakes his head, incredulous. "But that scream. . . . Chief, that poor son of a bitch was tied to that damn post and burned alive."

It's such a bizarre notion, I can't get my head around it. But I know what I saw. The wire. The post. The wood piled high and set afire. . . .

"Smelled like diesel fuel, too," I say.

He nods. "So, whoever did this used an accelerant."

I turn my attention to Mona. "Let's get this scene taped off. Twenty yards in every direction. Keep an eye out for footprints or anything else that doesn't belong here. If you see anything unusual, mark it and preserve it."

Nodding, she starts toward where our vehicles are parked.

"Skid, take a look around. See if you can find tracks or tire marks."

He tips his hat at me. "You got it."

The sirens are close now. Through the trees, I see the red and blue lights of a fire truck or ambulance. Mona's Maglite sweeps from side to side as she disappears into the trees.

I look down at the victim and feel a twinge of nausea. "What the hell happened to you?" I whisper.

The only answer is the song of the wind serenading the night.

CHAPTER 3

An hour later, the area is crawling with law enforcement. The paramedics arrived first and pronounced the victim deceased. The scene was taped off and secured. The fire department extinguished the remaining coals. Once they deemed the area safe to enter, control of the scene was passed to the coroner.

Light snow angles down from a lowering night sky. I'm standing just outside the caution tape, waiting for Doc Coblentz. Forty feet away, the blackened post stands in macabre testament to what transpired. Earlier, I was able to locate the wire I had removed from the victim's wrists and torso and placed all three pieces in evidence bags. It's the first evidence I've retrieved in an expansive outdoor scene that promises to be difficult.

A few yards away, a Holmes County sheriff's deputy is talking to one of the EMTs. The wind has picked up and I can see the EMT shivering beneath her coat.

"Chief?"

I glance over my shoulder to see Dr. Ludwig Coblentz and a young male technician approach. It's been a couple of months since I saw the doc; he's gained a few pounds. He's wearing a heavy coat with a faux-fur-lined hood. Khaki trousers with the hem tucked into duck boots. Both men are carrying large medical cases at their sides.

"Hey, Doc." I cross to him and we shake hands, not bothering to remove our gloves.

"The older I get, the colder these Ohio winters get," he says with an exaggerated shiver.

"I think that's why they invented insulated coveralls."

"I think that's why they invented Florida."

His mouth curves briefly, and then his eyes flick toward the victim, and the burned post. He's a seasoned doctor; he's seen plenty of unusual scenes in the years he's been coroner. He's calm and professional with a mindset that keeps the darker aspects of his job in perspective. I don't miss the flash of shock or the quick downturn of his mouth.

"I was perplexed initially when the call came in," he tells me. "I kept trying to make sense of what I was hearing." He sighs. "Now I understand why none of it made sense."

"Sometimes, even when you know what happened it doesn't make sense."

"That is the truth."

I relay to him what little I know.

"Skid and Mona heard a scream?" he asks. "Are you sure?"

I nod. "A scream or shout."

"So unless the scream came from someone else, the perpetrator of the crime or a witness, this victim was alive just minutes before they got to him."

I watch as his doctor's mind works through the possibilities. "Because

21

of the nature of the scream, they believe it was likely the victim," I tell him.

He nods. "How long ago was that?"

I glance at my watch. "About an hour and a half."

Grimacing, he sets down the case and bends to open it. He retrieves two individually wrapped gowns, two pairs of nitrile gloves, and shoe covers. He hands one set of each to me.

"The fire department extinguished the fire?" he asks.

I nod.

"Even so, we'll do our best to keep the scene as uncontaminated as possible."

We don't speak during the awkward dance of suiting up over the bulk of our coats and boots. When we're finished, I lift the tape for him and his technician, duck beneath it myself, and we enter the scene. I'd photographed both the victim and scene earlier. Seeing the corpse through the camera lens of my cell phone somehow gave me the distance I needed not to get caught up in what I was seeing. I zoomed for close-ups, but didn't get *too* close. As we cross to the body, I feel an unpleasant quiver in my stomach that tells me I'm not quite prepared for what comes next.

"Were you able to ID the victim?" Doc asks.

I shake my head. "Too much heat and smoke. As you can see, he's pretty badly burned."

"Accelerant?"

"We smelled diesel fuel," I tell him, aware that it's still discernible.

One of the EMTs has replaced the thermal blanket from earlier with a plain white sheet. Atop that she draped a waterproof blue tarp to prevent the lightly falling snow from soaking through and damaging any potential evidence.

Kneeling, the doc grasps the upper corners of both drapes. I brace as he peels them back. For a moment, I can't catch my breath. I've been exposed to several burn-related fatalities over the years. The car accident off the highway last summer. The barn fire a few years back. The house fire that killed an elderly couple shortly after I became chief. All deaths are disturbing, but there's something particularly gruesome when it comes to death by fire.

This victim is burned beyond recognition. When Skid and I laid the corpse on the ground a short time ago, he was supine. Now, the arms and legs have bent slightly. The knees are apart, likely from the muscles contracting. The flesh is blackened and peeling. The feet appear shrunken. The upper part of the body is rust colored and interspersed with black-looking flakes, either burned clothing or flesh or both. But it's the face that disturbs me. The forehead is bloodred and moist looking. The hair has burned away, especially around the face. The mouth is open, the tongue protruding like a piece of rotting fruit. The smell is an awful combination of singed hair, burning fabric, and overcooked meat.

I pull my scarf up over my nose and mouth, and try not to breathe.

"I'm not going to be able to tell you much, Kate, until I get the body on the table," he begins. "But I know you have an investigation to get started on, so I'll tell you what I can. All of it is preliminary at this point and subject to change, okay?"

"I'll take anything you can give me." I force my gaze back to the deceased. "Probably the most important thing at this point is to get him identified."

"Let's see what this poor soul has to tell us." Giving a decisive nod to the technician, the doctor kneels, his knees cracking in protest. "I think it's safe to say this individual was likely male. We have extensive thermal injuries with charring, particularly on the lower extremities and torso." He looks at me over the tops of his glasses. "Where did you find the victim exactly?"

I'd seen him looking at the post; I can tell by his expression he already knows. "He was wired to the post."

He swivels his gaze to the post, the thick pile of ash around it, the pieces of kindling and branches at the periphery that hadn't yet burned.

"Just so all of us are on the same page here," he says. "Are you telling me this victim was tied to that post and burned?"

"I don't think anyone can say that with certainty," I say, "but that's what it looks like."

"Good God," he mutters.

He turns his attention back to the dead man and tugs the sheet to mid-thigh. I force myself to look at the victim, this time my cop's brain looking for useful information. I see a scrap of what looks like denim sticking out from beneath the victim's hip. The brass glint of a belt buckle seemingly cooked into a blackened and peeling torso. Flakes of material that's indeterminate in nature.

Removing a swab from his case, Coblentz indicates a small flap sticking out from beneath the victim's hip. "This is what's left of a belt," he says.

"Can we check to see if there's a wallet?" I ask.

"Most males keep their wallet in a rear pocket." The doc's brows knit. "Was this victim's back to the post?"

I nod.

"That might work to our advantage," he says. "At least in terms of identifying him."

"The post may have protected the back side of his body."

"Exactly."

It's the first suggestion of good news I've had since my arrival. "Hopefully, his wallet is intact."

"Fortunately, leather doesn't burn as readily as one might believe."

He nods at the technician. "Let's roll him onto his right side," he says. "Away from us. Watch for slippage."

The technician kneels, back straight, and sets his hands on the victim's shoulder and hip.

I get to my feet and step back, watching as the two men logroll the body onto its side. The blackened surface gives way to singed denim and small patches of blue that's left on the buttocks and the backs of the victim's thighs.

"Extraction forceps," the doc says.

The technician swivels to the bag and hands him what looks like a medical pliers.

The doc presses the tip to a place where the denim hasn't quite burned away, then inserts the head between two layers of fabric, opens the small jaws, and pulls out a partially burned wallet.

"Here we go," he says.

The wallet is a bifold, much like the one Tomasetti carries. "It doesn't look too bad," I say.

He tosses me a ye-of-little-faith look.

With a gloved hand, I take the wallet. The technician is ready with a large sterile pad and sets it atop the tarp. Muttering a thanks, I set the wallet on the pad and use my index finger to open it. A quarter inch of a driver's license peeks out at me. The corners are blackened and melted, but the license is intact.

"Bingo." Carefully, I pinch the corner and ease the plastic from its nest.

A quiver of recognition kicks as I read the name. "Milan Swanz," I say. "He was Amish."

The doc looks at me a little closer. "You knew him?"

"I went to school with him. Arrested him. Twice." My eyes skim down to an address I'm familiar with. "Shit."

Reaching into my pocket, I pull out my cell phone and photograph the front and back of the ID. I go back to the wallet. There are no credit cards, which isn't unusual for the Amish. A five-dollar bill. A single. "Whoever killed him didn't take his cash," I murmur, and make a mental note to check to see if he had any credit or debit cards.

Finding nothing else of interest, I remove an evidence bag from my pocket, drop the wallet into it, and put it in my coat pocket.

I look at Doc. "We'll still need to cross-identify with DNA," I say. "To make sure someone didn't put Swanz's wallet on the body of someone else."

"DNA will be easy enough," the doc tells me. "Dental, too."

We stare at each other a moment. The doc's glasses are fogged. The tip of his nose is red and runny. I see disbelief and abhorrence in his expression, right alongside the steely determination I know will get him through. I feel the sum of those emotions roiling inside me.

"Is there any way to tell if this person was alive when he was burned?" I ask.

"Well, the autopsy will tell us if he died from thermal injuries or soot and smoke inhalation. Once we get him to the morgue, I'll run a test to check the level of carbon monoxide in the blood. Check for soot in the airway. In most arson cases, the cause of death is attributed to smoke inhalation. In the case of immolation, it's thermal burns."

We fall silent, as if the thoughts running through our heads are too dark to entertain.

"Anything else?" I ask.

"As you can imagine, this will likely be a complicated and difficult case," he tells me. "I'll probably bring in a forensic pathologist to assist."

I look down at the corpse, the blackened and peeling skin, the patches of burned denim, and I feel sick to my stomach. Milan Swanz was a troubled man who made plenty of mistakes in the thirty-six years he'd been on this earth. But he was a human being with a wife and children and parents who'd loved him despite his flaws.

My most pressing—and difficult—responsibility lies with notifying the family that Milan Swanz is gone. When that is done, I'll be able to focus on what I do best. Find the son of a bitch who killed him and bring him to justice.

•   •   •

I fish my cell phone from my pocket as I duck beneath the crime scene tape and hit the speed dial for Dispatch. My third-shift dispatcher picks up on the first ring.

"Hey, Chief."

"I need you to run Milan Swanz through LEADS," I say, referring to the Law Enforcement Automated Data System. "Run his wife, Bertha, too."

"You need the address?"

"I know where he lives." I sigh. "I need the names and contact info for his parents. Get me the names of any known associates you can come up with. Find out if there's a vehicle registered to him."

"You got it." I hear the click of her fingertips flying over the keyboard.

"They're Amish," I add. "There may not be much out there on the parents. Call me."

I disconnect, spot Holmes County sheriff Mike Rasmussen, and head that way.

He spots me and starts toward me. "Just got the call half an hour ago," he says. "What the holy hell happened?"

I reach him and we shake. He's wearing an official parka over insulated coveralls. His coat is open at the collar and I'm pretty sure he's wearing plaid pajamas beneath the coveralls.

I recap what little I know so far.

Mike Rasmussen is a seasoned cop. Like me, he's been around the block a few times and isn't easily surprised. When I'm finished speaking, he stares at me blank faced as if waiting for me to break into laughter and admit the whole thing is a sick joke.

"Are you shitting me?" he says. "Burned at the stake? Like some kind of fucking witch?"

"We just IDed him. Milan Swanz. He's local. Amish."

His eyes narrow. "Why is that name familiar?"

"Because he's got a record."

"What charges?"

I shake my head. "Just in Painters Mill and off the top of my head: Drunk driving. Disturbing the peace. Drunk and disorderly."

He looks at me a little more closely. "You know him?"

"Not well. I went to school with him. Arrested him twice myself in the last two or three years. He led a troubled life, I think."

"Any ongoing disputes?"

"I don't know. I'm going to go speak with his family now."

"Damn." He grimaces. "Is he married?"

I nod. "I'll probably speak to his parents, too."

"Jesus." He scrubs a hand over jaw stubble. "I'm still trying to get my head around this one."

"Not easy, is it?"

He looks past me, toward the post just inside the crime scene, and shakes his head. "Look, this is your jurisdiction, Kate, but if you need a hand . . ."

"I'll take all the help you can spare. This is an extraordinarily heinous crime. I thought it might be a good idea to bring in BCI. Maybe set up a task force."

"Whatever you need." He offers up a small smile. "Since you and Tomasetti are married now, can you work together?"

"As far as I know there aren't any rules against it." I shrug. "Painters Mill falls inside his region. We'll see."

"That's good. I think the three of us make a pretty good team."

I look past him, see Mona and Skid standing a few yards away, talking. "First light we need to set up a search grid of the immediate area. Metal detectors. Dogs. The whole nine yards. Expand from there. Chances are this happened just a few hours ago. We did a preliminary search, but it was dark. We might've missed something. Killer could have dropped something, left something behind."

"There's a pullover on the other side of those woods." He motions toward the trees beyond the crime scene. "I'll get a deputy out there, see if there are any tire marks or prints."

"That's good." I sigh. "Snow isn't helping."

"Never does. This one's going to be a tough scene to process all around."

"I'll call Tomasetti," I tell him. "Have your guys get with Skid and set up that search."

"Will do."

"Can you spare a few guys to start a canvass?" I ask. "Not many houses in the area, but we should check."

"I'll do it," he says. "Never know when you might get lucky."

• • •

Back in the Explorer, I call Tomasetti as I pull onto the road.

"I appreciate your getting me out of that meeting with the suits," he says by way of greeting.

Despite the disturbing images still playing hide-and-seek in my brain, I smile. "So you heard."

"Came over my Spillman a few minutes ago," he says, referring to the software system used by law enforcement and other agencies to record dispatch activities for police, fire, and emergency medical services.

"Where are you?" I ask.

"Just outside Painters Mill. Crime scene tech should be pulling in there about now. What about you?"

"I'm on my way to Swanz's residence to do the notification."

"Shit."

"Yep."

"Want some company?"

Usually, it's protocol to have a fellow officer present at a notification. You never know how someone is going to react. Some departments even keep a chaplain on call. In this case, however, since the family is Amish, I opt to do it alone.

"I'd rather have you at the scene," I tell him.

"I won't take it personally." He makes the statement lightly, but we're still thinking about the notification. "Call if you need me."

"I will," I say. "I'll meet you at the scene as soon as I finish up."

CHAPTER 4

It's after seven A.M. when I pull into the gravel lane of the home Swanz shared with his wife, Bertha. The house is a timeworn two-story frame that sits a scant fifty yards from the railroad tracks that run through Painters Mill proper two miles down the road. The tired-looking siding is pickled gray from the elements, the window screens dark with age. I catch a flicker of yellow light in a downstairs window as I idle around to the rear of the house and park.

A beaten-down flagstone walkway takes me to the front porch. I go up the steps and knock. I hear the chatter of children inside, and then heavy footsteps sound on a wood floor. The door swings open and I find myself looking at a pale-faced Amish woman in a blue dress and gauzy white *kapp*, a black cardigan wrapped around her shoulders. I've met her at some point. In fact, I'm pretty sure she works at LaDonna's Diner in town and has served me more than my share of coffee.

She blinks, surprised to see the chief of police at her door this early in the morning. "Can I help you?"

I have my badge at the ready. "Mrs. Swanz?"

"Yes?"

"I'm sorry to bother you so early. I'm afraid I have bad news."

Her eyes go wide as if she's expecting me to rush in and attack her. "What do you mean?"

"Milan Swanz was killed earlier, ma'am. I'm very sorry."

For an instant, she doesn't react. Simply stares at me as if she doesn't quite believe me and is thinking about arguing. "Milan?" she whispers. "Killed?"

"I'm afraid so," I say. "I'm sorry."

She looks past me as if expecting another person with more authority to be standing behind me to dispute my claim. "How on earth did it happen?"

"I don't have all the details yet. We're still investigating. But we believe he was murdered."

"*Murdered?*" She presses her hand against her chest in the first show of sentiment. "*Ach du lieva.*" Oh my goodness. "I can't believe it."

"If you have a few minutes, I'd like to come in and talk to you."

"Oh. Well. Of course." Squaring her shoulders, she opens the door wider and ushers me into a dimly lit living room. "Kids are getting ready for school. I'd rather them not hear this just now. We can talk in the kitchen. I've got coffee on the stove."

She leads me through the living room, past a gas floor lamp and a sofa draped with an olive-green afghan. The sound of a whisper draws my attention. I glance up to see four children at the top of the staircase, hands holding the rails like bars, faces trained on me. They look as if they're preteens, already dressed for school. I don't know if they heard the exchange between me and their mother. If so, they're remarkably stoic.

"Would you like coffee?" the Amish woman asks.

"I could use some."

The kitchen smells of bacon, last night's meat loaf, and burned toast. There's a window above the sink, snow pellets tinking against the glass. Pale blue cabinets. Big gas cookstove hissing in the corner. And Formica counters the color of butter.

I watch as she collects two mugs from the cabinet and pours coffee from an old-fashioned percolator that's blackened from soot and dented from years of use.

"I've seen you at the diner in town," I say.

"Been working there almost a year now." Turning to me, she hands me a cup and motions for me to sit. "So what happened to Milan?"

As chief of police in a small town, I've delivered more than my share of bad news. I've seen reactions ranging from stone-cold shock to complete physical and emotional collapse. Oddly, Bertha Swanz doesn't appear to be unduly upset. While it's true that the Amish tend to be a little more stoic than their English counterparts, I don't see grief on her face. There are no tears. Or shock. Tucking the observation away for later, I take the cup and sink into a chair.

"I don't know the official cause of death yet." I don't want to get into too much detail this early in the game. For one thing, I don't know enough about what happened. Secondly, everyone is suspect, including her.

"Mrs. Swanz." I remove my notepad and pen from my breast pocket. "When's the last time you saw your husband?"

That stare again. Not blank, but . . . unmoved. I gaze back at her, trying to get a handle on it. Then she says, "You know he's not my husband anymore."

The records check done on Milan Swanz indicated he was married. "I'm confused," I tell her. "You're married to him, aren't you?"

"Well, I was. We're divorced, you see. I haven't changed my name yet. It's a legal thing, I guess."

It's rare for an Amish person to get divorced. There's no provision for it. In fact, it's taboo. In the rare instance an Amish couple *does* divorce, the spouse who initiated it is usually excommunicated.

"*Sell is kshpassich.*" That's unusual. I say the words in *Deitsch* to remind her that I'm familiar with Amish customs and traditions.

"I remember you now. You're the police used to be Amish."

I nod. "The address on Milan Swanz's ID card is this address."

"He hasn't lived here for a time." She shrugs. "I reckon he hasn't updated his card is all."

"How long have you been divorced?"

"Almost five months now. He's the one wanted it."

I nod. "Was it amicable?"

"I wasn't happy about it." She lifts her shoulder, lets it drop. "You know how it is. When you're Amish, you make your vows in the presence of God and you marry for life. Milan didn't want to be married anymore. I didn't have a choice in the matter."

"Do you mind if I ask why you divorced?"

"I suppose it had something to do with all those loose girls he liked to run around with."

"Do any of those girls have a name?"

"I wouldn't know," she says. "Just women he meets."

"English girls?"

She hits me with a what-do-you-think frown.

"What about you?" I ask. "Is there a boyfriend involved?"

For a moment, I think she's going to laugh, but she's too well-mannered. "Lord no. I need a boyfriend like I need another no-gooder husband. I know that's not a nice thing to say and the Amish sure wouldn't approve, but there it is."

I let my eyes stray to the staircase, but the children are gone. "You have children together?"

34

"Four," she tells me. "Two boys and two girls."

"How old are they?"

"Danny is thirteen. He's my oldest. Lizzie's the baby. Just turned seven."

I write everything down. "When's the last time you saw or talked to Milan?"

"He came over to the house a week or so ago." The laugh that follows ends with a bitter note. "I figured he might want to see the kids. Or have some money for us. For groceries or whatnot. All he wanted was his tools. He took them and left and I haven't seen him since."

"How was your relationship with him?"

"Well, he was my husband for fourteen years. He sure wasn't perfect, but . . . I guess we got on okay." She sighs. "I know this doesn't sound right, but I sure didn't like what he did with the whole divorce thing. That just wasn't right."

Something askew, the little voice sitting on my shoulder whispers in my ear.

"Did you have disagreements?" I ask. "Or argue?"

"There was nothing left to argue about. In the end he wanted to be gone, and I didn't argue too hard about it." Her mouth tightens. "To tell you the truth, Chief Burkholder, I just wasn't too broken up about him leaving. I know that's a sad thing, but he really was a no-gooder."

"How so?"

"How was he a no-gooder?" She laughs ironically, her resentment obvious to me. "Well, he was a two-timer for one thing. He didn't like to work too much. What little money came to him, he drank it away like a fool, spent it on things he didn't need. Didn't pay the kids any heed. I don't know how it is that he was raised by good Amish parents because Milan barely had a decent bone in his body."

I look down at my notes, keep going. "Did Milan have any enemies that you know of? Did he have any ongoing disagreements with anyone?"

She sips coffee, studying me over the rim. She's got pale blue eyes that are red-rimmed. Not because she's been crying, but as if she doesn't get enough sleep.

"Milan was the kind of man to argue with a lot of people," she tells me. "Held his opinion in high esteem. Had a high opinion of himself, too. Thought he was smarter than everyone else and a lot smarter than what he actually was."

"Anyone in particular?"

"Last one I recall was with our neighbor there on the south side. Lester Yoder. Milan bought half a dozen cows out to the auction in Kidron a couple years back. Put up a wire fence. Yoder came over the next day and told him the fence was five feet over on his property. They went at it for a time. In the end, Milan had to move the fence and he didn't like it one bit. A week later, Milan was out welding. It was windy as the dickens that day. Next thing you know Yoder's cornfield caught fire. All twenty-two acres of it burned. It was an accident, of course. But Yoder blamed Milan. Accused him of doing it on purpose to get back at him for having to move the fence."

I don't recall hearing about the incident, but I ask the question anyway. "Did anyone call the police?"

She shakes her head. "Only English got called that day was the fire department."

I make a mental note to talk to Yoder. "Where did your ex-husband work?"

"Last I heard he was working down to the cabinet shop on the highway there between Killbuck and Painters Mill. Stutzman's, you know. I heard he got fired a while back."

My cop's antenna perks up. "Do you know why he was fired?"

"You'll have to ask them, I reckon."

"Did he get along with the people he worked with?"

"I wouldn't know."

"What about his friends?" I ask. "Was he close to anyone in partic-ular? Was there someone he might've confided in or talked to?"

She thinks about that a moment. "He used to run around with a guy from work. Another no-gooder, so they must've had a few things in common."

"Name?"

"I don't know." For the first time, she looks ashamed. "I heard Milan slept with his wife. They weren't friends anymore after that."

I write it down. *Slept with his friend's wife.* Underscore it. "Did he have a cell phone?"

"I wouldn't know."

"Did he leave any of his belongings here?" I ask.

"Didn't have much, really," she says. "Some clothes. A few tools. Took the last of it when he was here."

"Do you know where he was living?" I ask.

"Last I heard he was renting that old double-wide out on Township Road 104. I got the address around here somewhere." Rising, she goes to the counter and opens a drawer. "Never been there, but the kids vis-ited him there a time or two. They said it's a dumpy old place. Smells bad. A bunch of feral cats."

The lonely wail of a train whistle sounds outside as she rummages in the drawer. "Here we go." She recites an address.

I write it down.

"His parents lived there for a time," she says. "I think they still own it. Milan didn't have a place to go after he left here. I reckon he needed something to tide him over until he could get on his feet."

"Did Milan get along with his parents?" I ask.

"I suspect you'll have to ask them, Chief Burkholder. They're real nice folks. Did their best to help him out when they could. Get him straightened out, you know." She shakes her head. "Course that was a tall order for Milan. The man squandered every chance God ever gave him and he wasn't the least bit thankful for any of it."

•   •   •

I call Dispatch as I pull out of the Swanz lane. "I need you to run Bertha Swanz through LEADS." I spell the name. "NCIC, too."

"You got it, Chief." The reply is followed by the rapid click of the keyboard.

"Is Glock on this morning?" I ask, referring to my first-shift officer.

"He's on his way to the scene."

"Tell him to hold off. I need him to write up an affidavit for a search warrant for Milan Swanz's residence. Take it to Judge Siebenthaler and let him know we need it yesterday." I recite the address from memory.

"Sure."

"Get with the rest of the team and ask them to come in. We need all hands on deck until we get a handle on this."

"You got it."

"Can you text me the address of the Stutzman cabinet company? It's located in Killbuck, I think."

"Yes ma'am." A pregnant pause and then she adds, "Chief, I hate to lay this on you with so much going on this morning, but word's out about the murder. Steve Ressler over at *The Advocate* has been calling every fifteen minutes and asking for you. Radio station down in New Philly called. TV station out of Columbus. Tom Skanks over at the Butterhorn Bakery told me people are saying there was a witch burned at the stake out in the woods there by Painters Creek."

The rumor mill is the one thing you can always count on in a small town, I think, and sigh. "If you get any more media inquiries, tell them we'll be putting out a press release within the hour. Tell Ressler I'll call him as soon as I can."

"You want me to get started on that press release, too?"

I laugh at the absurdity of how much needs to be done. "Thanks. I'll fill in the blanks later."

•   •   •

Milan Swanz's parents, Orla and Ella Mae, live on a well-kept farm three miles south of Painters Mill. Weeping willow trees line both sides of the ruler-straight gravel lane. In the summertime, it's a pleasant sight to behold. With a gray sky spitting snow and promising more, it makes me long for sunshine and warmth. A big red bank barn with a Galvalume roof stands proud to my right. On the downhill side, several dozen Holstein cows huddle next to a round bale of hay. Beyond, double silos seem to blur in the snow slanting down.

The farmhouse is grand for an Amish home, with two brick chimneys and half a dozen tall, narrow windows. A few years ago, I recall a rumor that the bishop talked to the Swanzes because their home displayed "too much pride." As a result, Mr. Swanz removed the shutters from the windows. Ella Mae tore out her beloved flowers from her garden, leaving only the vegetables. It was a silly thing in my opinion and one of a hundred other reasons I never quite fit into the world of the Amish.

I park at the side of the house and take a narrow concrete sidewalk to the front. I'm crossing the porch when the door swings open. Ella Mae Swanz holds a broom in one hand, a dustpan in the other, and startles at the sight of me.

"Oh!" When she laughs, I catch a glimpse of a missing canine tooth before she self-consciously raises her hand to cover her mouth. "Katie

Burkholder! Didn't expect to see anyone out here so early and in all this snow!"

"Sorry to startle you." I offer a weak smile, then hold up my badge, letting her know this is an official visit.

"Well, that'll get my heart pumping for all those chores ahead of me!" Laughing, she tilts her head, curious as to why I'm here. "Is everything okay?"

"Mrs. Swanz, I'm afraid I have bad news," I tell her. "Milan was killed last night."

Her smile falls, her mouth open, her expression going blank. For the span of several seconds, she simply stares at me, blinking. "Milan?" she says after a moment. "Killed?"

"Yes, ma'am," I say. "I'm sorry."

"Well. My goodness." She says the words quietly, then looks down at the broom and dustpan in her hands as if wondering how they got there. "I can hardly believe that. He's so young."

That she takes the news with such calm surprises me. I recall my earlier conversation with Bertha Swanz and I experience an odd moment of déjà vu.

Brows knitting, she raises her gaze to mine. "What happened to him?"

It's as if she's asking about the death of a stranger rather than her son.

I tell her as much as I can without getting into the horrific details. "We're still investigating, but we believe he was murdered."

"Someone *killed* him?" she asks.

"We're still trying to figure out what happened." I pause. "I know this is a bad time, but can I come in and talk to you and your husband for a few minutes?"

"Orla's out feeding the cows, but he'll be back in a bit." She shakes her head as if trying to wake up from a bad dream. "My goodness this is going to be a shock to him. *Kumma*." Come.

She takes me through a living room where a cast-iron stove pumps heat and the pleasant smell of woodsmoke throughout the house. In the kitchen, she motions me to a chair at the table, then goes to the counter. She leans for a moment as if trying to gather her strength, then goes to an old-fashioned percolator, pours coffee into mismatched mugs, and brings both to the table.

I give her a minute to shore up her defenses, but I'm ever aware of the tick of the clock inside me. The one reminding me that there's a killer on the loose in my town and I haven't the slightest clue who he is or what else he might have planned.

I pluck the notepad from my jacket pocket and set it on the table in front of me. "When's the last time you saw your son?"

"Been a little while." Taking the seat across from me, she sips from her cup. "A month or so. Came over to borrow some tools once or twice."

"I understand he'd been excommunicated," I say.

"Six months ago. It's been tough on him."

"Was he excommunicated because of the divorce?"

"So they say."

My interest cranks up a notch. "What do you mean by that?"

She stiffens her shoulders as if at some point she'd made the decision not to be ashamed of her son. "I'll not speak poorly of my son. I'll surely not speak ill of the bishop. I won't do it. But I will tell you this truth: Bishop Troyer was too hard on Milan."

"How so?"

"I'll be the first to admit Milan made a few mistakes in his time. Started when he was a boy. Jumped into everything with two feet, and never tested the water first. Got him into a lot of trouble." She picks

41

up her mug, sets it down without drinking. "I don't think he was the only one wanted out of that marriage."

I recall my conversation with Bertha Swanz.

Milan didn't want to be married anymore.

I didn't have a choice in the matter.

. . . all those loose girls . . .

"Are you saying both of them wanted a divorce?" I ask.

"I'm saying she wanted it too. I'm betting she's the one put him up to it. She knew he'd get excommunicated and she sure didn't care."

Among the Amish, it's common knowledge that in order for a member of the church district to be excommunicated, a vote from the congregation must be unanimous. Whatever Milan Swanz did, it must have been a serious offense. I make a mental note to follow up and see if I can find someone else to corroborate.

"Was there a lot of animosity between Milan and Bertha?" I ask.

"She's an awful woman and she was a terrible wife. She drove him to the divorce if you ask me, and then made sure he got the blame. Told everyone she knew that it was Milan's idea. Well, I doubt that's exactly the way it happened."

I'm well aware that sometimes the parents are the last to accept the flaws or wrongdoing of their children. Even so, I write all of it down, press on.

"Do you know if Bertha was seeing anyone else?" I ask. "Was there someone courting her? Anything like that?"

"Wouldn't put it past her. She's a sneaky thing." She tightens her mouth. "My goodness, I probably ought to stop right there. I'm just so upset about all this."

"Mrs. Swanz, did Milan have any enemies that you know of? Any ongoing disagreements? Can you think of anyone who might've wanted to harm him?"

The back door swings open. An Amish man steps into the kitchen with a swirl of snow and the smell of cow manure. As he stomps snow from his boots, his eyes travel from me to his wife and back to me.

"What's all this?" he asks in *Deitsch*.

I can tell by the way he's looking at me that he knows I've come bearing bad news.

"Mr. Swanz." I get to my feet and tell him the same thing I told his wife, again leaving out as many details as possible.

"*Mein Gott.*" My God. The Amish man blinks rapidly, then goes to the counter and leans as if he's suddenly not certain of his balance. "*Murdered?* That's crazy. I can't believe it. Are you sure?"

I nod. "I'm sorry."

"Oh, dear Lord," he mutters.

"Mr. Swanz, I know this is a shock, but I'm trying to figure out what happened to your son and I need to ask you some questions."

Orla Swanz removes his barn coat, then crosses to the table, drapes it over the back of a chair, and sinks into it. For a moment, he looks as if he's going to throw up.

I divide my attention between the two of them. "Do either of you know of anyone who might've wanted to harm your son?"

Orla shakes his head. "I can't think of a soul who'd want to do something bad to him," he says.

Ella Mae sets her hand over her husband's, gives it a pat. "What about those people over to the cabinet shop?" she asks.

I recall Bertha Swanz mentioning Milan's former workplace and my interest stirs. "Are you talking about Milan's former employer?"

"They treated him poorly," Orla says.

"Milan liked to work with his hands," Ella Mae says proudly. "Made us some nice furniture back in the day." She gestures to the cabinets. "Made these for us, too. Installed them. He was good at it."

"What kind of problem did he have at the cabinet shop?" I ask.

"They were always accusing him of things he didn't do," the Amish woman snaps.

Orla raises his eyes to mine and nods. "They had a fire out there a few months back. Accused Milan of setting it. He didn't, of course."

"It was an electrical fire is what it was." Ella Mae huffs. "They got caught using electricity. Didn't want to fess up, and they sure didn't want the bishop finding out, so they said it was a kerosene heater and blamed Milan for it."

I jot the central points, make a note to visit the cabinet shop and fire marshal. "Who exactly blamed Milan?" I ask.

"Old man Stutzman, I reckon. That brute son of his. *Hochmut.*" She spits out the word. High-minded person.

"Do you have their names?" I ask.

"Gideon owns the place," Orla tells me. "He's decent from what I can tell. Noah Stutzman is his son."

"Noah's a mean one," Ella Mae adds. "Fancies himself the boss. Made life hard for Milan."

"Milan was one of their best cabinetmakers," Orla says. "Heard they lost some business after they let him go."

"Did Milan have a cell phone?"

Orla nods. "Called him once or twice down to the shanty." He recites the number from memory. I write it down.

"Did Milan have a best friend?" I ask. "A coworker maybe? Or childhood friend? Someone he might've confided in if he was having any problems?"

The couple stare at me as if they're at a loss—and all too aware it is a question they should have been able to answer readily. After a moment, Ella Mae jerks her head. "He was tight with Clarence Raber,

I think. They grew up together. Played together as boys. Worked together for a time."

I write down the name. "Were they close?"

Orla begins to answer, but Ella Mae interrupts him. "They were like brothers when they were youngsters," she says. "Clarence thought highly of Milan. Far as I know they were still friends."

"Does Clarence still live in the area?" I ask.

Orla takes it from there. "Last I heard Clarence was working down to the grain elevator in Coshocton."

Ella Mae pulls a tissue from her pocket and blots her eyes. "Going to be heartbroken when he finds out about Milan. They was close as boys can be. Loved each other like brothers, I tell you. Brothers."

CHAPTER 5

I roll to a stop at Dogleg Road to see that the Holmes County Sheriff's Office has blocked the intersection. I lower my window and flash my shield at the deputy standing guard and he waves me through. I spot Tomasetti's Tahoe as I park behind the BCI crime scene van. I've just gotten out when someone calls out to me.

"Chief!"

I glance over my shoulder to see Tomasetti striding toward me. Despite the circumstances, the sight of him sends a small thrill up the center of my back.

We meet next to his Tahoe. I see him glance toward the trees where the lights of the crime scene team flicker. There's another deputy walking toward the tree line, but his back is to us. Leaning close, Tomasetti brushes his lips against mine.

"You're a sight for sore eyes," he says.

"You, too." I kiss him back, take in the familiar scent of his after-shave, the smell that is distinctively his.

Sighing, he straightens, takes a step back. "You know this is highly inappropriate between a police chief and BCI agent."

"I won't tell if you don't."

A smile whispers across his features, but he sobers quickly, slips back into professional mode as he looks toward the crime scene. "How did the notification go?"

I recap my conversations with Bertha Swanz and the parents. "I got a bit of an odd vibe."

"How so?"

"Neither his ex-wife nor his parents seemed terribly broken up when I told them about Swanz."

His gaze narrows on mine. "Seems odd."

"I thought so, too. I mean, it's not unusual for the Amish to be a little more reserved, but in this case they seemed almost . . . aloof. Granted, Swanz and his wife were divorced, but for his parents to be so subdued. It was strange."

"Especially since you got similar reactions from both parties," he says.

"I'm getting the impression Swanz's relationships were complicated."

"How so?"

"Evidently, he had some problems with his employer." I tell him about the fire and Swanz being terminated. "There's a best friend, Clarence Raber down in Coshocton, who might be helpful to talk to."

I notice the work lights set up on the gravel pullover. "You guys find anything?"

"I think we've got tire-tread imprints."

"You know Mona and Skid and I were parked on the shoulder."

"We marked their tracks as well as yours straightaway." He motions toward the work lights. "A little farther down, there's a short two-track with enough room for a vehicle to pull nose-in. Agent spotted tire impressions there when we did the grid search. One of the techs is trying to cast them now."

"Snow probably isn't helping."

"Doubt if we'll be able to get a decent plaster, but worth a shot."

I want to see the crime scene. I want to walk it. Study every square inch of it. I want to know what's being done, what's been found. If there's anything new. I have enough experience to know that during this early phase of the investigation it's extremely important to limit the number of people allowed.

"I'm going to run by the cabinet shop where Milan Swanz worked." I need to speak to Clarence Raber, too, but in light of the suspicious fire and termination, his employer comes first. "Do you have time to run over there with me?"

"Not much to do here until the scene is processed. Evidence is being couriered and expedited, but we're still going to have to wait for it."

"In that case, I'll drive."

• • •

The village of Killbuck is a scenic twenty-minute drive from Painters Mill. Stutzman's Cabinetry and Woodworking is located on a side street just off of US 62 due east of the village proper.

I park in the gravel lot and we head inside. The workshop is housed in a newish steel building. The main entrance is a large overhead door that's been closed against the cold and snow. Next to it, a sign above the smaller main door reads OFFICE/CUSTOMER SERVICE, so we go through.

We enter a small office with a plywood floor, cheaply paneled walls, and a wood desk straight out of the 1980s. A matronly-looking Amish woman wearing a navy cardigan over a wine-colored dress looks up at us from her place at the desk, gives my uniform a quick once-over. "Can I help you?"

I have my shield at the ready. "I'm the police chief in Painters Mill," I tell her. "Is the owner or manager around?"

"Is there a problem?"

She seems more curious than concerned, so I don't elaborate. "We just need a few minutes of their time."

Never taking her eyes from us, she picks up an old yellow rotary-type phone, uses a pencil to dial a couple of numbers, and speaks into the mouthpiece. "Mr. Stutzman, please come to the office."

Her voice echoes over a speaker system in another part of the building. Behind her, a large plate-glass window looks into a busy workshop where a dozen or so Amish men stand at workbenches or are bent over pneumatic saws. Though the door that opens to the shop is closed, I can hear the hiss and sigh of air tools.

I'm thinking about helping myself to a cup of coffee at the coffee station in the corner when the door swings open. I've never met Gideon Stutzman, but Tomasetti pulled up his information during the drive and I recognize him right away. He's fifty-three years old. Married and resides here in Killbuck. Wearing a charcoal-colored barn coat over a blue work shirt and suspenders, he's short of stature with a wiry build and a too-bright smile that's probably reserved for customers.

As he closes the door behind him, I see him take in my uniform and his smile falls. "Can I help you?" he asks.

"Mr. Stutzman, we'd like to ask you some questions if you have a few minutes."

His eyes flick to Tomasetti, who is holding out his ID, and then he jabs a thumb toward the workshop. "One of my guys do something wrong?"

"No, sir."

"Well, I got a few minutes." The Amish man nods at the woman. "We'll be in my office."

As he leads us through the door and into the workshop, the noise level increases to just below deafening. The tat-tat-tat of a nail gun. The whirr of a saw. The hiss of air tools. The smells of fresh-cut lumber and the oily tang of wood stain hang in the air.

We pass by battered wooden shelves, an array of ancient-looking tools—handsaws, hatchets, and scythes—neatly arranged by type and size. "If your son is available," I say amicably, "I think it would be helpful if he joined us."

Nodding, Stutzman puts two fingers to his mouth and emits a loud whistle. "Noah!"

Across the room, a bear-size Amish man straightens, takes our measure, and shoots us a thumbs-up.

Stutzman stops at an industrial-type door with a glass panel embedded with security wire. A punch-card time clock is mounted on the wall, reminding me once again that the business is Amish owned.

Stutzman ushers us inside. "A little quieter in here." He motions us into chairs adjacent to his desk. "You guys look kind of serious. I'm thinking you're not here to buy cabinets." He settles into the chair at a beat-up metal desk.

"I understand Milan Swanz worked for you a while back," I begin.

"Milan Swanz." The Amish man grimaces as if he's bitten into something sour. "Is this about the fire?"

"You know what happened?" I ask, surprised.

His eyes narrow. "How could I not know about it? It's my business that burned down."

Realizing we're not talking about the same incident, I clarify. "Mr. Stutzman, Milan Swanz was killed last night."

"Oh." He recoils with so much force that his chair scoots back a little. "Well, I'll be. I didn't know." His brows knit. "How'd it happen?"

"We believe he was murdered," I say.

50

"Holy cow!"

"What can you tell me about Mr. Swanz's time here at the cabinet shop?" I ask.

"He worked here a couple years, I guess." He assumes a pained countenance. "Milan was good with his hands. He knew his wood, too. Knew his tools. But there were some problems."

"What kind of problems?" Tomasetti asks.

"Well, he didn't get along with the other guys." Stutzman shrugs. "I mean, there were no fights or any such thing. He just hit people the wrong way." He pauses as if he's getting warmed up. "And while Milan was good with his hands and all, he didn't have a very good work ethic. He missed a lot of work. Came in late. He was a drinker, I think. That's the one thing I can't abide. I put up with it for a time, thinking he might pull out of it. But you got to be able to count on people. I got a business to run."

"Is that why you fired him?" Tomasetti asks.

Stutzman gives him a steady look. "Final straw came the day I sent him out to deliver cabinets to a builder down to Coshocton County. Milan got into an argument with the customer, if you can believe it. Almost cost me that sale and it was a big one. I fired him the next day."

"How did he take it?" I ask.

He tightens his mouth, reluctant to answer, but acquiesces. "Cussed me up one side and down the other. Demanded his check. I know a man's job is a serious thing and getting fired like that can hurt his pride, but I never seen anyone get so riled up. Milan had a temper on him."

"Did things get physical?" I ask.

"No."

"Did he threaten you?" Tomasetti asks.

"He might've said a thing or two." It's a typical Amish answer when they don't want to make a negative comment.

"Like what?" Tomasetti asks.

The Amish man shrugs. "Aw, he said I wouldn't get away with it. Said it would come back on me. I didn't think too much about it at the time."

A pregnant silence ensues, goes on too long. Stutzman fidgets, looks down at his hands.

"I understand there was a fire," I say.

"A year ago. Our workshop was in a hundred-year-old barn back then. A lot of dry old wood and she went up like kindling. Took the tools. Equipment. Everything."

"You think Swanz had something to do with it?" Tomasetti asks.

Expression grim, Stutzman looks from Tomasetti to me. "I'll not speak poorly of an Amish brother. Not one who's died. Even an excommunicated one."

Another typical Amish response. One that's drilled into the heads of children from the time they're old enough to understand. "If you don't have anything good to say about someone, don't say anything at all."

Especially to an Englischer.

"All we need is the truth, Mr. Stutzman," I say quietly. "We're not looking for gossip or anything like that."

"Well." Shaking his head, he continues with a reluctance that's palpable. "After the fire, the Amish came, like they always do. They built this here building. Put their money together and paid for some of the equipment we'd lost. God saw us through."

"Did you go to the police with your suspicions about Swanz?" I ask.

"I didn't have any kind of proof." His eyes skate away from mine. "Fire marshal said a kerosene heater started the fire. Someone left a jacket on the back of their chair, which was left too close to the heater. Fabric caught and there you go."

I hear the door latch click. I glance over my shoulder to see the man

Stutzman had whistled at earlier standing in the doorway, looking at us. He's wearing a blue work shirt, dark trousers, and suspenders. Sawdust covers the brim of his hat.

"This is my son, Noah."

Noah Stutzman is as large as his father is small. I guess him to be about six four, two fifty, with biceps the size of Christmas hams.

Brown eyes land on me and Tomasetti and then flick to Stutzman. "*Was der schinner is letz?*" he says. What in the world is wrong?

"*Kumma inseid,*" the elder Stutzman says patiently. "Close the door."

Noah does as he's told. There's no chair for him, so he goes to the wall, leans against it, and folds his arms at his chest while his father makes introductions and fills him in on the death of Milan Swanz.

I watch the younger Stutzman carefully as his father speaks, looking for any indication that he already knows what happened, but the younger man gives nothing away.

"I wish I could say I'm surprised," he says when his father finishes.

"That Swanz is dead?" I ask. "Or that we're here, talking to you and your *datt* about it?"

His gaze sharpens on me at my *Deitsch* pronunciation, but he doesn't ask. "All I'm saying is Milan rubbed a lot of people the wrong way."

"How's that?" I ask.

"He was loud and mean and didn't much care one way or another."

"Anyone in particular he rubbed the wrong way?" Tomasetti asks.

The large man lifts a shoulder and lets it drop. "Just about everyone he met, I imagine."

"Where were the two of you last night?" Tomasetti asks.

Both men look more surprised than offended by the question.

Noah scoffs, all but rolling his eyes.

"You don't think we done that, do you?" the older man asks.

53

"Just checking you off our list," I put in.

"I was home with my wife," Gideon says.

Noah frowns. "Same. You can check."

After a moment, the younger man looks at his father. "You tell them about the fire?"

The elder Stutzman nods. "Of course I did."

Sighing, Noah turns his attention back to me and Tomasetti. "I reckon he didn't tell you the heater that caught belonged to Milan Swanz, did he?"

"No," Tomasetti tells him. "But we appreciate the information."

•   •   •

"What do you think?" I ask.

"I think we're probably going to have quite a few persons of interest to check into before all is said and done."

Tomasetti and I are sitting in the Explorer. Snow pellets tink lightly against the windshield. Disquiet sits in my belly like a stone. Frowning, I reach for the radio mike and hail Dispatch.

"Get me background checks on Noah and Gideon Stutzman." I spell the first and last names.

"You got it."

"Anything come back on Bertha Swanz?" I ask.

"She's clean, Chief."

"Did Glock get the search warrant?"

"Yes, ma'am."

"Email me the PDF, will you? I'm going to try to swing by there and take a look on my way back to Painters Mill."

"Sending it your way now."

I rack the mike and look at Tomasetti. "Do you have time for a quick look at the victim's residence?"

Before he can answer, my cell phone chirps. I glance at the dash display and see **HOLMES COUNTY CORONER**.

"Hey, Doc."

"We've got our victim cleaned up, Kate. I'm waiting for the forensic pathologist to arrive to assist with the autopsy. I don't know much at this point, but there is some limited information to be gleaned if you have the time."

I feel a creeping dread in my chest, but I quickly suppress it. I don't let myself react because Tomasetti is watching me. "I'm on my way."

CHAPTER 6

Most cops don't attend autopsies. It's rarely necessary in these days of high tech and probably a good rule of thumb anyway, especially if you're squeamish. As a general rule, I don't attend the actual autopsy. I do, however, make it a point to see the victim's body after it has been cleaned up and is in a clinical atmosphere with good lighting and the coroner present to answer questions. The body is an integral piece of evidence. Every aspect of the case begins and ends with the victim.

Of course, there's a human element involved, too. The loss of a life, especially violently and at the hands of another, is profound. A good investigator will never lose sight of that. Whether on a quest for information, a personal ritual, or to pay homage—or any combination thereof—those torturous minutes I spend with the dead establish a connection. It's an important dynamic, because when I walk out of that room I'm not looking into the death of some random stranger. I'm one step closer to knowing them. I've seen what happened to them, the ugliness and the brutality of it. In the days and weeks that

56

follow, as I come to know my victim on an almost intimate level, I will remember that part of them. And I'll be all the more driven to find the person responsible.

Tomasetti and I don't speak as we ride the elevator down to the morgue, which is located in the basement of Pomerene Hospital. He uses those scant seconds to check his cell, his texts and emails. But I know the brunt of his attention is on me. I pretend not to notice and I use that small span of time to shore up and slip a little more securely into my thick-skinned cop persona.

When the floor indicator bell dings, I'm ready. As the door swishes open, Tomasetti brushes his fingertips across my knuckles. "You got this?"

"Yep."

Doc Coblentz's administrative assistant, Carmen, looks up from a desk that's jammed with manila folders, and smiles. She's wearing a suede skirt with brown riding boots and a cream-colored sweater with a coordinating scarf tied at her neck.

"Morning, Chief!" she says brightly. "Agent Tomasetti."

Not for the first time I wonder how someone who spends so much time in close proximity to the dead can remain so upbeat. "I think you're one of the best-dressed women in Painters Mill," I tell her.

"I appreciate that, Chief." Beaming, she laughs. "To be honest with you, I don't get many compliments down here."

"Can't take that too personally," says Tomasetti as we sign in. "Your clientele tend to be pretty quiet."

She hefts another hearty laugh. "Doc's expecting you. Go right in."

We go through the door and enter the medical section of the facility. To my right is an alcove where supplies and sterile biohazard gear are stored. Doc Coblentz's partially glassed-in office is on the left. As usual, the blinds are pulled, but the door stands open. An old Simon

& Garfunkel song pours into the hall and I feel some of the tension leach from my shoulders.

Doc Coblentz sits at a desk that's heaped with folders, binders, and papers, staring at a computer monitor the size of a TV. A bagel loaded with cream cheese and chives is nestled next to a mug that reads I PRESCRIBE COFFEE.

"Hey, Doc," I say by way of greeting.

"That was quick." Blotting his mouth with a napkin, he rises, and the three of us exchange handshakes.

"Thanks for putting a rush on this," I tell him.

He waves off my thanks. "Considering what we're dealing with, I cleared my schedule. The forensic pathologist should be here within the hour." His expression turns thoughtful. "My technician and I photographed and preserved everything, including what was left of the clothing, before cleaning up the victim. I took several dozen X-rays as well as CT scans. In terms of confirming the victim's ID, extracting DNA is not a problem. The teeth are completely intact and there are several unique dental features present."

Though an ID was found on the victim, the possibility that it was planted to mislead the police remains. It's always prudent to confirm a victim's identity via DNA if possible.

"The extensive thermal injuries will prevent us from retrieving fingerprints," he tells us. "I'm confident we'll be able to get toxicology."

"I'll expedite," Tomasetti says.

"Any idea as far as time of death?" I ask.

"We can usually rely on the core body temp to at least come up with a ballpark. Because the decedent in this case suffered significant thermal injuries that may have raised the core body temp, we can't do that. All I can tell you at this point is that there was no livor or rigor present. Rigor begins approximately two hours after death."

I think about the scream or shout that Skid and Mona reported hearing and juxtapose that with the timeline of the discovery of the body and its arrival here at the morgue. "So, it's likely the murder had just happened."

"That's a good guess."

"What about cause of death?" Tomasetti asks.

"Unfortunately, I can't tell you much at this point. Once we get him on the table, we should be able to determine if this individual's death was caused by thermal injuries or smoke inhalation or something else."

Tomasetti sighs. "Wouldn't be the first time someone tried to conceal evidence by burning the body of their victim."

"Or tried to make it appear to be something else," I add.

Grimacing, the doc looks from Tomasetti to me. "As you can imagine, the autopsies of burn victims are extremely difficult and complex, particularly if we're dealing with extensive thermal injury. That's why I called in the forensic pathologist."

He shakes his head. "Much of what I see in here in the morgue is bad. Trauma from car accidents. Suicides. Drowning victims. Bodies that aren't discovered in a timely manner. This one is one of the worst I've seen."

I think about the things we saw at the scene, and I feel the familiar scrape of cold fingertips at the back of my neck. That weird quiver in the pit of my stomach.

The doctor brings his hands together. "I guess the good news is that there's plenty of information to be gleaned preliminarily. Hopefully, you'll find at least some of it helpful as you delve into this case."

"On that note, let's suit up," Tomasetti says.

Doc ushers us to the alcove, where we don disposable gowns, shoe covers, masks, hair caps, and gloves. This is usually the time when Tomasetti cuts loose with some wisecrack or inappropriate one-liner, the cornier the better. Not in a show of disrespect, but to help deal with the stress of what we're about to see. This morning, he's reticent, and it's not until we're leaving the alcove that I'm reminded he lost his wife and children in a fire, to arson. I try to catch his eye as we leave the alcove, but he's ahead of me and reaches the corridor first.

Doc is waiting and takes us past the yellow and black biohazard sign and a plaque that reads MORGUE AUTHORIZED PERSONNEL. At the end of the hall, he pushes through double swinging doors. The autopsy room is brightly lit and uncomfortably cold, with floor-to-ceiling tiled walls. I see a counter lined with boxes of sterile gloves, glass jars, and stainless-steel containers the size of pet bowls. A large scale hangs down from the ceiling. Everything is clinically clean, the pong of formalin and antiseptic strong, but the repellent smell of burned and decaying flesh hovers.

Doc's assistant stands at a counter, his back turned to us as he unwraps sterile tools and sets them on a paper-lined tray. Beneath a large pull-down light, the victim lies on a stainless-steel autopsy table. A blue paper sheet is draped over the body, a dark circle of moisture where some liquid has soaked through.

I'm aware of Tomasetti beside me, and I'm trying not to acknowledge the fact that my heart is beating too fast as we cross to the table.

"Morning, guys," says the technician.

A mask conceals his mouth, but I discern the smile in his eyes and I'm reminded that this is business as usual for him.

Reaching up, Doc adjusts the overhead light. "Put the X-rays up on the board, Jared, will you?"

"Sure." The young man flicks on the X-ray light box mounted on the wall.

The doc goes around to the other side of the gurney, reaches for the drape, and pulls it down. Though I saw the victim at the scene and have a pretty good idea of what to expect, the sight of the body shocks me anew. The flesh is an awful mosaic of black interspersed with purple, red, and pink. The flesh of the face is blackened and peeling. The mouth is open, the pink and brown tongue protruding between teeth that are shockingly white. The sight of it is almost too much to bear.

Next to me, Tomasetti mutters something unintelligible beneath his breath.

"The clothing was removed and preserved," the doc says. "The shoes and belt as well. Everything was couriered to the BCI lab in London, Ohio."

The flesh of the lower torso and extremities is blackened, cracked, and peeling in areas. The upper torso, ostensibly where the skin was farther away from the heat source and protected by clothing, is singed brown and swollen looking with raw, red patches. A strip of skin around the waist, likely where the belt was worn, is intact, but bright pink in color. The feet appear swollen and purplish-pink, as if they were baked inside the shoes. . . .

"Jesus," Tomasetti mutters.

"As you can see, the thermal injuries are severe, particularly on the lower half of the body," Doc Coblentz tells us. "That is likely due to the position of the body and its proximity to the heat source." He looks first at me over the tops of his glasses and then at Tomasetti. "Both of you viewed the victim at the scene, correct?"

"Yes." The word comes out like a croak, so I clear my throat, say it again.

The doc continues. "Preliminarily, I found no evidence of any incised wounds. I did not see any gunshot wounds. Both of those assessments may change once we do the internal examination."

"Sexual assault?" Tomasetti asks.

"We were able to get an anal swab," the doc tells us. "No indication of assault."

"I'm just going to say what all of us are thinking," Tomasetti says. "At the scene, it looked like this guy was tied to that post and burned alive. Dr. Coblentz, do you have any way of knowing if that's what happened? Was this victim burned at the stake? Or was he posed after he was already dead?"

"Without internal examination, I can't answer that," Doc responds. "I can, however, share some observations. Preliminarily, of course." Reaching around behind him, he removes a long wooden swab from a tray and indicates the victim's hands. "As you mentioned, the victim was bound to a wooden post with wire. According to my notes, Kate, you sent the wire to the lab?"

I nod. "Correct."

He shifts the swab to the wrist. "See this?"

I don't want to look, but I do, and for the first time since walking into the room, I see the victim through the eyes of a cop instead of a woman who is nearly overcome with horror.

Doc Coblentz continues. "The flesh *appears* to be cracked, apparently from thermal injury. I believe that is actually an incised wound, ostensibly caused by restraints. I took a look at the radiographs, which I believe will confirm that because there is a fracture of the right radial styloid."

"In layman's terms?" Tomasetti says.

"A small bone that's part of the wrist is broken. Most often that type of fracture happens during a fall or some sports activity." He tightens his mouth. "It's rare, but that kind of fracture has been documented as occurring during handcuffing."

"Or in this case, wire?" I ask.

The doc nods. "Exactly."

Tomasetti narrows his eyes. "So the victim was bound while conscious and struggled with so much force that he broke his wrist?"

Doc Coblentz nods. "Another scenario is that he was bound and then dragged by his wrists."

I glance at Tomasetti. "I didn't see any drag marks."

"We'll take another look." He grimaces. "Doc, if the victim struggled with that much vigor, could that indicate something like panic or pain? That he'd been alive and under extreme duress when the fire was set?"

"That is certainly a feasible theory," Doc Coblentz replies. "During autopsy, we will look for soot from inhaled smoke in the esophagus and respiratory tract. We'll also screen for carboxyhemoglobin levels in the blood. That will tell us if he was breathing during the fire. Even then, I will not be able to tell you if the victim was conscious, only if he was or was not breathing. Sometimes, much can be determined by the amount of soot on the mucous membranes. In this case, however, the thermal injuries are so extensive, we can't see that with the naked eye."

Doc Coblentz turns to his assistant. "Put the X-ray from the C3 vertebra level on the board."

"Sure." His assistant jumps into action, finding the radiograph quickly, and snapping it into place so that the X-ray is visible to all of us.

"The victim also suffered a broken hyoid bone," the doc says.

"Isn't that usually associated with a strangulation?" I ask.

He nods. "It's usually a postmortem finding in victims of strangulation and sometimes hanging."

"Are you saying the victim was strangled first?" Tomasetti asks.

"I cannot explain it. I do know that injury to the hyoid bone is rare. In survivors, it's usually caused by trauma. If I may." Doc rounds the gurney and, with a fresh swab, indicates a shadowed area on the screen. "The hyoid bone is this U-shaped bone situated in the anterior portion of the neck. The angle we're looking at is between the mandible and the thyroid cartilage."

"Is it possible he was struck in the throat area?" I ask.

"Or subdued by something looped around his neck," Tomasetti murmurs.

"Yes and yes." I see the smile in his eyes. "Suffice it to say, I'm hoping to narrow all of this down once we get a more complete picture. That's the best I can do at this point."

• • •

"So, did the killer stage the scene?" Tomasetti poses the question in brainstorming fashion, not expecting an answer, but to put forth a premise. "To conceal evidence? Or somehow muddy the investigation?"

"Or was this some kind of bizarre pseudo-symbolic execution?" I add. "Was he burned at the stake?"

We're standing next to the Explorer in the hospital parking lot. Light snow drifts down from a slate-gray sky. It's cold, but the wind has picked up. Traffic from Wooster Road hisses in the near distance. Despite the chill, neither of us is ready to get in the vehicle. As if by unspoken agreement, we need a few minutes to let the air wash away the remnants of the things we witnessed in the morgue.

"The killer went to a lot of trouble," Tomasetti says, his breaths puffing out in front of him. "He had to dig a posthole. Set the post. That took some time."

"Not an easy task when the ground is frozen," I say. "Unless he had help."

"Something to consider," he tells me. "We'll look at all of it." He pauses. "Do we know where the pallets came from?"

"There's a pallet manufacturer in Millersburg. Pickles is looking into it. So far, no way to tell if these particular pallets were made at that facility or elsewhere."

"This has the hallmarks of something that was planned," he says.

"In advance," I add. "The killer—or killers—were determined."

He nods. "Burning someone at the stake is such a bizarre way to kill someone. Why would anyone go to all that trouble? They could have simply shot him and buried the body. Or weighted it down and tossed it in a lake? Dumped it in a remote area or woods."

"He wanted the body to be found." As I make the statement, I feel something else scratching at the back of my brain.

"To what end? Prove a point? Send a warning? What?"

I'm still thinking about the mentality behind the method of death. "There's something symbolic about burning a person at the stake."

"The European witch trials." He shrugs. "If you look at history, particularly European history, people who were considered heretics were executed that way."

"Dirk Willems was burned at the stake." I say the name even before the thought fully materializes, swing my gaze to Tomasetti's, feel my eyes go wide. "From *Martyrs Mirror*."

Tomasetti arches a brow. "The book?"

"A lot of Amish families have it in their homes," I tell him. "Most do, I would say. It's a huge tome, something like eleven hundred pages, and tells the stories of the persecution of Christians who believed in the doctrine of nonresistance, or pacifism, and adult baptism. Those people were basically the religious predecessors of the Anabaptists."

"You mean the Amish?"

"And the Mennonites and Hutterites. They are three distinct denominations that fall under the Anabaptist umbrella, so to speak."

"That hits a little closer to home." He tilts his head, looks at me a little closer. "I'm not quite up to speed on my Anabaptist history."

I take a moment to fill him in. "The Anabaptist movement began in sixteenth-century Europe during the Reformation. They believed in things like nonresistance or pacifism, separation from the rest of the world, and adult baptism. They were considered heretics and perse- cuted for their beliefs. Hundreds were tortured and executed, includ- ing being hanged, drowned, or burned at the stake." I pause. "Willems was a believer."

"What happened to him?"

"He was captured and imprisoned for his beliefs. But he escaped. While being pursued on foot, he crossed a frozen pond. The man pur- suing him fell through the ice and Willems went back and pulled him out. Willems was recaptured and burned at the stake."

"Light reading for a ten-year-old," he says dryly.

I nudge him with my elbow. "It's a loose connection, but there it is."

"If we were to start building a profile of Swanz's killer," he says slowly. "Let's look at Willems first. He was Amish. He was executed by individuals who did not approve of his religion. If you follow that precept, Swanz's killer would have to be non-Amish."

"Most non-Amish people don't know about Willems."

"True," he says. "In addition to that, the Amish are pacifists."

"They're also human," I say, "which means they're susceptible to all the same weaknesses as the rest of us."

"Including homicidal rage." His brows pull together. "What about an individual or group who has it out for the Amish?"

"Can't see it," I say. "I mean, the whole persecution thing is tough for us to even understand. The Anabaptists were horribly tormented in Europe; they were tortured and murdered. And so they came here for the freedom to worship without persecution. But that was centuries ago and, of course, the world is a different place now. We're tolerant."

"All of that said, there may be something there," he says. "Not only could what happened to Swanz be some sort of reenactment, but there are a lot of Amish and Mennonites in the area."

"It means something to murder an individual in that manner," I say slowly, thinking as I speak. "It makes a statement about the killer. His motive. His mindset."

"You mean aside from his being a crazy son of a bitch?"

I nod. "He'd have to know such an unusual and violent murder would generate a lot of interest. A lot of media coverage."

"A psychopath looking for his fifteen minutes of fame?" Tomasetti frowns when his cell chirps.

He's reaching for it when my own cell erupts. Holding Tomasetti's gaze, I fish it out of my pocket, see HOLMES COUNTY SHERIFF on the display. "Hey, Mike."

"Chief, where you at?"

The urgency in his voice gives me pause. "Just left the morgue."

"Look, one of my deputies just found a second set of tire tracks. There's a two-track off the township road north of where the body was found. It looks like the killer came in that way, not via Dogleg Road."

I tighten my grip on the phone. "Tread marks?"

"I got better than that. The son of a bitch dropped a pair of pliers."

I reach for the door handle, slide into the Explorer, see Tomasetti do the same. "Fingerprints?"

"We can hope. Deputy is personally delivering those pliers to BCI as we speak."

"On my way," I tell him, and disconnect.

•   •   •

Township Road 3423 is a desolate stretch of timeworn asphalt that runs parallel to Dogleg Road, with a three-hundred-yard stretch of woods between. The lights of two sheriff's department cruisers light up the naked treetops. The overgrown pullover is already cordoned off. The BCI crime scene van idles just outside the perimeter. I park behind the van.

Tomasetti and I disembark simultaneously and start toward a deputy who's unrolling a line of yellow tape from tree to fence post to tree in an effort to protect as much of the scene as possible.

"We're not going to be able to get in there." Tomasetti states the obvious as we approach the tape.

"Might be able to get a look if we're lucky," I say.

We stop a few feet from the tape. From where I'm standing, I can see the opening in the trees, demarking the mouth of a trail. In the summertime, raspberries flourish in these woods. I've picked them myself a time or two. Families come here to pick berries or hike along the creek. It's a pretty, private tract, surrounded by eighty-foot-tall trees. At night, teenagers come here to drink. Lovers come to park.

Looking frustrated, Tomasetti sighs. "How well do you know the area?"

"Walked it plenty of times." I fish my cell from my pocket, tap a few keys, and tilt the screen so that Tomasetti can see the map I pulled up. "We're here." I indicate the spot with my index finger. "There's a trail that cuts through the woods and goes all the way to the township road. Probably half a mile or so. Small creek there." I slide my finger slightly right. "Body was found about here."

He gestures to the pullover behind us. "Why would the killer park here, when Dogleg Road is closer to where the victim was burned?"

"More private on this side," I tell him. "Both roads are quiet. Lots of trees for cover. It's part of a floodplain, which means no farms or houses."

"So the killer is likely familiar with the area," he murmurs.

"Or he did his homework."

He raises his gaze from the phone, looks around. "Any idea how the victim spent his last hours?"

"Not yet."

"So let's say the killer brought him here. Parked in that pullover. They got out of the vehicle. At that point, the killer marched or dragged the victim through the woods, along the trail, all the way to the clearing. Once there, he tied the vic to the post. Set the fire."

"Dragging the victim would explain the broken bone in his wrist." I think about that a moment. "If the victim was conscious, how did the killer subdue him? Control him? Did he carry him? Drag him?" Not for the first time I entertain the possibility that there were two of them.

"We also have the broken hyoid bone," he says. "Maybe the killer overpowered him. Strangled him to unconsciousness."

"Tomasetti, if Mona and Skid are right about the scream they heard, the victim was still alive. The killer may have seen them coming and left. Or been on his way out."

"Or watching the victim burn to death," he says darkly.

"If Skid and Mona *did* interrupt him, he probably left in a hurry."

"Might explain the pliers."

"Kate!"

I glance over to see Sheriff Mike Rasmussen slide from his cruiser and stride toward us, his expression grim.

"Anything?" I ask.

The three of us exchange handshakes. "Nothing yet."

"You get a photo of the pliers?" I ask.

"Coming your way." He tugs out his phone, taps a few keys. "They're common fence pliers."

I look down at my cell, study the photo. "A tool anyone who lives in a rural area keeps on hand," I murmur.

"Were they new?" Tomasetti asks. "Rusted?"

"New, I'd say," Rasmussen tells him.

"So the killer may have purchased them recently," I say.

"You got someone looking into the pliers?" Tomasetti asks.

"We're stretched tight." Rasmussen looks at me and raises his brows.

"I'll put someone on it." I hit the speed dial for Dispatch.

My first-shift dispatcher, Lois, picks up on the second ring. I can tell by her tone the station is a madhouse. I don't ask. "I'm emailing you a JPEG of pliers," I tell her. "I need to know where they were purchased. Who's on?"

"Everyone."

"Tell T.J. to check with the hardware store here in Painters Mill. Farm store, too. Send Pickles up to Millersburg. Tell him to check with Walmart and Tractor Supply while he's there. Any feedstores in the area. I need the names of customers who purchased a shovel or posthole digger, wire, and/or fence pliers in the last two months."

"You got it."

I glance at the time, feel the thump of urgency against my chest. "Is anyone there at the station?" I ask.

She pauses as if looking around. I hear the din of voices in the background. The chime of the switchboard. "Mona's still here."

"Tell her to meet me at Swanz's place." I tell her the address. "I'm headed that way now."

CHAPTER 7

Every homicide investigation possesses a unique personality, but there's one theme all of them share: urgency. The sense that everything should have been done yesterday. It is the lifeblood of forward motion and pulses through a cop's veins like mercury. The stakes are high, there's no room for error, and you sure as hell don't waste time on anything extraneous. You do what needs to be done, you move on to the next thing, and you'd damn well better do all of it with forethought and caution.

We're nine hours into the case and not one of my five W's has been answered. Who? What? When? Where? Or why? I have no suspect. I know little about my victim, who was close to him, or how he spent his final hours. I don't know for certain exactly where he was killed and I have no idea what the motive was.

One step at a time, Kate. . . .

The trailer home where Milan Swanz lived is located on a narrow track off of Township Road 104. The clock on my dash tells me it's four minutes past noon when I make the turn onto the gravel drive. A 1980s-era double-wide sits in a weed-riddled lot covered with patches of snow. There are no vehicles in sight. No visible tire tracks. No lights on inside.

Eyeing the windows for movement, I kill the engine and pick up my mike. "Ten-twenty-three," I say, letting Dispatch know I've arrived on scene.

"Roger that."

"Mona, ETA?"

"Six minutes, Chief."

"Ten-four."

Bracing for the cold, I get out and start toward the mobile home. In the summertime, this area is probably beautiful, surrounded by sixty-foot-tall trees with a good-size pond at the rear. In the dim winter light, the structure looks abandoned. The scene is as dismal as a junkyard. The battered gray siding is striped with rust. The skirting at the base is hit-or-miss. A few feet away, a charcoal grill lies on its side, ashes spilling onto the ground. The back side of a riding mower sticks out from beneath a blue tarp. Half a dozen tires lean against the base of the wood deck. I see two fifty-gallon drums shot full of holes, a five-gallon bucket, and a satellite dish that's been broken in half.

I take the steps to the front deck, open the screen door, and knock. "Painters Mill Police Department!" I call out.

Stepping aside, I wait, listening for movement. The only sound comes from the snow softly hitting the roof.

"Police department!" I knock again, using the heel of my hand. "Come out and talk to me!"

I wait a full minute before trying the knob. I'm not surprised when it turns easily. I push open the door and let it swing wide. The stink of cigarettes and two-day-old garbage greets me. There's a wall switch to my right, so I flip it on. Yellow light shines from a ceiling fixture. There's a retro kitchen to my right. Almond-colored Formica counters piled with dishes, a cereal box, an accumulation of mail, and a bag of chips. A newish fridge that's too small for its space huddles in the corner.

"Painters Mill Police Department!" I call out. "Is anyone home? Show yourself! Come out and talk to me!"

No answer.

I walk into the small living room, leaving the door open for not only light, but fresh air. Gold carpet beneath my boots. A peninsula-type bar of sorts to my right separates the living room from the kitchen. A good-size TV sits atop an entertainment center. Floor lamp next to a recliner. Coffee table covered with what looks like more mail, a can of Budweiser lying on its side. A brown sofa sits beneath the window, a wadded-up blanket on the center cushion.

I take it all in and find myself looking for signs of a struggle. At this point, I don't know if Swanz was killed at the scene or elsewhere, his body moved. I don't know how much time has passed since he was last here.

Resting my hand on my .38, I cross the living room and start down the hallway that I'm assuming leads to the bedrooms and bathroom. I spot the switch on the wall, flip it on. Nothing.

"Police department!" The last thing I want to do is surprise some sound sleeper who just happens to have a shotgun next to his bed. But there's no response and I'm pretty sure I'm alone.

My senses hum as I pass by a small bedroom. One window. A ratty-looking mattress on the floor. No sheets. I enter, go to the closet, open the door. Nothing of interest. Backing from the room, I continue down the hall, my boots muted against the carpet. Bathroom to my left. The smells of mildew and dirty towels offend my nose as I cross to the cabinet, open it. Shave cream. Box of condoms. Disposable razor. Bottle of Tylenol.

Back in the hall, I pass by an exterior door to my right and enter a larger bedroom at the rear of the trailer. The bed is a tangle of mismatched sheets and blankets. The smells of unwashed linens and dirty hair poke at me as I go to the closet. A few shirts. Sneakers. A pair of boots. Jeans wadded up on the floor.

More relaxed now that I know I'm alone, I go back to the living room and look around. There's no sign of a struggle. Nothing broken or tipped over or out of place. Just a messy house kept by an unmarried guy. Pulling on my duty gloves, I go back to the kitchen. There's a small dining table. A vintage toaster on the counter. I pick up the mail, page through, notice the post date from two days ago. Most look like bills, a few marked "Past Due" and left unopened. I open the nearest drawer, find an array of mismatched flatware and utensils. Below that, a stack of kitchen towels. In the next drawer I find two well-used beer koozies from McNarie's bar. I stare at them a moment, wondering if Swanz was a regular, and I make a mental note to check.

In the cabinets, I find a dozen or so thrift-store dishes. Canned goods. Boxed pasta meals. Before I open the fridge, I glance out the window. No sign of Mona.

In the living room, I check the coffee table first. More unopened mail. State Bank of Painters Mill. Past-due bill from the local gas company. A few advertisements. Classified section of a newspaper. Nothing.

Pounding on the door draws my attention. I look over to see Mona standing in the doorway. "Did you find the body in the freezer yet?" she calls out.

"Striking out, mostly." Straightening, I go to her. "I thought you were going to go home and get some sleep."

"Too much going on." She gives me a sheepish grin. "Didn't want to miss any action."

"I'm glad you decided to stay."

I recap what I've found so far. "I'm getting the impression Swanz was here recently—say twenty-four to forty-eight hours ago." I motion toward the living room. "I'm going to finish up here. There's a shed outside. I could use a hand."

"No problem," she says. "I'll take the shed. Want me to check under the trailer, too?"

"Sure."

Her brows pull together. "We looking for anything in particular?"

I shake my head. "Hopefully, we'll know it when we see it."

"Gotcha."

Turning, she crosses the deck and trots down the steps.

I go back to the sofa, remove the cushions, run my hands into the creases. Crumbs and specks of dried grass. A lone dollar bill. Nothing. Nothing. Nothing.

Sighing, I look around, take the hall back to the main bedroom. In the closet, I pick up the boots, but there's nothing tucked away inside. I pull a shoebox off the overhead shelf. Empty. I see an Amish-type hat. Two baseball caps. A belt dangles from a wire hanger.

I go to the bed, lift the mattress, but there's nothing there. There are built-in drawers next to the closet, so I check them next. Empty. Frustrated, glad that I'm nearly finished, I go to the nightstand, kneel, open the top drawer. A deck of cards. A wrinkled edition of *Sports Illustrated.* Box of tissues. Eyeglasses.

I tug open the next drawer. A spiral-bound notebook. A pen. A lightbulb. I pick up the pad, page through—and my hand freezes. Most of the pages are blank, but toward the middle, I come upon half a dozen addresses scrawled in blue ink. I skim the addresses. The final one at the bottom of the page stops me cold.

14652 TOWNSHIP ROAD 16

PAINTERS MILL

I stare at the address, my brain trying to make sense of it. It's the address of the farm where I grew up. My brother, Jacob, inherited it when our parents passed away. Why would Milan Swanz have my brother's address written in a notebook? Who do the other five addresses belong to? What is the connection to Swanz?

Chances are, this is nothing more than some benign list. Maybe these people bought cabinets from the shop where Swanz worked. Maybe Swanz did some casual labor for them.

Pulling my cell from my pocket, I photograph the page. Then I pluck an evidence bag from my duty belt, drop the notebook into it, and start toward the door.

•   •   •

The police station hums with barely contained chaos when I arrive. A NewsCenter 7 van idles in my spot, forcing me to park across the street. On the sidewalk in front of the station, a young woman in a snazzy yellow coat faces a bearded cameraman, sleek microphone in hand as if they're about to go live.

Spotting me, she catches the eye of her cameraman and charges. "Chief Burkholder! Can you tell us anything about the murder? Have you IDed the victim? Is it true that he was burned at the stake?"

I offer her a tight smile, but I don't stop walking. "Press release in a few minutes. Stay tuned, okay?"

I push through the door to find a dozen people jammed into the small reception area. My team has already arrived for the briefing I was supposed to start twenty minutes ago.

"Chief Burkholder!" I spot Tom Skanks from the Butterhorn Bakery pushing through the crowd, his eyes on me. Joe Neely from Mocha Joe's is gesturing animatedly to a reporter I recognize from a Dover radio station. Lois stands at the reception desk, a headset clamped over her head, a landline pressed to one ear, a cell phone to the other. She looks at me wild-eyed, so I head her way first.

"Chief! Kate! Hold up!"

I turn to see Mayor Auggie Brock rush toward me. He's breathless, his hair mussed, tie askew. The urge to keep going is strong, but I stop and turn to him. "Auggie."

He doesn't bother with niceties. "A man burned at the stake?" He whispers the words with the drama of a high school girl, as if everyone in the entire room doesn't already know. "Are you shitting me? Did that seriously happen?"

"Unfortunately, that's what it looks like," I tell him.

"Do you know who the victim is?"

I tell him.

"Holy shit, Kate."

"Auggie, I'm about to brief my officers now. I'm late. Look, you should probably come to the briefing."

"Aw, hell." He looks around. "What about all this press?"

"They can wait." I glance toward Lois, notice the blush of stress in her cheeks. My officers are gathered in the hall outside the meeting room. "You should probably say a few words."

He makes a sound of incredulity. "I have no clue what's going on."

"Welcome to the club."

He frowns at me. "Kate, people are freaked out about this. People are talking about frickin' witches. Could this be the work of that devil-worshipping cult that's down in McConnelsville? Do you have a suspect?"

"We're working on it." Over the top of his head, I make eye contact with Lois.

"My phone has been ringing off the hook since six A.M.," he hisses. "Janine Fourman called and said tourists are canceling B and B reservations left and right—"

"Nothing I can do about that," I cut in.

"You called in BCI?"

"You know I did. Sheriff's department, too."

Someone shouts Auggie's name. When he turns, I make my escape and head directly for Lois. "Hey," I say.

Mouthing a curse, she glances my way, gives a tight smile as she speaks into her mouthpiece. "Ma'am, if you see a prowler, call 911," she tells her caller.

I try not to notice the sweat beaded on her forehead as she shoves a handful of pink message slips at me. "Sorry," she mouths, and makes a hand signal for crazy.

I page through messages as I stride toward my office. Quickly, I unlock the door, slip inside, and take the drastic measure of locking it. I spend two minutes pounding out a press release and an abbreviated version of what we know so far. It's a rough draft, scant on details, and filled with poor grammar and abbreviations because I'm rushed. Lois has enough experience to edit before broadcasting it. I make a few notes at the bottom of the document, asking her to set up a tip hotline, and I hit Send. Then I'm out of my chair, through the door, and striding down the hall toward the "war room."

Through the doorway, I see Skid sitting at the table, nursing a grande-size coffee from Mocha Joe's.

"Hey, Chief," he says as I enter.

The small room is crowded, ten degrees too warm, and smells of aftershave, body odor, and coffee. Sheriff Mike Rasmussen is sprawled on a chair next to my podium, talking animatedly into his cell. I spot Tomasetti leaning against the wall, doing the same, but his eyes are on me, and we exchange a secret smile. Glock, Pickles, and T.J. are seated across from Skid. I see a detective with the Ohio State Highway Patrol. My second-shift and floater dispatchers, Jodie and Margaret, are embroiled in a head-to-head conversation. No sign of Mona, so I'm assuming she's finishing up the search of Swanz's residence.

Taking my place at the half podium, I tap the mike some misguided soul has already turned on. "Heads up."

The room quiets. "We've only got a few minutes, so let's make them count." I set down my notebook, glance at my barely legible notes, and flick off the mike. "Here's what we know so far. Painters Mill resident Milan Swanz was killed last night at approximately three A.M. in the woods due south of Dogleg Road. He was thirty-six years old. Amish, but recently excommunicated. Divorced. Father of four. He had a misdemeanor arrest record, which includes drunk and disorderly. Next of kin have been notified."

I recite Swanz's address, the names of his ex-wife and parents, and recap the pertinent segments of my conversations with them. "Swanz was unemployed. He'd been fired from his job about a year ago." I name the cabinet shop. "I do not know if his termination is related to this case in any way, but there was a fire at the shop, which was ruled accidental by the fire marshal. The owners, Gideon and Noah Stutzman, were suspicious of Swanz." I look at Rasmussen. "Any chance your department can get with the fire marshal and take a look at that?"

"Consider it done," the sheriff says.

I nod. "We will not have the cause or manner of death until after the autopsy, but I think it's safe to assume this was a homicide. Preliminarily, it is believed that Swanz was tied to a post and burned. According to the coroner, preliminarily, the victim suffered severe thermal injuries and possibly asphyxiation caused by strangulation. The victim also suffered a broken wrist, possibly from struggling against the wire binding his wrists, or because he had been dragged."

"Hell of a way to go," Pickles mutters.

The door opens and the mayor slinks in. I nod at him as he takes his place in the nearest chair and I continue. "I searched the victim's residence earlier." I recite the address. "Officer Kurtz is there now with a warrant and finishing up. There was no sign of a struggle. Nothing amiss. Inside the trailer home, I *did* find a list of five addresses that may or may not be related to the case."

"Local?" Glock asks.

I nod. "I'll get the names of the property owners and take a look at all of them for a connection." I glance at Tomasetti. "Might be a good idea to get a CSU to the residence to process."

"You got it," he says.

"Mike." I look at the sheriff. "Anything on the canvass?"

"Deputies checked four homes within a three-mile radius of the location where the body was discovered," he says. "None of the homeowners saw anything unusual as far as vehicles or buggies or pedestrians."

"What about CCTV cameras?" I ask. "Any game cams in the area?"

"None of the homeowners have security cams. We did look at two game cams. Nothing but white-tailed deer and skunk."

I turn my attention to Tomasetti. "Any luck on the tire-tread imprints you guys found at the scene?"

"No go," he says. "Too much snow and too wet to plaster."

"Lovely." I look at Pickles. "Did you check with retailers on the pliers found at the scene, posthole digger, and/or shovel?"

The old man is at the ready. "I got seven names from the Walmart in Millersburg. Six more from Tractor Supply. I'm about halfway through my list. So far, I got nothing."

I turn my attention to T.J. and raise my brows.

"I got three names from the hardware store here in Painters Mill," he tells me. "Two more from Quality. Two didn't pan. Still checking the other three."

"Keep on it." I scan the faces in the room. All of them have been up most of the night, tromping through snow and cold and wet, and yet I've not heard a single complaint. I can tell by the energy in the room, the air of restlessness, that they're itching to get back to work.

"A couple more items," I say. "According to Swanz's parents, he had a cell phone, which was not found on his person or at the scene. Now that we've searched his residence, I think it's safe to assume that cell phone is missing."

Tomasetti pipes up. "You called the number?"

"Goes directly to voicemail." I recite the number.

He taps it into his cell. "Carrier?"

"I don't know."

"I'll figure it out," he says. "Any other devices?"

"Not that we've found. Nothing at the house."

"Vehicle?"

"According to his ex, Swanz drove a 2014 Ford Mustang. It's not at the residence. Not at the scene. At this point, we have to consider it missing as well."

"We'll put out a BOLO." The Ohio State Highway Patrol detective speaks up for the first time.

"Do we know how Swanz spent his final hours?" Glock asks. "Or who was the last person to see him alive?"

Both are questions I feel I should have been able to answer by now.

"No." I look down at my notes. "His ex-wife claims she hasn't seen him for a week. His parents say they saw him about a month ago."

"Seems like a long time for an Amish family," Rasmussen says.

"We have to bear in mind that he was excommunicated," I tell him. "It's my understanding that Swanz liked to go to bars and he liked women. Might be worth checking." I give Glock a pointed look. "Go to the Brass Rail. Talk to whoever's there. Find out if/when Swanz was there. If he's a regular. Who he hung out with."

He gives me a mock salute.

"T.J.," I say. "Same for Miller's Tavern."

"Stay away from the hot wings." Skid pats his belly.

A round of chuckles ensues, but it's short-lived. Recalling the koozies I found in Swanz's trailer, I decide to swing by the remaining bar on my way to see my brother. "I'll hit McNarie's," I tell them.

"Chief." Auggie uses the folder in his hand to fan his face. "There are all sorts of crazy rumors floating around town about witches and cults in the area. Is that something our citizens need to be worried about? If not, how do I reassure them?"

"There is a known pseudo-cult down near McConnelsville," the Ohio State Highway Patrol detective puts in. "Don't know much about them, but they're on our radar."

I look around, realize I'm out of personnel to whom I can assign the task. "I'll ask Mona to look into it," I say. "See if we can find any connections."

The state highway patrol detective rattles the report in his hand. "One more thing, Chief Burkholder. Spillman that came over indicated the body was discovered by two of your officers." His brows knit. "The crime scene is sort of an out-of-the-way location, especially in the middle of the night. Did a citizen call it in? Or did your officers just happen upon the scene?"

I look at Skid and nod, giving him the floor. "Skidmore?"

Something in the way his gaze shifts away from mine gives me pause. Skid's not shy. He doesn't mind the limelight and will be the first to cut up or utter some uncouth joke, even during the most serious of situations.

"I was on patrol," he says, then assumes a sheepish countenance. "Got out to take a leak. Officer Kurtz must have seen my taillights and rolled up behind me. We got out to talk and we heard what sounded like a scream or shout. At that point, we also discerned smoke. So, we scaled the fence and immediately observed the fire through the trees. Within a minute, we spotted the victim and made efforts to extinguish the fire."

In the seconds that follow, half a dozen questions occur to me, and I can't help but wonder what they were doing in that area at that hour. I don't say anything because we've more important concerns to deal with at the moment.

"We'll have statements from both officers available end of day," I tell the detective.

I've been so absorbed in the case, I hadn't realized until now that not all of the details add up. For one thing, it's against department policy for any officer to pull over to take a leak, even on a back road at three o'clock in the morning. And what the hell was Mona doing there? Even if she'd stayed late and was on her way home, she would have been traveling in the opposite direction.

•   •   •

The press conference is an overcrowded free-for-all of shouted questions, outlandish theories, an overzealous media, and the flashing of cell phone camera lights, all of it fielded by me, Mayor Brock, Tomasetti, and Sheriff Rasmussen. The mayor is still speaking when I make my exit and steal away to my office.

It doesn't take long for me to find the names that go along with the addresses I found in the notebook at Swanz's trailer. The first are Amish bishop David Troyer and his wife. The second is Noah Stutzman, the son of Swanz's former employer. The third address belongs to Monroe Hershberger. I don't know him personally, but recall he's a well-thought-of Amish elder here in Painters Mill. The fourth address is for Swanz's neighbor Lester Yoder. The man who accused Swanz of burning his cornfield. The final address, of course, belongs to my brother and sister-in-law, Jacob and Irene. I know Swanz had disputes with Stutzman and Yoder. Since Swanz had been excommunicated, it's likely he was not a fan of Bishop Troyer, either. If memory serves me, I believe Monroe Hershberger is one of the *Diener* of the Amish church district. If that's the case, he may have been involved with Swanz's excommunication as well.

So why is my brother's address included? Did he have a beef with Swanz?

"Only one way to find out," I mutter, and reach for my keys.

CHAPTER 8

The farm where I grew up isn't quite pretty. The fence along the driveway needs paint. The ground surrounding the barn and outbuildings is trampled to mud. The barn could use a new roof. But this place is rich in memories, some good, some bad, and when I was a kid, it was my universe. As I drive up the long gravel lane, past the cherry tree I helped my *datt* plant when I was twelve, it strikes me that I've finally come to terms with not only my past and the things that happened here, but the relationship I share with my Amish family.

I park in the gravel area at the rear of the house. I sit in the Explorer for a moment and watch the snow flutter down from a brooding sky. The cop inside me is cognizant of the ticking of the clock. The part of me that remembers so well what it was like to be that Amish girl who never quite fit in relishes being surrounded by the place that will always be the foundation of me.

I take the narrow sidewalk to the back door and knock. It's quiet; my nephews are likely still in school. The cattle and hogs have long since been fed. The sound of boots on the wood-plank floor sounds just inside the door and then my brother is there, looking at me as if his own memories aren't too distant, and yet the woman standing before him is a stranger he doesn't quite recognize.

"Katie." He looks past me, taking in the lightly falling snow, and then he steps back. "*Kumma inseid.*" Come inside.

Taking off my hat, I follow him through the mudroom and into the large kitchen. A welcome blast of heat from the stove hits me in the face as I enter. My sister-in-law, Irene, stands at the sink, washing a big Dutch oven. She looks at me over her shoulder and smiles. "Katie!" she says. "How's married life treating you? My goodness, you're right on time for date pudding and coffee. I just made both if you've got the time."

"I'm afraid I'm here on official business," I say to her, but I'm looking at Jacob. "Do you have a few minutes?"

He studies me intently, as if he discerns something in my eyes. He addresses his wife in *Deitsch*. "We'll be in the big room," he says.

I follow him into the living room, where a woodstove crackles and pops from its place next to the window. A gas-powered floor lamp shines brightly in the corner. All of it giving the room a cozy, well-used countenance.

"You look tired." He motions me to the sofa. "And troubled."

"Have you heard about what happened to Milan Swanz?" I ask as I take a seat.

He nods. "Heard about it down to the feedstore this morning. Everyone's talking about it, especially the Amish." Holding my gaze, he settles into the armchair. "Is it true?"

I nod. "How well did you know him?"

"Not well." He shrugs, nonchalant, but looks away a little too quickly. "You know how it is when you're Amish. Everyone knows everyone."

I stare at him, not liking his answer—or his demeanor.

"Did you have any business with him?" I ask.

"Milan fell on hard times for a while. After he lost his job, you know. I hired him to help me with the cross fence. He helped me dig postholes, drive T-posts, and stretch wire." He shrugs. "Three or four days of work. That's it."

I nod, watching him carefully. "Did you have any problems with him?"

"No."

"Was he a good worker?"

"Milan liked his breaks. Smoked cigarettes." He offers a half smile. "Not exactly a workhorse, but he got the job done."

"Jacob, did you have any disagreements with him?" I ask. "Any arguments or misunderstandings?"

"No."

"What about Irene?"

"Of course not."

"When did he work for you?"

"A week or so ago, I think."

"For how long?"

"Four days." He raises a shoulder, lets it drop. "When the fence was finished, I had nothing else for him to do and he moved on."

"Any problems with pay? Anything like that?"

His eyes narrow. "Why all of these questions?"

I look past him and through the fogged-up glass and see a dozen or so head of cattle gathered at the round bale of hay, their backs covered with snow. "I searched Milan Swanz's residence this morning," I tell him. "There was a list of addresses. Swanz had had disputes with almost everyone on the list."

"I don't see what that has to do with me."

"Your address is on the list."

For the first time he looks surprised. "I don't see why that would be so surprising," he says. "Milan worked for me."

I nod, watching him closely. He gives me nothing. "You know Milan was excommunicated," I say.

"Of course I do."

"Bishop Troyer's address was on the list, too."

He blinks, looks down at his hands. "I don't know what to say to that."

"Did he have some kind of argument or dispute with the bishop?" I ask. "Maybe when the excommunication was taking place?"

"You'll have to ask the bishop."

"Do you have any idea why your address is on the list?"

He shakes his head. "I cannot know the answer to that."

The list of names isn't the be-all and end-all of the investigation. Swanz was the victim, and I can't imagine any of the people whose names are on the list murdering Swanz, especially by burning him at the stake. Still, my gut tells me to keep pushing; the list may be relevant.

I look at my brother, try to see past the stoic façade. The secrets I see in his eyes. "I'm trying to get a handle on what kind of man he was."

Jacob says nothing.

"Do you know who he was close to?" I ask. "Friends? Enemies?"

"I don't think I'm the person to answer those questions, Katie. He was little more than a stranger to me."

"Was there any gossip about Swanz going around?" It's a flimsy question. But I can't shake the sense that my brother knows more than he's letting on.

He looks at me a little more closely. "He was fair game. The way he lived his life. That he'd been excommunicated."

"What did you hear?"

He tightens his lips, looks away. Inwardly, I smile at the irony. Generally speaking, the Amish don't hesitate to partake in gossip. The one thing they will not do, however, is gossip about an Amish person who has passed away, especially to an *Englischer*.

"Jacob." I say his name firmly. "I'm trying to find out what happened to him. If you know something—anything—please talk to me."

He sighs. "I heard Milan had . . . some problems. A temper, for one thing. He had a mouth on him. Cursed like a demon. Wasn't a very good worker. Or a good father for that matter. I heard he liked his women, too. Then he has the gall to ask his wife for a divorce. No wonder he was excommunicated." He shrugs. "Whether all of that is gossip or fact, I can't possibly know. But that's what people were saying."

Something there, I think. Something he doesn't want to talk about.

"What else?" I ask.

"That's enough, don't you think?"

"Who were his friends?"

He stares at me for a long time, his eyes probing mine. "All I can tell you about that, Katie, is that I wasn't one of them. He worked for me for a short time. I paid him. We parted ways. And that is all."

•   •   •

The conversation with my brother follows me all the way back to the highway. After a great deal of discord following my leaving the Amish, Jacob and I had landed in a comfortable space. We've come a long way in the years I've been back in Painters Mill. But I know the Amish mindset well enough to understand that my decision to leave will never allow us to be as close as we once were. In terms of the case, I don't think he was lying to me. Not outright, anyway. But I do believe he's holding back. When you're a cop, holding back and lying are one and the same.

I'm so embroiled in my thoughts I nearly miss the gravel turnoff into the parking lot of McNarie's bar. Though it's barely four P.M., the lot is crowded with a hotchpotch of pickup trucks, half a dozen cars, and a dump truck with the Painters Mill Sand and Gravel logo on the door. I idle around to the back of the lot, looking for Swanz's Mustang, but it's not there. Back in front, I park next to a souped-up muscle car and slog through two inches of slush to the entrance. I hear the thrum of music before I open the door. When I step inside, the bass vibration of an old Lynyrd Skynyrd headbanger boxes my ears like fists.

It's been a couple of years since I've crossed this particular threshold. The memories of my troubled past wash over me. Not much has changed, but I take a moment to let my eyes adjust to the dim light and take in my surroundings. To my right, the bar is a beat-up slab of oak the size of a railroad car. A mirrored wall sits behind it. To my left, a row of booths, replete with red vinyl and stainless-steel trim, line the wall. Beyond, a jukebox from another era judders like an imbalanced washing machine spinning out of control. Farther back is a pool table where two men and a young woman are engaged in a game of eight ball.

The barkeep, a man I only know as McNarie, stands behind the bar, pouring amber liquid into a shot glass. He's staring at me, frowning. I don't take it personally and head that way. I take one of six stools, as far away as possible from the other two patrons.

"Ain't seen you around," McNarie says.

"Been behaving myself, I guess."

"That's disappointing." A smile whispers across his face, but doesn't quite reach his eyes. "You used to be one of my best customers."

I smile. "Nothing personal, McNarie, but I'm glad those days are over."

That earns me another frown. "What are you drinking these days, Chief?"

"You got coffee made?"

"How far we fall." But he laughs. "This morning's okay?"

"It'll do."

A basketball game flickers on the TV screen in the corner. The other two patrons pretend to watch, but I can tell their attention is on me. Wondering why the chief of police is sitting at the bar in a place like this.

"Here you go."

The bartender slides a restaurant-style cup and saucer in front of me, two containers of half-and-half on the side. "You here about Swanz?"

"You heard?"

"Who hasn't?" He shrugs. "Craziest shit I ever heard. You know that son of a bitch was here till close that night, right?"

I set down the cup. "A phone call would have been nice."

He lifts a shoulder, unperturbed. "I knew you'd figure it out and show up sooner or later."

An acerbic retort teeters on my tongue, but I tamp it down, keep my eye on the ball. I pull my notebook from my pocket, flip back the cover. "What time was he here?"

"Got here around six. Stayed till close, which is two A.M., as you know."

"Who was he with?"

"No one."

I squash exasperation. "Did he drive?"

He shakes his head. "To tell the truth, I think he walked. Lives just a couple miles down the road."

"Did he talk to anyone while he was here?"

"He talked to whoever he thought might buy him a drink." He motions with his eyes to the pool players in the back. "Those fools are here just about every night, too. If I recall, Swanz played a game of pool with them. Had his eye on that girl. Like everyone else, I guess."

I look over my shoulder at the group. The two men stare back at me, beers in hand, curious. The woman is nowhere to be seen. Shit. I turn back to the barkeep. "Do you have security cameras?" I ask.

He cuts me an are-you-kidding look. "No one who spends his time here is a fan of Big Brother, if you know what I mean."

"Was Swanz a regular?" I ask.

"Came in two or three times a week."

"Ever have any problems with him?"

"All's I know about Swanz is that he drank like a damn fish and he couldn't handle his booze."

I glance over at the pool players. They've gone back to their game. Still no woman.

"Did anything suspicious or unusual happen the night Swanz was killed?"

"I didn't notice anything out of whack."

"He ever argue with anyone?" I ask. "Get out of line?"

"Swanz got loud when he drank. Got handy with the lady patrons, if you know what I mean. To tell you the truth he was a belligerent sot. Always begging for a free drink or a ride home."

"He get belligerent with anyone in particular?"

"He was kind of an equal-opportunity asshole."

"Any fights?"

"I might've heard a rumor or two."

"Does the rumor or two have a name?"

"Nope."

One of the things I used to appreciate about McNarie was his discretion. The man knows how to keep his mouth shut and prides himself on not being a stool pigeon. Even if you were the police chief, you could come here, drink away your troubles, and not have to worry about your escapades being bantered about all over town. This afternoon, his discretion is irritating.

"I don't know the names of everyone who comes through that door." He gives me a knowing look. "People like it that way."

Keeping an eye on the pool players, I take him through some rudimentary questions, but he doesn't seem to know much. "Is there anything you can tell me about Swanz that might help me figure out what happened to him?"

"Not that I can think of." Looking at the TV, he picks up a shot glass and runs his towel around the rim.

I lay a ten-dollar bill on the bar and get up without thanking him.

I feel the stares burning into my back as I start toward the pool table. More curious than hostile, but I remind myself to stay on my toes since I'm here alone and there's a killer on the loose.

Eric Clapton croons about all the illicit benefits of cocaine as I reach the pool table. The two male players are in their late twenties or early thirties. Blue jeans and flannel shirts with work boots. I glance toward the restroom down the hall, but the woman still hasn't reappeared. I wait while one of the men bends and sets up for a shot.

"Who's winning?" I say by way of greeting.

They ignore me for a beat too long, which annoys me, but I hold my tongue and wait.

The man with longish brown hair sticking out of a skullcap gives me a slow once-over. He's tall and lanky, with two days' growth of a beard and callused hands. "You here wanting to know about Swanz?" he asks.

I show him my badge. "I understand you guys talked to him last night."

"We talked to him." He squints at my badge. "Heard someone killed him out in them woods down the road. Is that true?"

"I think that's what happened." Reaching into my pocket, I trade my badge for my notebook. "What's your name?"

"Marco Ellison." He spells the last name and I write it down.

The man who'd made the last shot straightens and sets his cue against the pool table. "We both talked to him. Bought him a beer. Played a game of pool."

"What's your name?" I ask.

"O'Dell," he says. "Rick."

The second man is a few inches taller than me, with the build of a professional wrestler, all of it wrapped in red-plaid flannel, a puffer vest, and worn jeans.

I cover some of the same questions I covered with McNarie, mentally comparing the timelines. "How well did you know Swanz?"

O'Dell speaks up first. "Never really sat down and talked to the guy. I mean, I seen him around here a lot. A regular, you know."

Not wanting to be left out, Ellison takes it from there, motions toward the bar. "Usually sat right there, drank his beer, and watched whatever game was on."

"Was Swanz with anyone last night?" I ask.

The two men exchange looks and shake their heads. "Came in alone, I think," O'Dell replies.

"He was friendly enough," Ellison adds. "You know. Talked to people, but never really saw him with anyone in particular."

"How was his frame of mind?" I ask. "While you were with him? Anything bothering him?"

"He was kind of smashed," Ellison tells me.

"Complained about his old lady if I recall," O'Dell puts in.

"His ex-wife?" I ask. "What did he say about her?"

"Just called her fat and shit," he says. "Disrespecting her mostly."

"Did Swanz ever get into any fights with anyone?" I ask. "Or have any problems? Arguments?"

Once again, the two men exchange looks, shake their heads. "Never saw it," Ellison says.

"What about your lady friend?" I ask.

"What about me?"

At the sound of the crisp female voice, I look over my shoulder to see the woman approach from the rear exit door. She's in her twenties, slender and pretty, with a mountain of red hair that tumbles over her shoulders like silk. She's not wearing a coat. Too much makeup. Big boobs with no bra. Navel piercing winking at me below the hem of her sweater. I catch a whiff of marijuana as she joins us and realize she'd gone out back to smoke.

Marco intervenes as if she requires handling with kid gloves. "She's asking about Swanz," he tells her.

I can tell by the way the woman's eyes light up that she's not too broken up about Swanz—and more than a little intrigued by the idea that she's being asked about his death.

"What's your name?" I ask her.

"Britney Gaines." She looks down at my notebook. "With one 't.'"

"I understand you played a game of pool with Milan Swanz last night," I say.

"Yeah, we did. Dude couldn't play for shit." Britney with one "t" rolls her eyes. "It was always a little weird to see an Amish dude in a bar. I didn't know they boozed it up like that. And that haircut of his always cracked me up!" She laughs, and then her mascara-laden eyes narrow on mine. "The girl at the nail salon told me Swanz was burned alive. That there's a group of witches living off the grid in those woods and they sacrificed him during some kind of ritual. Any truth to that?"

"There are no witches that I'm aware of," I tell her. "And we're still trying to figure out exactly what happened to Swanz."

"No way someone should get away with that shit," says Ellison.

O'Dell picks it up from there. "Milan might've been a loser, but he had a bunch of kids. And he sure didn't deserve that."

Feeling as if I'm spinning my wheels, I ask the woman some of the same questions I covered with her cohorts, ending with "Did you see him talking to anyone last night?"

For the first time, she looks at me as if her brain cells are firing and she's actually considering the question. "Now that you mention it, he was talking to a dude." She thrusts a red-tipped nail at the nearest booth. "They were sitting right there. I remember thinking it was odd because Milan usually sat at the bar."

My interest surges. "Do you know the man's name?"

"Never laid eyes on him before. That caught my attention, too. I mean, I come here pretty regular and I'd never seen him before."

"What did he look like?" I ask.

Her brows knit. "All I remember is that he was wearing black, a good shirt and slacks, which is kind of weird because most of the guys that come in here dress like slobs." She slants a look at the two men and laughs. "No offense."

"Was he Amish or English?" I ask.

The question garners more serious consideration. "That kind of got my curiosity going, too, because he kind of *looked* Amish, even though he didn't have a bad haircut like Milan. I think this dude had a pony-tail or man bun or something."

"Hat?"

"I think so. It was on the table between them. Black."

Which fits with the type of hat an Amish man would wear in the wintertime. "Beard?"

"Not sure. I mean, I wasn't really paying attention. But I *think* so."

"How old was he?"

"Gosh, I don't know. Not old. I mean, he didn't have gray hair and he wasn't all wrinkled or bent over."

I try not to roll my eyes.

Her brows draw together again and she takes a sip of her beer. "It was kind of weird. I mean, he was like one of those people you look at and yet you don't see their face."

"How long did Swanz sit with him?"

"Gosh, I dunno. Fifteen or twenty minutes?"

"Ms. Gaines, would you be willing to ride down to the station with me and sit down with a sketch artist?"

Her eyes widen. Her mouth opens enough for me to see the silver stud piercing in her tongue. "Seriously? Like . . . in the movies?"

"This individual may or may not have anything to do with what happened to Milan Swanz, but if we can identify him and talk to him, he might be able to help us figure it out."

"Um . . . well, I'm kind of drunk right now, Chief Burkholder," she says sheepishly. "Is that okay?"

She doesn't look exceedingly intoxicated. Since I'm desperate—and knowing it might take some time for Tomasetti to wrangle a sketch artist—I don't hesitate. "We've got coffee and bottled water at the station." Recalling her trip to the alley for a toke, I add, "That means if you have anything on you that you shouldn't take into a police station, you should go into the ladies' room and flush it."

"Oh. Um . . . now that you mention it, I do need to make a quick pit stop."

"Take your time."

CHAPTER 9

Ensconced in darkness and falling snow, he sat in the parking lot of the bar and watched from the anonymity of his vehicle. He'd known there would be fallout for what he'd done. There always was, and dealing with the aftermath was a calculated risk he had to take. Usually, he was more adept at getting things done and then getting out quickly. This particular situation was a little more complicated than usual. There'd been some disagreement about how to handle it. No one was happy about the delay, least of all him.

He'd dealt with plenty of law enforcement over the years. No one had anticipated a formerly Amish cop. Burkholder had insights the others did not. Combined with her reputation, that made her dangerous. He would have to exercise added caution this go-round. Maintain a safe distance, but keep an eye.

For now, it was just him and her. All he could do was watch and wait and do his best to make sure she didn't get out of line. If for any reason the situation deteriorated or she became a threat, he would have no choice but to handle her, too.

The thought troubled him more than he wanted to admit. The notion of taking such a risk left a bitter taste in his mouth. If he was forced to act, it would have to be quick and discreet. There would be no satisfaction. There would be no pleasure. Just a keen sense of purpose and the personal sacrifice that went along with it. It would be one more sin heaped upon a hundred others and adding to a long list of transgressions for which, when the time came, he would not be forgiven.

CHAPTER 10

I give Britney a ride to the police station with the assurance that I will also make sure she gets a ride home. I call Tomasetti on the way.

"Any chance you can get me a sketch artist?" I say by way of greeting.

"That's an interesting request," he says. "I take it you have a witness?"

I tell him about my trip to McNarie's bar. "It's a long shot, but I thought it might be worth pursuing."

"I think that's a good call." A beat of silence, and then he adds, "I got a guy who owes me a favor. Let me see what I can do."

•   •   •

I'd known walking into this that Britney Gaines wasn't going to give us much in terms of identifying the man who'd been talking to Swanz. Not because she was intoxicated or didn't try hard enough, but because she simply didn't notice enough details to make a sketch a viable tool. Unfortunately for me, it takes nearly three hours to go through the motions. By the time I drop her at her apartment in Painters Mill, it's seven thirty, fully dark, and aside from my brother—and Noah Stutzman, whom I'd spoken to before I found the list—I've yet to speak with the remaining individuals whose addresses are on the list.

That said, the list itself isn't much of a lead; if I wanted to be perfectly honest, it's not a lead at all. But at this point in this lackluster investigation, it's the best I've got, and desperation obliges me to follow up.

It's too late in the evening for me to visit the bishop and his wife. Not only are they known to rise early, but they're elderly—well into their eighties. They've likely already called it a night. Of course, I'm going to buck conventional decorum and talk to them anyway. With the clock ticking and not a single solid lead, it won't wait until morning.

I haven't seen the bishop since my wedding just over two months ago. He didn't officiate at the ceremony. While we've had our differences over the years, and will never see eye to eye on my belief system or the way I live my life, his being there meant the world to me. As I pull into the gravel lane of the Troyer farm, I find myself hoping that milestone meant something to him as well and might grease the wheels of cooperation.

As I park in the gravel area at the back of the house, I notice there's no light in the windows. Snow brushes against my face as I take the walkway to the porch. Opening the screen door, I knock, knowing it may take him a while to answer. As I wait, I listen to the yip of coyotes in the field behind me. The whisper of wind through the treetops. The hushed tap of snow against the siding. I'm thinking about knocking a second time when the door creaks open.

The wrinkled face of the bishop's wife, Freda, peers out at me through the gap. "Katie Burkholder? What on earth are you doing here at this hour?" she asks in *Deitsch*.

101

"I'm sorry to bother you so late, Mrs. Troyer," I respond in kind. "This is an official visit. I need to speak with the bishop. Is he around?"

"This is about Milan Swanz." It's not a question.

"Yes, it is."

She stares at me, unspeaking, for a beat too long, then opens the door the rest of the way. "*Kumma inseid.*" Come inside.

Freda Troyer may be a scant five feet tall, but despite her diminutive stature, she's formidable, a woman who is comfortable in her skin, knows her mind and doesn't hesitate to speak it. She makes no effort to engage in small talk as I follow her through the mudroom to a large kitchen. The room is dark, the only light coming from the lantern in her hand. I'm thankful when she lights a second one on the counter. As a kid, having grown up without electricity, I wouldn't have noticed the lack of light. Now that I'm English, I'm aware of how much I've come to rely on it.

The Amish woman motions to the table and chairs. "*Sitz dich anne.*" Set yourself there. She goes through the doorway and disappears.

I slide into a chair at the table, glad for the warmth, taking in the smells of lantern oil and something that was baked earlier in the day. To my relief, the bishop doesn't keep me waiting. He's dressed in black—shirt, suspenders, jacket, and a flat-brimmed felt hat. He leans heavily on a four-prong walker as he enters the kitchen.

"Now that you're a married woman, I thought you might set all of this police business aside," he says.

No matter how many years of life experience I have under my belt—that I'm now a grown woman and the chief of police—invariably the nerves of the Amish girl I'd once been tense at the low timbre of his voice, and I find myself sitting up a little straighter.

"I'm sorry to bother you so late, Bishop, but there's been a homicide and I need to ask you a few questions."

His hair is mostly silver with a few black strands throughout, and unevenly cropped. His beard is white, unkempt, and dangles to the waistband of his trousers. He seems smaller than when I last saw him, his posture stooped, his legs bowed. The frailty doesn't detract from the steel in his eyes.

"I heard about Milan Swanz." He shakes his head. "It's a terrible thing."

"I'm trying to find the person responsible." I pull out the copy I made of the list of addresses. "I went to Milan's house and found this." I slide the sheet in front of him. "Do you have any idea why he might've had your address written down?"

Reaching into his breast pocket, he pulls out wire-rimmed glasses, looks down at the paper, and shrugs. "I have no way of knowing such a thing."

"Did he ever do any work for you?" I ask. "Cabinets? Odd jobs? Anything like that?"

"No."

"Do you see any connection between these other addresses, your own, and Milan Swanz?"

"No."

"Has Swanz been to see you here at the house?" I ask.

"No."

"Bishop, I know he was excommunicated. Was he upset about that?"

"He wasn't happy about it, of course. No one would be. But Milan knew the rules and he broke them."

"What about before he was excommunicated?" I ask. "When you initially placed him under the *bann*?"

"That was a long time ago." The old man shrugs. "More than a year now."

"Anger can fester over time," I say.

The bishop says nothing, his eyes holding mine, his expression impassive.

In the Painters Mill church district, an Amish person who has been placed under the *bann* can make things right by changing his or her behavior and confessing to the congregation, in which case he or she will be reinstated. If they refuse to change the offending behavior or confess, however, they will be permanently excommunicated, a status from which there is no return.

I rephrase the question. "How angry was Milan when you excommunicated him?"

"He did not wish to be excommunicated. He was upset. But he broke the rules not just once, but many times."

An adroit skirt of the question. "Did he lose his temper?"

"I don't recall that."

"Did he threaten you?"

He holds my gaze, silent and unapologetic.

"What about Monroe Hershberger?" I say, referring to the Amish elder whose address also appears on the list.

A quiver moves through the bishop's gaze. A nerve, I think, and I set my index finger to Hershberger's address. "Why would Swanz make a list of addresses that contains both yours and Monroe Hershberger's?"

"Monroe is one of our *Diener*," he says, using the proper Amish term for "servant" and referring to the elected officials who oversee the church district, usually the bishop, the deacon, and one or two ministers or preachers. "He is our deacon," he finishes.

Again, he's avoiding the question, so I give another push. "The deacon sometimes conveys messages of excommunication."

"Perhaps."

"Was Monroe Hershberger involved in the *bann* or excommunication of Milan Swanz?"

The old man gives a curt nod. "He was there."

"Was he upset with Monroe?"

"If he was, he didn't say."

"Did Milan become angry with the deacon?"

Nothing but a deadpan stare.

Impatiently, I tap my index finger against the sheet on the tabletop between us. Under normal circumstances, I wouldn't bring up the names of other individuals who may or may not be involved in the case. But Painters Mill is a small town and the Amish community is close-knit. This man is the bishop, which means he knows most of his congregation personally. He has his finger on the happenings inside the community. I broach that invisible line without regret.

"Has Lester Yoder ever had any kind of disagreement with Swanz?" I ask.

"Maybe you should ask Yoder about that," he says.

"I'm asking you."

He doesn't respond, but I think I see a hint of temper in his eyes.

"When's the last time you spoke to Milan Swanz?" I ask.

"I've only spoken to him a couple of times since the excommunication. I don't recall the date. A time ago."

"Did you argue?"

The old man tightens his mouth, glances toward the living room, where I think I hear the whisper of his wife moving around in the darkness.

"I'll not discuss my personal business with you," he snaps. "Not this."

I curb my own anger and press on. "Bishop, if you know—"

105

His eyes home in on mine like lasers, knowing and hard. "There's another address on that list you didn't ask about, Katie."

He says my name as if I'm fifteen years old and in trouble because I didn't follow some rule that nobody gives a damn about.

I reach for the list and tuck it into an inside pocket of my coat. "Has my brother had any disputes with Swanz that you know about?"

"I think you should ask him about that. That's all I can tell you."

I stare at him, wondering what he knows and why he won't reveal it. "Bishop, if you had information that might help me find out who's responsible for the death of Milan Swanz, you'd share it with me, wouldn't you?"

The old man stares at me for a long time before answering. "Talk to your brother," he says. "That's all I have to say to you."

"You know something and you're withholding it from me," I say. "Why is that?"

"No more questions." Grunting, the old man sets his arthritic hands on the walker and heaves himself to his feet. Instead of turning away, he faces me, looks down at me. "I think we may be in for some bad weather, Kate Burkholder. You should be careful out there, on the road. Do you understand?"

I look past him to see Freda standing in the doorway, watching us from the shadows of the living room, and for the first time in my life, I feel as if the bishop isn't being completely truthful with me.

"Who are you protecting?" I ask quietly.

"Give your brother my best," the old man says, and then he's gone.

• • •

There are times in the course of an interrogation when an individual's evading a question is as telling as an outright lie. Had my conversation with Bishop Troyer gone differently, I would have waited until morning before approaching Monroe Hershberger. When I initially discovered the list of addresses at Swanz's home, I honestly didn't feel it was important or relevant to the case. Now, I'm not so sure.

Monroe Hershberger and his wife live on a small farm off of Township Road 102 between Painters Mill and Millersburg. The clock on my dash tells me it's after 8 P.M. when I make the turn into the rutted lane. As I near the house, I discern the golden light in the windows, and I'm relieved at least one of the elderly couple is still awake.

I park in a circular turnaround in front and wade through snow to the porch. Before I can knock, the door squeaks open and I find myself looking at a tall, rail-thin man wearing typical Amish garb sans the hat. I recognize him as Monroe Hershberger, though I don't recall the circumstances of our meeting. Such is the way of small-town life.

"Mr. Hershberger?" I have my badge at the ready and introduce myself.

"Yes?" He looks past me as if expecting a horde of cops to converge.

"I'm sorry to bother you so late, but I'm working on the Milan Swanz case and I'd like to ask you a few questions."

"Oh. Milan." His eyes widen and for a moment he seems tongue-tied. "Just heard about what happened this afternoon. Awful thing."

"I thought I heard voices down here." A female voice interrupts.

I look past him to see a short Amish woman push past her husband. Ada Hershberger is as rotund as her husband is tall, with ruddy cheeks, and her green eyes look at me with suspicion.

"Katie Burkholder. I thought that was you." She slants a sideways look at her husband and frowns. "I see you've rendered him speechless already and he hasn't even invited you inside."

"Hi, Ada." I know her from the gift shop in town where she works. I bought a knitted afghan from her a couple of months ago. She's a talker. Amicable. And funny. She's also a little on the ornery side when she gets riled up. She's one of the reasons I go to that particular shop when I need a gift.

"I'm sorry to bother you so late," I tell her.

"Think nothing of it." She nudges Monroe with her elbow. "Where are your manners, Old Man?" She uses the nickname fondly and then motions me in. "I reckon we know why you're here." Taking her husband's arm, she ushers me into the living room. "Come on now. I just made tea. Let's drink it while it's still hot."

A few minutes later, the three of us are settled in the small, dimly lit living room. Ada and Monroe sit on a love seat–size sofa, the backrest of which is draped with a quilted throw. I settle into an overstuffed chair across from them, trying not to notice the broken spring poking my backside. An old gas lamp hisses at us from its place in the corner.

"*Da tay is goot,*" I say, unable to place the unusual flavors. The tea is good.

She waves away the compliment. "It's an old recipe my *mamm* used to make for my *datt.* Chamomile for sleep. *Heregraut* for the things that worry you." St. John's wort. "And *hollerbier* for that nice flavor." Elderberry.

I sip again, let my eyes slide to Monroe. "I understand you were involved in Milan's excommunication."

The couple exchanges a look. Ada pats her husband's hand, which seems to relax him, and he speaks. "Well, we took the vote and it was done. Milan was excommunicated."

"How did he react?" I ask.

"As you can imagine, he was none too pleased." The old man picks up his mug and takes a long drink, as if for fortification. "He was a troubled man, you know, constantly struggling with one problem or another. If it wasn't his wife, it was his employer. If not his employer, then the children or maybe fate. It was a sad thing to witness, time and time again. And as is always the case, the excommunication made everything worse for him."

"Tell me about the excommunication," I say.

Monroe heaves a sigh. "Milan had been under the *bann* on and off for years. He was making cabinets at the time, and doing woodworking on the side. Course, once he was put under the *bann,* no one would do business with him and he lost his Amish customers. His relationships suffered, especially with his wife. His reputation suffered, too, and Milan became angry."

"How do you know that?"

"A few weeks after he was excommunicated, he came to me. He was upset . . . drinking, you know. Said he would change. Begged me to let him come back. Of course, by then it was too late. He'd been given many opportunities to make things right so he could come back. But he'd taken things too far, too many times, and the decision had been made. When I told him that, he fell to *grisha.*" Shouting. "And *fluch-vadda.*" Curse words.

"Did he threaten you in any way?" I ask.

The old man shifts in his chair. "He said all sorts of crazy things. But that's the way Milan was. Said things he didn't mean."

"Mr. Hershberger, what did he say exactly?"

"He tossed around some blame. Blamed everyone but himself, I think." The old man's eyes flash to his wife, to the cup of tea in his hands, then back to me. "Milan said he'd get back at us. For what we'd done to him, you know. That we didn't understand. That we'd ruined his life. It was a sad thing to behold, really."

"Did he say *how* he would get back at you?" I ask.

"No. I don't think he even realized what he was saying. Just a sad man talking." But his eyes skate away from mine, a small tell that niggles the back of my brain. "I don't think he meant anything by it."

He falls silent and for the span of several heartbeats the only sound comes from the hushed patter of snow against the window and the hiss of the lamp. Watching them, I get the sinking suspicion that there's more. That they're struggling with it because they don't want to speak ill of a dead Amishman. Not to me, whom they consider an *Englischer* despite my birthright.

Finally, Ada heaves a sigh and speaks up for the first time. "Tell her the rest, Monny."

The old man tosses her a sour look. "I don't see how that will help anything," he snaps. "Milan is gone to God now. It's over."

"Mr. Hershberger, this isn't really about Milan; it's about finding the person who murdered him. This is about keeping them from hurting anyone else." I pause. "If something happened, I need to know about it."

The silence that follows stretches on for so long that I think they're not going to open up. Finally, Monroe looks down at his cup and shakes his head. "We had some problems here at the farm a few months back."

"What kind of problems?" I ask.

"Someone drove a vehicle through our cornfield," he says. "Took a joyride. Circles, you know. It was after a big rain and there was a lot of mud. Tore that field up something awful. I only had about thirteen acres and whoever done it ruined most of the crop."

"It was a total loss," Ada adds. "Did the soybean field, too."

"Was it Milan?" I ask.

"We don't know for sure," the deacon replies. "No one saw him."

"We have our suspicions," Ada puts in.

I would have remembered a vandalism incident of that magnitude. "You didn't call the police?"

"Well." Sheepish, the Amish man looks down at his hands. "No."

110

Ada sets her hand on her husband's arm. "Tell her about the pigs."

"Pigs?" I look at him and raise my brows.

He frowns, his expression stubborn and pained, as if he knows there's no escaping the inevitable. "We raise hogs, you know. Do a pretty good business." He sighs. "A few weeks after the fields were torn up, someone came in the night and let the hogs out of their pen. Twenty-two of them. They got into the garden."

Ada presses her lips together. "Someone opened the gate," she said. "Herded them in. Then shut them in. The pigs destroyed everything."

"You believe Milan Swanz was responsible?" I ask.

Monroe looks down at his hands.

"Oh for goodness' sake." The Amish woman jerks her head. "I was upstairs, reading, when I heard the ruckus. I looked out the window and I'm pretty sure it was Milan Swanz getting into that English car of his and pulling away."

"The Mustang?"

"*Ja*," Monroe replies.

"Was there anyone with him?" I ask.

"Didn't see anyone else," she replies. "Man didn't have many friends left. In fact, I don't know a soul who'd want to spend any time with him. Milan Swanz was one of those people you steer clear of if you've got a brain in your head."

CHAPTER 11

I was a homicide detective with the Columbus Division of Police for two years before becoming chief in Painters Mill. During that time, I worked with a number of cops, and most of them were a lot more experienced than me. It was a difficult and intense time, and a period of rapid professional growth. I learned more during that two-year period than in the entirety of the six I'd spent in patrol. One of the detectives I partnered with during that time was Bud Lawrence. He was a thirty-year veteran, six months from retirement, and the last thing he wanted to deal with was a rookie detective young enough to be his daughter who was under the impression she knew more than he did. That young female detective was me.

I disliked Bud from day one. He was blunt, openly rude, and seemed to go out of his way to make my life miserable. When I screwed up, he ridiculed me—and not in a good-natured way. At the time, I had no way of knowing that of all the people who had mentored me, it would be Bud whose teachings I would come to value the most. After a few rocky weeks and a lot of stress, I learned to keep my mouth shut; I learned to pay attention to the right things, and I began to learn. Bud shared something more important than anything you'd get from a classroom, and a hell of a lot more valuable: his experience. He taught me how to think like a cop, how to push when I didn't have any push left, and how to think outside the box.

It's eleven P.M. and I'm sitting in my office at the police station. The switchboard has quieted. The last sheriff's deputy left an hour ago. It's just me and my second-shift dispatcher and the knowledge that I don't have squat in terms of a suspect. My brain squirms inside my head, but I'm intellectually spent and too tired to push.

When you hit that wall, put that voice inside your head on paper and let the damn thing talk.

It was one of Bud's favorite axioms, and to this day I keep a supply of legal pads in my desk. Tonight, at a loss and batting zero, I pull one out and I go to town on the page.

Symbolism of murder—burned at the stake—connection to Martyrs Mirror?

Victimology: Swanz led a troubled life. Divorced. Misdemeanor convictions. Alcohol abuse. Excommunicated. Not well liked. Ex-wife—lying about boyfriend? Parents—not close to him. Something off?

Argument with neighbor—burned cornfield.

Bishop Troyer—cagey? Something to hide?

Stutzman's cabinetry—fire—lost everything. Revenge? Noah Stutzman?

Monroe Hershberger—destroyed crops & garden—reluctant to speak poorly of fellow Amish?

Still need to speak with best friend—Clarence Raber.

I scrawl in longhand, fast, stream-of-consciousness. I fill two pages before I settle into a rhythm, and finally my cop's brain kicks in and I dig deeper.

> List of addresses. Relevant? Bishop Troyer—bann/excommuni-
> cation. Noah Stutzman—termination. Monroe Hershberger—
> excommunication. Lester Yoder—neighbor—burned cornfield.
> Jacob? Did Swanz have a beef with my brother?
> Regular at McNarie's. Excessive drinking. Unidentified
> male? Made contact with Swanz. Looked Amish. Need to ID him!!

I stop writing. Look down at my notes. Read through them from start to finish. I underscore Jacob and Unidentified male.

You got nothing, Kate, a little voice reminds. *Go home and get some sleep or you're not going to be worth a damn in the morning.*

"Shut up," I whisper.

But I close the legal pad, tuck it into my briefcase, and call it a night.

• • •

Everything I know about the case plays in the back of my mind as I back out of my parking spot and head for the farm. I'm tired and troubled and in need of a hot shower and a few hours of undisturbed sleep. I have every intention of turning onto the county road that will take me north toward Millersburg and Wooster.

I don't make the turn. Two miles down the road, I pull into the parking lot of McNarie's bar. For the span of a heartbeat, I consider going inside and slugging back some temporary reprieve. To my credit, I've outgrown the destructive behavior of my younger self. Eyeing the vehicles—all six of them—I circle the lot, then stop at the exit, kill the engine, and get out.

Around me, the night is misty, cold, and so quiet I can hear the bass drum of music from the bar fifty yards away. I stand there a moment, listening, thinking, trying to put myself in Swanz's head. I walk to the shoulder and look in the direction of his trailer home, which is about two miles away. It's a long walk, especially if you're intoxicated, but it's doable.

Less than twenty-four hours ago, Milan Swanz was in the bar, drinking. According to witnesses, it was common for him to be without a vehicle. If he'd been unable to get a ride and decided to walk home, he would have passed over the very ground upon which I'm standing.

"Did you walk home?" I whisper, my voice sounding strange in the silence of the night. "Or did someone drive you?"

No one in the bar noticed Milan leaving with another individual. But I can't ignore the mysterious man he'd been seen talking to. Did he leave with Milan? Drive him home? If so, what happened during that short, two-mile jaunt?

The questions nag as I get back into the Explorer. I start the engine and creep along the route he would have taken. I roll down my window, and a blast of cold air washes over me. It would have been a cold walk, I think. If someone had offered a ride, an intoxicated Milan would have jumped at the offer.

Absently, I engage my seat belt, find myself looking down at the strap. . . . *suffered a broken hyoid bone* . . . Doc Coblentz's words come at me from the recesses of my mind.

"Was there a struggle?" I say. "In the vehicle? Or alongside the road?"

Milan Swanz was not a small man. He was muscular and tall with a generous amount of weight. How could someone subdue such a strong man? I stare down at the seat belt in my hands; I glance over at the passenger seat next to me.

115

"He was intoxicated," I whisper. "Or there were two of them."

It's not the first time the possibility has occurred to me. A scenario plays out in my mind's eye. A deserted back road late at night. An intoxicated Swanz is walking home and offered a ride. He gets in. While the driver converses with him, a second individual hides in the back seat. When the time is right, he loops a rope or strap over Swanz's head, tightens it around his throat, and strangles him to unconsciousness.

And the hyoid bone is broken in the process. . . .

Leaving my window down, I idle along the road, keeping my eyes on the ditches, the fence, the trees beyond. In the yellow glow of the headlights, intermittent snow slants down from a black sky.

I reach the crime scene and stop. The shoulder and roadway are scarred with tire ruts. I pull onto the shoulder, snag my Maglite off the seat, and get out. I stand there a moment, listening to the inhale and exhale of the forest. I take it in. Put it to memory. Try to imagine what might've happened and somehow absorb the memory of this place.

To my left, I can see where the fence was cut, both sides peeled open for the first responders. I start that way. The thin layer of snow is wet and soft, my feet silent as I enter the trees. I'm not exactly sure what I'm looking for. I spent a good chunk of my day here; I've seen every inch of it. Still, I was compelled to return. Earlier, it was teeming with law enforcement, crime scene investigators, and, nearer the road, journalists. Now, alone and in the dark, I have a better sense of what it was like the night Swanz was killed.

I follow the beaten-down path through the woods to the place where the body was found. The wooden stake was removed and sent to the lab for testing, as were samples of the lumber and ash. New snow coats everything that remains. I stop ten feet from the remaining pile of ash and wood. I walk around it, trying to imagine, yet at the same time, trying not to. I pull out my notebook and write: *Where did the pallets come from?*

116

I've circled the fire area a second time when a sound from the woods startles me. Not the snapping of a twig. More like a muffled thud. An odd sound for the woods. I stop walking and look that way, feel the hairs at my nape stand on end. There are plenty of deer out this way. There are possum and raccoon, rabbit and coyote, all of which are nocturnal. There's also a killer on the loose, and while it may be cliché that a criminal always returns to the scene of the crime, it holds true.

Without changing my gait, I stride toward where I heard the noise. I'm aware of the .38 in my holster beneath my parka. Casually, I tug down the zipper for quick access. I sweep the Maglite along the trees. Eyes penetrating as far as the light will allow. No movement. Nothing there.

So why are the hairs up at the back of your neck, Kate?

I break into an easy jog. Sweeping my light left and right. Fifty yards and I stop. Listen over the low thud of my heart. The scrape of a branch across fabric sounds to my left.

"Stop!" I call out and launch myself into an easy, ground-covering jog. "Painters Mill Police Department!"

I maintain the speed for another hundred yards, then stop and listen, my breaths puffing out in front of me. I stand still, the beam of my flashlight digging into the darkness. All the while I try not to think about the rumors of a devil-worshipping cult living off the grid in these woods.

"Is someone there?" I call out.

The only sound that comes back at me is the hiss of my labored breathing and hard thud of my heart.

CHAPTER 12

It's after seven A.M. when I walk into the station. My floater dispatcher, Margaret, mans the switchboard with the cool head of a seasoned war correspondent. She catches my eye as I walk past, chirps out a cheerful "Morning!," and shoves a dozen or so message slips into my hand.

"Get me everything you can find on Clarence Raber." I spell the last name for her. "Background. Known associates. Check for warrants."

She scribbles on a pad. "Got it."

"Who's on?" I ask.

"Glock."

"Tell him to—"

"I'm right here, Chief."

I turn to see the man in question come around the corner of his cubicle. Despite the fact that he likely worked through the night, his uniform is clean and crisp, his eyes are clear and focused. "You had any sleep?" I ask.

"As much as I needed," he says.

I tell him about Clarence Raber. "According to Swanz's ex, they were best friends. He works at the grain elevator in Coshocton. I thought I'd run over there."

"You want some company?"

I smile. "I'll drive."

•   •   •

Sweet Feed and Seed is located off County Road 68, across from a field of cut corn, the yellow stalks covered with snow and shivering in the wind. A mishmash of steel buildings lines the west side of the lot. Ahead, a beat-up elevator juts sixty feet into winter haze. The gravel parking area is populated with half a dozen pickup trucks and a semi rig parked alongside the road, the dirty snow all around crisscrossed with tire ruts.

Glock and I slog through slush to a low-slung building where a sign above the door reads OFFICE. An old Alan Jackson number oozes from a 1990s-era boom box on the counter where a woman wearing insulated coveralls pages through her phone.

"Morning." I cross to her, thankful for the warmth, and hold up my badge. "We're looking for Clarence Raber."

Her bored expression transforms to startled when she notices I'm a cop. "Oh."

"Is he around?" I ask, aware that Glock is hanging back, keeping an eye on the parking lot.

"This about that weird murder up in Painters Mill?" she asks.

"This is about me talking to Clarence Raber." I say the words amicably, but she gets the message.

"I think he's out in the elevator this morning." She reaches for an old-fashioned desktop phone that is ostensibly part of a paging system. "Let me check."

I raise my hand and stop her before she can speak. "If you could just point us in the right direction, we'll get out of your hair."

She hauls herself to her feet and points. "He's greasing the bearings on the elevator this morning. Walk straight out then go left. Can't miss it."

"Thank you."

Tipping his hat at her, Glock opens the door, and we go through.

"Bet the farm she's calling him right now," he says as we cross the short distance to the larger building.

"Bet you're right."

We look at each other and grin.

The elevator is a massive structure fabricated of corrugated steel that's striped with rust. Despite the cold, the overhead door is raised about five feet. The rumble of what sounds like a generator emanates from inside. I duck under the door, and find myself in a cavernous space packed with equipment and machinery. Ahead, the elevator conveyor belt slants upward toward the ceiling at a thirty-degree angle. A young male matching Raber's description stands on a catwalk of sorts, twenty feet up, cranking a wrench the size of a man's arm.

"Clarence Raber?" I call out.

He stops cranking and looks down at us. "Help you?"

I hold out my badge and identify myself. "I'd like to talk to you about Milan Swanz."

Eyes flicking from me to Glock and back to me, he tosses the wrench in an open toolbox beside him and trots down the steel-mesh stairs. "I wondered when you guys were going to come talk to me."

He's wearing an insulated coat over duck coveralls, which are open just enough for me to see the blue work shirt and suspenders beneath. Not exactly Amish, but close, as if he's not quite sure himself. He's blond haired and blue eyed with the barely-there beard of a newly married Amish man.

120

"Yeah?" I say pleasantly. "Why is that?"

"Milan and I used to be friends." He shrugs as he crosses to us. "Crazy what happened to him, isn't it? Heard it on the news this morning. I still can't hardly believe it."

He reaches us and the three of us exchange handshakes. "You guys figure out who did it?"

"We're working on it." His grip is warm, callused, and strong. "We were hoping you might be able to shed some light."

"Sure. Whatever you need."

I pull out my notebook. "Tell me about your relationship with Milan."

"We knew each other since we were little kids. Practically grew up together. Used to play in that old barn out to his parents' farm." He offers a self-deprecating smile. "Got into plenty of trouble together as teenagers."

"What kind of trouble?" I ask.

"Nothing serious." He laughs, Mr. Happy-Go-Lucky. "You know, the usual kind of *rumspringa* stuff. Drinking and raising hell." His expression softens as if the words rekindle fond memories. "Terrorizing the girls. The way a couple of teenaged idiots do."

I can tell by his *Deitsch* pronunciation of *rumspringa* that he's Amish or at least grew up Amish. "When's the last time you saw Swanz?"

A flicker of something I can't quite identify in his eyes. "Been four or five months now," he says.

Curiosity pings. "Did you have a falling-out?"

"Well." He scrubs his hand over his beard, looks back toward the scaffolding as if he'd rather be up there greasing bearings instead of down here talking to me. "I guess I walked right into that one, didn't I?" He smiles sheepishly.

"Clarence." I say his name firmly, wait until he stops fidgeting and meets my gaze. "We're trying to figure out what happened to Milan Swanz and you're wasting our time. If something happened between the two of you, you need to tell me about it. Right now."

"We had a falling-out about four and a half months ago." As if realizing the statement might be misinterpreted, he raises his hands, chokes out a laugh. "Not *that* kind of falling-out! I mean, I didn't *kill* him."

"What kind of falling-out?" I ask.

"Look, the problems between me and Milan had nothing to do with what happened to him. Can we just leave it at that?"

"Let me put it this way, Mr. Raber. We can do this here all friendly-like, or we can drive you to the station in Painters Mill and do it in an interview room. It's your call."

He heaves a sigh, shakes his head. "Milan had a tendency to over-react when something didn't suit him. When he was a kid, it was all fun and games. Everyone thought he'd straighten out as he got older. Truth of the matter is, it got worse."

"How so?"

"He had a temper. Everything was a slight, you know? He took things personal and then he couldn't let it go. It's like he'd dwell on it and stew. When he got pissed, you'd best look out because he didn't exactly have a lot of self-control. Sometimes he got mean." He shakes his head. "Especially when he drank."

"Did he have any problems with anyone in particular?" I ask.

"I know he had some problems with the people he worked for." He recaps the story about the fire at Stutzman's cabinet shop, which corresponds with what I already know. "Milan took it bad when they fired him. Said they humiliated him. And he sure didn't have no soft spot for the dude's son."

"Noah Stutzman?"

He nods.

"Did Milan start the fire?"

"He said he didn't. I believed him. But everyone else sure had their suspicions."

"Did Milan have any problems with anyone else?"

"That's about all I know about." He shrugs. "Pulled him off a guy in a bar once, but that was a long time ago up in Canton."

Glock speaks up for the first time. "What about your falling-out with him?"

"It wasn't good." Shaking his head vigorously, he swears beneath his breath. "Damn, I hate to trash him now that he's dead. It just don't feel right."

"If it's any consolation," I say, "you don't have a choice."

"Right." He shoves both hands into his pockets. "I was over at his house one afternoon, drinking a beer like we'd done a hundred times before. His wife was there. The kids." He heaves a sigh. "His son runs into the kitchen and accidentally knocked something over, made a mess." Raber's jaw tightens as if he's bitten into something unpalatable. "One minute Milan was sitting there chilling and the next he grabbed that kid. Just fucking . . . yanked him around way too rough. The little guy squealed and started crying. I'm no fighter, but I swear to God I just about tore into Milan."

I write it down. "What's the child's name?"

"Aaron. He's the middle kid."

"Did anyone call the police?"

"No."

"Was Milan abusive to his children?"

"Never thought so. I mean, I'd never seen it. Until that, anyway. A few days later, when I saw them at worship, I saw a cast on the kid's arm."

A swell of outrage tightens my chest, but I bump it back. Stay on topic. "So Milan broke his son's arm?"

"Yeah. When I asked him about it, he said it was an accident. But I was frickin' there. I saw it and I didn't like it." For the first time, Clarence Raber doesn't look quite so happy-go-lucky. "That was the last time I talked to him. I never went to his house or returned his calls. Far as I was concerned, he no longer existed."

"How did his wife react to her son being hurt?" I ask.

"She filed for divorce shortly thereafter. I mean, even with her being Amish and all, who could blame her?"

In the back of my mind, I recall Bertha Swanz specifically telling me Milan was the one who'd initiated the divorce. "Are you sure it was Mrs. Swanz who initiated the divorce?" I ask. "Not Milan?"

"She told me she's the one done it."

I think about that a moment. "Do you know if she has a boyfriend?"

"Last I heard she was seeing that Yoder dude lives next door to her."

"Her neighbor?" Surprise quivers in my chest. "The one whose field caught on fire?"

"That's the guy."

"Mr. Raber, can you tell me where you were night before last?" I ask.

He gawks as if I've sucker-punched him, then shakes his head as if resigned. "I was home with my wife and our new baby. You can ask her."

"Were you there all night?"

"Yes, ma'am, I was."

"You know we're going to check," Glock puts in.

"Knock your socks off," he says. "I gotta get back to work."

At that, he turns and walks away.

•   •   •

When you're a cop and you need information from the Amish, taboo is a slippery slope to maneuver. There are certain subjects the vast majority of the Amish simply won't broach. Homosexuality. Sexual assault. Child abuse. When you're Amish and you finally muster the courage to confide or ask for help, you speak only with a trusted friend, only in whispers, and you never talk to an outsider, especially a cop.

Crimes such as domestic violence, sexual assault, and child abuse are no more prevalent among the Amish than other cultures or groups, but because of the wall of silence that exists between the Amish and English, such incidents are less likely to draw the attention of law enforcement. The victims are far more likely to suffer in silence without recourse.

As I pull into the driveway of the farm where Milan Swanz's ex-wife lives, I don't ponder the reason why she didn't tell me about Swanz breaking her son's arm. I already know the answer. I understand her hesitancy because I'm well versed on Amish taboo. Of course, that doesn't excuse her for withholding information in the course of a homicide investigation.

The snow has stopped, but the air presses down cold and heavy and wet as I take the walkway to the porch. In the distance, the whistle of an approaching train wails, a lonely sound that makes me wonder how many times a day this house is rattled by railroad cars barreling past.

The door creaks open. Bertha Swanz glares at me through the foot-wide gap, a wily cat peering out at a pit bull intent on harming her. "Well, I don't know why you're here again," she says.

"I'm here to ask you about the things you lied to me about last time we spoke," I return evenly.

I can tell by her expression she knows exactly what I'm referring to. She doesn't want to talk to me, but knows she doesn't have a choice. "I guess that means you're going to want to come inside."

"I guess it does."

Frowning, she turns away and heads for the kitchen. "I got coffee."

I follow her. "I'll settle for some honesty."

She clucks her tongue, a sound of annoyance.

The aromas of woodsmoke and kerosene fill the overwarm air as we make our way to the kitchen. Breakfast dishes from earlier are stacked next to the sink, not yet washed. A cast-iron skillet sits on the woodstove, a thin layer of grease inside.

"The children are at school?" I ask.

"Of course they are." Bertha snatches up a gas-blackened percolator and pours into mismatched cups.

I take a chair at the table without being asked. "Why didn't you tell me your ex-husband broke your son's arm?"

She looks calm on the exterior as she brings cups to the table, but I don't miss the slosh of coffee that spills over the rim as she hands one to me. "I didn't know it was important." She shrugs. "You didn't ask."

"It is and I'm asking now."

She takes the chair across from me. "Milan lost his temper sometimes. With the kids, you know. I don't think he meant to actually break—"

"Did he ever hurt the children?"

"No."

"He broke your son's arm, ma'am."

"Just that one time," she snaps. "Grabbed him too rough. That's all."

"What about you?" I ask. "Did he hit you?"

She looks away, but quickly raises her gaze back to mine. "He might've slapped me a time or two."

"In the face? Your body?"

"Face."

"How bad?"

"Bad enough."

I stare at her, feeling my temper rise, my heart beating a little too fast. "You know it's against the law to strike someone."

"I didn't like it much. Just tried to keep things calm."

"You should have called the police. We would have helped you."

Her laugh has a sour tone. "You don't know anything."

We stare at each other silently.

"Is that why you filed for divorce?" I ask after a moment.

She shivers as if her filing for divorce is worse than her husband breaking a young boy's arm. The cup she's holding quivers, so she sets it on the table. "I told you. Milan's the one filed."

"Do not lie to me," I snap.

She looks down at the cup, wraps her hands around it as if to warm them.

"Bertha, I'm not here to judge you. I don't care who filed. But I need the truth because I'm trying to find out who murdered your ex-husband. The more I know about him, the better. Do you understand?"

"I don't want them to know," she whispers.

She's referring to the Amish, of course.

I give her a moment, think about possible implications of domestic abuse. A protective brother or father. "Did you confide in anyone about what was going on in your marriage?" I ask. "That Milan had hit you? That he injured your son?"

"I told no one."

"What about your family? Do any of them know what was happening?"

As if realizing where I'm going with this line of questioning, she sighs. "We don't speak of such things."

I switch gears, go at her fast and hard. "Why didn't you tell me you're in a relationship with Lester Yoder?"

She opens her mouth, makes a sound that resembles a dog choking on a chicken bone. "Because it's a private thing," she says.

"Last time I was here, I specifically asked you if you were involved with anyone."

She shakes her head. "My seeing Lester so soon would have been condemned. You were Amish once. You know how it is."

"How long have you been involved?"

Her body seems to sag and when she raises her gaze to mine, misery swims in her eyes. "Seven months now. He's a widower, you know. Going on two years for him."

Before the divorce. "Is it a sexual relationship?"

I don't miss the color that climbs up her neck and enters her cheeks. "Not at first." She lowers her eyes to the tabletop. "I was having so much trouble. With Milan, you know. Lester caught me crying one morning. I had a cut lip. Milan had smacked me a good one and left the house. I was out in the barn so the kids wouldn't see, and Lester came over to borrow that old crosscut saw."

"What did you tell him?"

She tightens her mouth as if she doesn't want to answer. But she knows she doesn't have a choice. "He saw the cut, asked me about it, and everything just poured out. I confided in him and . . . over the next few weeks . . . one thing led to another."

"Is Lester protective of you?"

Her eyes narrow. "Not particularly."

"Did he have anything to do with Milan's death?"

"Oh, dear Lord, no!" She slaps a hand over her mouth, a sound of distress escaping. "You can't possibly think such a thing. The man is kind and wouldn't hurt a flea."

"Where were you the night your ex-husband was killed?" I ask.

"Here," she says. "With the kids. Like always."

Finishing the last of my coffee, I dig into my coat pocket for my card and write my cell phone number on the back. "If you think of anything else, will you call me?"

She stares at me a moment, then motions toward the door. "I think we're finished here."

*   *   *

I'm mulling my exchange with Bertha Swanz and nearly to the station when Sheriff Mike Rasmussen calls. I know the instant I hear his voice that the news isn't good.

"You need to come in," he tells me.

"What's up?" I ask.

"Kate, I got a witness here claiming your brother had some kind of altercation with Swanz four days before Swanz was killed."

For the span of several heartbeats, I'm so taken aback that I can't find my voice. I just talked to Jacob and he didn't mention an argument.

"Are you sure about that?" I ask.

"I'm sure, damn it."

"Who's the witness?"

"A neighbor," he tells me. "Guy by the name of Jim Bogart."

Something sinks inside me, a rock swiveling down to the bottom of a deep lake. I've arrested Jim Bogart twice for OVI. The second time, he caught a conviction, went to jail, paid a massive fine, and lost his driver's license for a year.

"You know I've got a history with him," I say.

"Yeah." Rasmussen lowers his voice. "Kate, Bogart called BCI before he called me. Your name came up, and now the agent liaison is all over my shit. Evidently, this Bogart character has already talked to the media, too, and they're running with it."

"Must be a slow news day," I mutter.

"Always is when it's that juicy." He sighs. "Look, the BCI agent is here now. So is Auggie. They want to talk to you."

"I'll be there in ten," I say, and smack my palm hard against the disconnect button.

CHAPTER 13

With a homicide investigation in the queue and spooling hot, the last thing I want to deal with is the reprisal of a disgruntled citizen. But when you're a public servant, community perceptions carry a lot of weight. Even if you've done nothing wrong, the precept of "innocent until proven guilty" goes out the window. If the situation appears suspicious in the eyes of the public, you are guilty, your career is in peril, and you'd damn well better set the record straight before the situation spirals out of control.

It takes me eight minutes to reach the station. By the time I pull into my slot, I'm officially worried. One look at Lois's expression when I walk through the door and I know it's worse than I thought.

"Hi, Chief!" She says the words with far too much enthusiasm and with a side-eye toward the two men standing in the hallway outside my office.

I follow her gaze to see Mike Rasmussen leaning against the wall, finger-pecking something into his phone. A man I don't recognize—a

BCI agent, judging by his attire and persona—stands across from Rasmussen, doing the same. Jim Bogart manspreads on the ragtag sofa and offers me a gotcha-bitch smile as I cross to the dispatch station.

Lois attempts to communicate something to me via a hand signal I don't understand.

"Messages?" I ask.

She plucks a dozen or so slips from the slot. I spot the sticky note she's placed on top of them and read her handwriting.

Bogart is claiming your brother is involved in the murder and he's accusing you of protecting him!!!

Good grief.

"Chief?"

I turn to see Mike Rasmussen shove his phone into his pocket and stride toward me. "If you've got a few minutes, we'd like to have a word."

"Sure, Mike." The words come out sounding surprisingly composed. Tucking Lois's note into my pocket, I glance over his shoulder to see the second man approach. No visible badge. Eyes direct and homed in on me. Mouth pulled into an indecipherable grimace.

Out of the corner of my eye, I see Jim Bogart get to his feet. "You want me in there, too?" he asks, looking a little too eager.

Rasmussen practically snarls at him. "Stay put, Mr. Bogart, we'll call you if we need you."

Looking disappointed, Bogart settles back onto the sofa.

"There's a little more space in the war room." I look past the sheriff, make eye contact with the BCI agent, and extend my hand. "I don't believe we've met."

"Agent Chambers," he says, giving my hand a too-hard squeeze. "BCI. Call me Neil."

"Appreciate your being here." I motion toward the war room and head that way. "We need all the help we can get."

Rasmussen makes a noise beneath his breath. "This won't take but a few minutes," he assures me.

Knowing I'm walking into an ambush, I take the hall at a brisk pace, push open the door, flick on the lights. "Did you get with the fire marshal about the blaze at Stutzman's Cabinetry?" I ask the sheriff.

"They're going to take a look at the case file," Rasmussen tells me. "Copy us on everything. As it is, the fire was not ruled arson. No accelerant. And the misplacement of the jacket near the heat source was deemed accidental."

I take the chair at the head of the table and sit. Looking like he'd rather be anywhere but here, Rasmussen takes a chair two spaces down. Chambers closes the door behind him and takes the chair next to the sheriff.

Symbolism, I think, and turn my attention to Rasmussen. "What's this about?"

"Citizen out there in reception, Jim . . ." He grapples with his notes.

"Bogart," I put in.

"Right." He heaves a sigh. "Kate, he called Agent Chambers this morning and made a statement saying he saw your brother, Jacob Burkholder, arguing with Milan Swanz a couple of days before Swanz was killed."

I stare at him, my pulse quickening because I realize I've already made my first mistake. While I mentioned the list of addresses I found at Swanz's residence, I didn't follow up by sharing the names of the property owners with my team, nor did I add it to the evidence log. "Okay."

"Were you aware of that?" Chambers asks.

"No," I say honestly.

"Have you talked to your brother about the case?" Chambers asks.

I don't hesitate; I know they already know. "Yes."

"When was that?" Chambers asks.

"Yesterday."

"It's interesting that he didn't mention the argument," Chambers says.

I think of the list I'd dropped in the drawer of my desk and feel sweat break out on the back of my neck. "My brother told me Swanz had done some work for him," I say.

"Did you document that, Chief Burkholder?" Chambers asks, but I know he already knows.

"Not yet," I return. "With all due respect, we've had our hands full and I haven't had a chance."

Chambers cocks his head, his brows knitting. "Why did you seek out your brother in the first place?"

There it is, I think, and take the plunge. "There was a list of addresses at Swanz's residence," I tell him.

Chambers looks at Rasmussen and raises his brows. "Do you know anything about a list of addresses?"

"Chief Burkholder mentioned the list during our first briefing," the sheriff replies.

Chambers turns his attention back to me. "Is there a reason why you didn't log that list into evidence?"

"I didn't consider the list evidence," I say.

"Why is that?"

"For one thing, it wasn't found at the crime scene." I shrug. "When I initially discovered the list of addresses at Swanz's home, I honestly didn't feel it was important or relevant to the case."

"Because you have so many other leads?" He adds a generous dose of sarcasm to the question.

"Because it's a list of addresses," I say evenly. "Swanz was known to do casual labor. It wouldn't be terribly unusual for him to have addresses written down. Even so, I looked up the names of the property owners and I was following up."

"So even though the list wasn't 'evidence'"—he makes air quotes—"you looked into it as if it was, indeed, evidence. Is that correct?"

"I looked up the owners of the properties," I say.

"Who's on the list?" Rasmussen asks.

I tell him.

"They're all Amish?" he asks.

I nod. "I talked to the individuals on the list and determined that each of them had had some kind of contact with Swanz."

"Well, that's really interesting." Chambers leans back in his chair. "And yet you didn't see fit to share the information with other law enforcement? Or even document it?"

Having already answered his question, I hold his gaze, saying nothing.

Chambers gives a helpless shrug. "At what point, Chief Burkholder, were you going to share the information with the rest of us?"

"I probably would have shared the names with the task force today. At this point, I'm still trying to determine if any of the individuals on the list are relevant to the case."

Chambers nods slowly, as if weighing the information for logic and honesty. "The witness also claims he saw your vehicle at your brother's farm yesterday. For the record, did Mr. Burkholder mention he'd argued with Swanz?"

"As I already told you, Swanz had done some work for him," I say. "He didn't say anything about an argument."

I can tell by his expression he's enjoying my discomfort. "Do you think that's suspicious? I mean, for your brother not to mention something like that?"

"I think it's worth asking him about," I say.

Chambers tosses a look at Rasmussen I can't quite identify, and my heart thumps in my chest.

"Does your brother have an alibi for the night Swanz was killed, Chief Burkholder?" Chambers asks.

"At the time I spoke to my brother, I didn't know about the argument, so I didn't ask if he had an alibi," I say. "I should remind you that none of the individuals on the list are suspects or even persons of interest."

Chambers laughs and cuts an I-told-you-so look at Rasmussen, then raises his hands in surrender. "There you go."

"Kate, as I mentioned earlier, Bogart went to the media." Growling beneath his breath, Rasmussen leans forward, sets his elbows on the table. "He insinuated that you're covering for your brother."

"Or maybe Bogart is disgruntled about the OVI conviction," I say, "and he's using this incident to get back at me."

"He's claiming you're covering not only for Jacob, but the Amish community," Rasmussen adds.

"I'd tell you that's ridiculous, Mike, but I think you already know that," I say.

"If some unflattering story runs, Chief Burkholder"—Chambers changes the timbre of his voice, assuming the faux persona of an ally playing devil's advocate—"it's not going to bode well for any of us. It's sure as hell not a good look for you."

Rasmussen frowns at the BCI agent. "Neil, that's the thing about being a cop in a town the size of Painters Mill. Everyone knows everyone. Sometimes, paths cross when they probably shouldn't."

"Okay." Chambers nods. "And then we have John Tomasetti assigned to the case. That's another crossing of paths that won't play well if the media decides to push it."

"Agent Chambers," I say slowly. "If you've got something on your mind, I suggest you put it on the table right here and now."

"Appearances matter, Chief Burkholder, especially in this day and age when law enforcement is under a microscope. I think we can all agree you used poor judgment that could easily be misconstrued by the public at large."

"I appreciate your concern, but my reputation speaks for itself."

"If we were in any other jurisdiction, you'd be off the case," Chambers says. "Guaranteed. Tomasetti, too. Lucky for you that's not my call."

"Let's not get ahead of ourselves," the sheriff says diplomatically. "We're not exactly drowning in manpower, for God's sake."

"This might be tough to swallow, but I'm not wrong," Chambers argues.

Rasmussen sighs. "Kate, Neil makes a valid point."

"I don't disagree with him," I admit. "That said, none of this has been verified. I don't believe we've reached the point in which I need to recuse myself from this case."

The sheriff turns his attention to Chambers. "She's got a spotless reputation. She has a good working relationship with the community as well as the local Amish. They trust her. That alone makes her uniquely valuable to this investigation."

"A good investigator is a good investigator," he says. "Whether they're dealing with the Amish or not."

Frowning, I lean back in the chair, and cross my arms in front of me.

"Let me put it this way," Rasmussen begins, with uncharacteristic testiness. "You show up at an Amish farm with questions about murder and you're going to get stonewalled so fast your head will spin."

Chambers all but rolls his eyes.

"Kate's a good chief and one of the best investigators I know," Rasmussen maintains. "I trust her. And we need her."

"Thanks for your vote of confidence, Mike, but any decision about my continuing to work on this case falls to Mayor Brock." I get to my feet, drill Chambers with a glare. "In the interim, I think all of us would be better served if we concentrated on the case."

Temper flashes in the agent's eyes.

Before he can respond, I reach for the intercom box in the center of the table. "Lois?"

"Yeah, Chief?"

"Can you send Mr. Bogart back here to the war room?"

"You got it."

Chambers sits up straighter. "What are you doing?"

"I'd like to hear from the witness," I say, and then turn my attention to Sheriff Rasmussen. "Since Agent Chambers is under the impression that I'm too personally involved, would you like to do the honors?"

He nods. "Sure."

Chambers mutters something beneath his breath.

Not quite comfortable with having relegated myself to a backseat position, I pull out my notebook.

A knock sounds and the door swings open. Jim Bogart stands at the threshold looking a lot less cocky than he had out in the reception area. He's fifty-two years old, with a salt-and-pepper goatee and the burly build of a man who's spent most of his life doing physical labor.

"Hi, Jim." Rasmussen motions him into the chair nearest the door. "Come on in. We appreciate your coming forward today."

Bogart eyes me warily as he slides into the chair. I stare back at him, keeping my expression as neutral as I can manage.

"I understand you have some information for us about the Milan Swanz case," the sheriff begins. "Can you tell us what you witnessed between Jacob Burkholder and Milan Swanz?"

The man scoots closer to the table. "Well, Swanz was putting up a cross fence near where my property borders Jacob Burkholder's place. My barn is close to where Swanz was working that day. I was on the second level, cleaning out my feed room. I heard an argument so I went to the window." Looking pleased with himself, he sets his gaze on me and pauses with drama. "Sure enough, Burkholder was out there arguing with Swanz."

"What day was that?" the sheriff asks.

"Five days ago," he says. "About two in the afternoon."

"What were they arguing about?"

"I missed some of it. By the time I got to the window, Burkholder was all over Swanz, yelling at him. I think he said something about the bishop." He shakes his head. "Let me tell you something, Burkholder was pissed. I swear I never seen an Amish guy so mad. I've lived in Holmes County my whole life and never heard any of them so much as raise their voice. I thought these two were going to come to blows."

"Did it get physical?" Rasmussen asks.

"Didn't see it if they did."

"Anybody get threatened?" Chambers asks.

"Not that I could hear," Bogart replies.

"Was anyone else present?" This from the sheriff.

"Just them two. And me."

Dread hovers over me as I write all of it down.

"How long did the argument last?" Rasmussen asks.

"Just a few minutes," Bogart replies. "Like I said, I missed the first part of it. But they were yelling their heads off."

The sheriff continues. "What happened next?"

"Burkholder jabbed his thumb toward the house and ordered Swanz off his property. We're talking foaming-at-the-mouth pissed. Swanz was cussing like a damn truck driver. Next thing I know, Burkholder tore the fence stretcher off the end post. For a second, I thought he was going to slug Swanz with it. Instead, he threw it on the ground. He told Swanz to get off his property and never come back. And Swanz ran."

Chambers poses the next question. "What made you decide to report it?"

"I didn't think too much of it until I heard what happened to Swanz. At that point I thought 'Oh shit' and made the call."

• • •

Ten minutes later, Sheriff Rasmussen and I are sitting at the table in the war room. Chambers left without commentary, but I know he'll be back. People like Chambers don't go away easily and usually don't go of their own accord. The only sound comes from the hum of the ceiling lights and a not-quite-comfortable silence that's as encompassing and cold as ice on a winter lake.

"Well, that was a clusterfuck," the sheriff says.

"Which part?" I ask.

He sighs. "All of it."

I nod, fingers of unease walking up my spine. The last thing I want to do is recuse myself from the case. The reality that I may have no choice in the matter sits like acid in my stomach. "Mike, do you think I need to sit this one out?"

"That's not my decision to make."

"That's not what I asked you."

"All I can tell you at this point, Kate, is that if your brother is involved, even in a peripheral way, you're walking a fine line."

"Have you talked to Auggie about it?" I ask, referring to the mayor, who is officially my boss.

His frown deepens. "That's out of my bailiwick."

"Has Chambers talked to him?"

"I don't know." He scrubs a hand over his jaw, looks at me over the tops of his fingers. "I think that's something we need to be prepared for."

"Prepared for what?" I ask.

"You know as well as I do that Chambers made some valid points. We can't ignore that. I'm not saying I agree with everything he said. What I *am* saying is that we need to keep the public eye in mind and be transparent about what we're doing."

A dozen questions dangle on the tip of my tongue, but I don't voice them. I already know what the answer is. What he's going to say. I also know that once things are said, they can't be taken back.

I look at Rasmussen, really look at him, and I let down my defenses, let him see what's really there, that I'm speaking from the heart. "We've known each other how long, Mike? Eight? Nine years?"

"We've known each other too long to be having this conversation," he mutters.

"Mistrust is the kiss of death when you're a cop."

"This is not a matter of trust."

I nod, but I'm aware of the tinge of doubt tweaking my chest, and it hurts a hell of a lot more than I want to admit. "I need to speak to my brother."

Rasmussen groans. "You know that's not a good idea, right?"

"I also know that he won't talk to you. He sure as hell won't talk to Chambers."

"I hate to say this, Kate, but your talking to Jacob at this juncture is going to be a problem. For him. For all of us."

"Is he a suspect?"

"He just became a person of interest."

"He didn't murder Swanz."

"Are you saying that as his sister, Kate? Or a cop?"

141

"Both," I tell him. "One is not mutually exclusive of the other."

He sighs unhappily. "What do you suggest?"

"Let me do my job."

"If you're asking for my blessing, it's not going to happen. I'm sorry."

I ignore the quicksilver twist of pain in my chest. "You know as well as I do that I've got a better chance than you or Chambers or anyone else of getting the truth about what happened between my brother and Swanz."

The friendliness falls away and his gaze grips mine. "You want a friendly word of advice, Kate?"

I stare back at him, my heart beating fast, an uncomfortable knot forming in my chest.

"If you go talk to your brother, I don't want to know about it." Eyes never leaving mine, he leans back in his chair. "If allegations of wrongdoing come to a head and the shit hits the fan, you're on your own. You got that?"

"I got it." Rising, I push the chair up to the table and leave the room.

CHAPTER 14

I barely notice the snow-covered field or the cattle huddled at the round bale of hay as I zip up the lane of my brother's farm. I've relived my meeting with Rasmussen and Chambers a dozen times during the short drive; I've picked it apart. Analyzed what was said. Critiqued my every response. None of what's happened sits well. The one thing I keep coming back to is the thin line between right and wrong and how easily that line can be blurred. On a professional level, I'm keenly aware that I'm not helping matters. On a personal level, it hurts that Mike Rasmussen, whom I've always considered a friend, waffled when it came to supporting me.

The pain of that pounds hard in my chest as I park adjacent the chicken coop and get out. The door to the barn stands open a few feet. Hoping to catch Jacob alone, I head that way.

I find him in one of the horse stalls, mucking. I watch him work for a moment, remembering that I did the same chore hundreds of times as a girl and that once upon a time—before the summer when

143

Daniel Lapp tore apart our lives—Jacob and I were as close as a brother and sister could be.

"Some things never change," I say.

Straightening, he looks at me, pushes up the brim of his hat with a gloved hand, and smiles. For an instant he looks so much like the brother I'd once idolized that a pang tolls in my heart.

"You were always better at this than me," he says.

"I was happy to pass the torch."

He goes back to work and for a few minutes, we simply enjoy the moment, being in each other's company, the earthy smells of the barn, content to remember without all the complications of our adult lives.

"I need to know what happened between you and Milan Swanz," I say.

The pitchfork freezes mid-toss; then he empties the tines and scowls at me as if he has no idea what I'm talking about. "I told you," he says. "Milan did some work for me. On that fence at the side of the property. I paid him. That was the end of it."

"I know you argued with him, Jacob. I know it was heated. I need you to tell me what that was about."

He stares at me as if trying to figure out how I could possibly know, and how I have the gall to ask him about it.

"A witness came forward," I tell him. "He overheard the argument. He saw you with Swanz. In fact, he went to BCI after I spoke to you, and he's claiming I'm protecting you. I need you to come clean and tell me what happened."

It takes a lot to anger my brother. Not because he's easygoing, but because he's good at keeping all those un-Amish-like emotions tucked away and locked down tight. In all my thirty-six years, I've only seen him truly angry a handful of times. As I stand in the aisle and look at him through the stall door, I see that temper peek out at me.

Without speaking, he sets the pitchfork against the stall divider and approaches me. "I'm sorry this has caused you trouble with your police work," he says. "I didn't mean for that to happen. But I'll not speak of what happened to you or anyone else."

"You don't have a choice," I tell him. "I don't have a choice but to ask."

"My argument with Swanz has nothing to do with what happened to him."

"That's not a good enough answer."

"It's going to have to do."

He tries to brush past me, but I reach out and grasp his arm. "Jacob, Milan Swanz is dead. You argued with him just four days before his death. Do you have any idea how that looks?"

"I don't care what the English think," he snaps.

"What about the police?" I say with equal vehemence.

He looks down at the place where my hand grasps his biceps through his coat. "I had nothing to do with Swanz's death."

"I know you didn't, damn it!" I release him with a little too much force, giving him a small shove in the process. "What I don't understand is why you lied to me. What are you hiding?"

He looks away, the muscles in his jaws working, as if he's grinding his teeth. "I think you should leave."

"I'm not leaving until you tell me what the hell is going on."

Stepping away, he picks up the pitchfork and goes back to the wheelbarrow. For the first time he looks upset in a way I didn't expect. "I can't talk to you about this, Katie."

"About what?" I snap. "What happened? If you have nothing to hide, why can't you talk to me?"

Tightening his mouth, he forks shavings, shakes off the excess, and dumps the manure in the wheelbarrow.

"Are you protecting someone?" I ask.

No response.

Not giving myself time to debate, I stride to him, take the pitchfork from his hands. He resists and for an instant we struggle for possession. Finally, I yank it from his hands, swivel, and throw it like a spear to the end of the aisle.

When I turn back to him, I'm breathing hard. Not from the physical exertion, but because I'm an inch away from losing my temper. "Talk to me," I say.

He looks down at his boots, shakes his head. "There are some things best left unsaid. You know that. Some things are . . . private and should stay that way."

"Jacob, if the police come for you, I can't protect you."

"I don't need your protection."

"You just became a person of interest in a murder case. That's not to mention there's a killer on the loose in this town," I hiss. "I saw Swanz's body. I know what he's capable of. If he takes another life, part of it will be on you."

Shoving his hands into his pockets, he closes his eyes, then lets out a long, pained breath. Misery suffuses his expression and in that moment I know whatever he's holding inside him isn't about him, but someone he loves.

"Who are you protecting?" I ask.

"It's . . . James," he says after a moment.

I blink at him, surprised. "James?" His eleven-year-old son. My nephew. I don't know the boy as well as I should; we're not close. What I do know about him is that he's a sweet kid with freckles on his nose and puppy-dog eyes. He's got a contagious grin and a happy-go-lucky personality that I've loved since the moment I laid eyes on him.

"James." Stupidly, I repeat the name and I feel myself bracing. Not as a cop. But a woman who knows too much about the world. And an aunt who knows that what comes next is going to hurt.

"What happened to him?" I ask.

Jacob's expression goes dark. Grimacing, he looks down at the ground. Then he lowers his head, runs his hands over his face. "James wanted to help with the fence. When Swanz was here. He likes working with his hands, you know, like all boys do. So I gave him my pliers. Some T-post clips. And I told him to help Swanz and work hard."

I nod.

My brother raises his head, meets my gaze. "They worked on the fence for two days. The second afternoon, James didn't come in for supper." He stops speaking as if he's run out of breath. An uncomfortable moment ensues as he struggles for composure. "They'd been working over by the old barn that day. When I went out to get him, there was no one there. They were nowhere in sight. But Swanz's car was still parked in the drive." His jaw goes taut. "I went to the barn. Found them in the loft."

The words hit me like a volley of punches. Involuntarily, I step back, press my hand to my abdomen. I feel sick inside. Outraged. Part of me doesn't want to hear the rest. I don't have a choice but to ask anyway. "Jacob . . . did he . . ." I can't finish.

"No." Jacob shakes his head. "Not that. But, Katie, I think if I hadn't gone out there when I did, something bad would have happened."

"James is okay?"

"He's eleven years old. He's innocent. He was . . . upset. Embarrassed and confused. He's a smart boy. He knew everything was wrong."

"And Swanz?"

"He got down the steps before I could stop him. But I followed, caught up with him over by the fence. Right next to my neighbor's property." He frowns, letting me know he's aware of who the unnamed "witness" is. "I haven't struck another human being since I was a boy myself. It's not our way. It's not *my* way." He shrugs. "It's certainly not something I want my son to see. I almost went after Swanz, but God reminded me it was wrong."

"What happened?" I ask.

"We argued. I told him I was going to go to the bishop and tell him everything. Then I paid him. I ordered him off my property. Told him not to come back. And he left."

I think of the story the witness described, acknowledge that the circumstances Jacob laid out match, and I utter a silent prayer because I believe him.

We fall silent. The only sound comes from the cooing of a pigeon in the rafters, and the hum of wind coming through the door.

"Did you go to the bishop?" I ask.

"I went that evening."

"What did the bishop say?"

"He listened mostly, but I could tell he was troubled."

I nod. "Jacob, I know you didn't murder Swanz. But I have to ask. Were you involved in his death in any way?"

"No," he says.

"Do you have any idea who might've done it?"

"All I can tell you about Swanz is that he was *veesht*." Evil. "None of the Amish were sorry to see him go, including me."

•   •   •

The weight of a troubled mind shadows me like a lumbering beast as I knock on the door of the house where Bertha Swanz lives with her children. I'm preoccupied, trying to figure out what to do with the information my brother just gave me, when Bertha's eldest son informs me his mother is working and won't be home until ten o'clock this evening. I thank him and go back to the Explorer. One of the things I like about being a cop in a small town is that you know a lot about the citizens you serve and protect. I happen to know that Bertha Swanz is a waitress at LaDonna's Diner. I know their coffee is good and I have a feeling that before all is said and done, I'm going to need the caffeine.

The diner is located just off of Main Street in a low-slung building that was a five-and-dime back in the 1970s. During breakfast and lunch, the restaurant is packed with everything from tourists to local merchants to farmers and even Amish families who come in for a meat and potatoes meal. But the diner is rarely busy in the evening, when most of the downtown area storefronts are closed for the day.

A welcome blast of heated air washes over me when I enter. The interior is a narrow space with a single row of booths, a counter appended with the requisite red-and-chrome stools. A smattering of tables at the front window looks out over Main Street. The lighting is too bright, the country music a tad too loud. The not-quite-pleasant aromas of grease and seared meat too strong. I spot Bertha Swanz taking someone's order in a nearby booth and I grab a stool at the counter, upturn the cup on the saucer in front of me.

"Hi, Chief Burkholder!" A second waitress clad in a pink uniform hustles up to the counter. "Cup of joe?"

"Yes, ma'am," I say. "Thank you."

"Need a menu?"

"Not this evening," I tell her.

With a wink, she hustles away, pushes through the double doors that will take her to the kitchen.

I've just taken my first sip of coffee when Bertha walks to the cook's window, snaps down the order, and chimes the bell with her palm.

"Mrs. Swanz?" I say when she doesn't acknowledge me.

Wiping her hands on a towel tucked into her apron belt, she approaches me with the enthusiasm of a woman about to walk the plank. "You're here for dinner?" she asks.

"I'm here to talk to you."

"Well, I'm working and I need my tips." She says the words amicably, but there's an edge in her voice that wasn't there last time we spoke. "Can it wait until tomorrow?"

"Mrs. Swanz, we're going to do this right now. We can do it here at the diner, or we can do it at the police station," I tell her. "It's up to you."

The Amish woman stiffens, gives me with a withering look.

I point at her counterpart. "Tell her you need a fifteen-minute break," I say. "Grab your coat. We can talk in the alley."

A few minutes later, the two of us are standing outside the door at the rear of the restaurant, looking out at two rust-scuffed dumpsters and a vintage pickup truck, all of which are dusted with snow.

"You find out who killed him?" she asks as she yanks the collar of her coat up to her chin.

"Still working on it," I say.

"Well, I don't know why you're bothering me again."

I think about my brother, my young nephew, and the disturbing account of what happened in the barn. "Are you sure about that, Mrs. Swanz? Are you sure there isn't something else you'd like to tell me about your ex-husband?"

"I told you everything I know," she snaps.

"Everything you know about your children?"

"I don't know what you're talking about," she huffs.

I can tell by her expression that she does. I lean closer to her, get in her face. "I think you do."

She backs up a step, putting distance between us, her eyes skating away from mine.

"Was your ex-husband ever inappropriate with the children?" I ask.

Blinking, she reaches into the pocket of her dress and pulls out a pack of Camel cigarettes. Smoking is considered "worldly" and therefore frowned upon by most Amish, but some of the more conservative groups still partake, especially the men.

With a shaking hand she taps one out and offers it to me. "It's not against the *Ordnung*," she mutters.

I know better than to take it, but I do and we light up. "Your secret is safe with me." It's a small, intimate bond that we now share.

We smoke in silence for a minute. I watch the snow come down. See the reflection of the traffic light against the brick façade of the building. I feel the passage of time pressing down.

"Bertha." I take her back to the question at hand. "Was he ever inappropriate with the children?"

"No. He wasn't." Her voice is so low, I have to move closer to hear her. "But I saw him . . . looking at them, you know. I kept them in my room at night."

I think about that in terms of Swanz's murder and I wonder if at some point he took things too far. What if someone caught wind of it? A loved one? An uncle or grandfather or family friend? What if they decided to do something about it?

"Are you sure?" I ask.

"I'm sure."

For a full minute neither of us speaks. I watch her smoke, take in the way her hand shakes. I see the wheels of her brain spinning. Something there, I think, and I give her another push.

"Bertha, is there anything else you can tell me that might help me find the person responsible for your ex-husband's death?"

"There was a rumor going around," she whispers. "A while back. About Milan. I don't know if it's true, but I heard it."

"What rumor?"

"A couple of months ago at worship, everyone noticed that the bishop's hair was all messed up."

"His hair? Messed up how?"

"Like it had been cut. Or hacked off, more like." She shrugs. "Some of us women talked about it and at first, we thought he might've had a cancer spot removed from his scalp. Something like that. But when we were cleaning up that day, some of the women were acting strangely. It was as if they knew something about me and didn't want to talk about it.

"At first, I was hurt. Felt left out. I mean, we're close. Friends, you know." She shrugs. "A few days later, I went to see Erma Miller's new baby. A few of us were having sweet coffee and I heard a crazy story about what really happened to the bishop."

The Amish woman looks to be on the verge of tears as she recounts it. "Milan had already been excommunicated, and I can tell you he wasn't happy with the bishop. Wasn't happy about anything, to be honest. He'd go down to Clarence Raber's place and they'd drink like fools."

She huffs. "Anyway, I overhead Erma telling the other women that Clarence and Milan got drunk one night, and drove over to the bishop's house." She presses a hand to her abdomen as if to ease a cramp. "She said Milan and the bishop had words and somehow the bishop ended up on the floor. Milan had a knife on him and hacked off a piece of the bishop's beard. Some of his hair, too. When Freda came out with that crop of hers—you know, the one she'll use on you if you get out of line—he pushed her down, tore off her *kapp*, and cut her hair, too."

When you're Amish, hair is an expression of your obedience and

152

submission to God. A man stops shaving upon marriage; his beard symbolizes his personal identity and his standing in the community. An Amish woman stops cutting her hair after she is married. To have such a personal piece of individuality stolen is an assault not only on their identity, but on their faith.

"It's the most awful thing I ever heard." Bertha puffs hard on the cigarette. "I was so ashamed."

"No one called the police." I don't pose it as a question.

"No. It was too much. To think an Amish man would bring that kind of shame onto his own. The bishop. Can you imagine?" She shakes her head as if trying to rid the images from her brain. "No one wanted anyone to know, least of all the English."

She tosses the cigarette to the ground, steps on it, grinds it into the asphalt. "That's just about all I got to say about that," she says. "Just thinking of it shames me all over again."

"Mrs. Swanz, do you have any idea who might've killed your ex-husband?"

"No, ma'am."

"Were you involved in any way?"

She cuts loose with a bitter laugh that's fraught with pain. "I might be a liar and a sinner, Kate Burkholder. The one thing I am not is a murderer. Even if that evil bastard deserved it."

CHAPTER 15

Almost everyone has something to hide, from the little white lie you tell to protect someone's feelings to the kinds of secrets that destroy lives. I think about the lengths to which people will go to keep certain information from coming to light. I know better than most that in the minds of a few, some secrets are worth killing for.

It's eleven P.M. and I'm behind the wheel of the Explorer, trying not to think of my own skeletons. It's been a long and unproductive day. I'm beyond exhaustion, but too wound up to go home. Instead of making the turn toward the highway that will take me to the farm, I make a left and head toward Dogleg Road.

Most murders are a far cry from the way they are depicted in movies and novels. They're not particularly complex, or thoughtful, or intelligent. Most are mindless acts of stupidity or rage or impulse committed by a psychopath or jackass for some fatuous reason no one gives a damn about. There is no reason or supposed justification. Just a life lost and a dozen more destroyed. And for what? Jealousy? Greed? Evil?

When it comes to the homicide investigation, I've always believed that once a cop understands the why, he can usually figure out the who. This case is different. The things I know about Swanz do not paint him in a positive light by any stretch of the imagination. He was physically and emotionally abusive to his wife and children. If he perceived he'd been wronged, he sought revenge. According to my brother, he was a child predator. His former employer suspected him of arson. His ex-wife asserts that he assaulted an elderly bishop and his wife. All of those things are the actions of a man devoid of a moral compass, a complete lack of self-control, and sociopathic tendencies. More than one person may have been compelled to do away with Swanz. And yet here I am, at the end of day two of the investigation, and I have next to zero in my investigator's tool kit.

I'm a hundred yards from the crime scene, thinking about my brother and so distracted I almost don't notice the vehicle in the ditch. I'm nearly past when I hit the brakes and come to a stop. Quickly, I throw the Explorer into reverse for a better look. It's a four-door, dark-colored sedan with Pennsylvania plates. No driver inside that I can see. The vehicle is nose down, the front tires in several inches of mud, the rear tires on the gravel shoulder. It doesn't look crashed or stuck. The engine isn't running.

Reaching for my mounted spotlight, I level the beam on the vehicle and pick up my mike. "Ten-eighty-five," I say, using the ten code for abandoned vehicle. "Jodie, can you ten-twenty-eight?" Check vehicle registration.

"You got it, Chief."

"Pennsylvania plates." I recite the number and give her my location. "I'm going to take a quick look around."

"Roger that."

Snagging my Maglite from its nest, I get out of the Explorer, and sweep the beam in a 360-degree circle. There's no one in sight. No voices or movement. Just utter quiet and light snow slanting down in a northerly breeze.

I set the beam on the driver's-side door and start toward it. There's no one inside, front seat or rear. The car is a newish-model BMW. Clean interior. The hood and trunk are securely closed. I set my hand against the hood, find it warm to the touch. It hasn't been long since the engine was running. I check the tires, but there's no flat. That's when I notice the footprints, partially obscured by snow, as if someone got out of the vehicle a short time ago. I set the beam on the prints, see that they go to the fence, over it, and into the woods.

Toward the crime scene.

The place where I'm standing is about fifty yards from where Milan Swanz was killed. The CSI technicians have long since released the scene. It's not unusual for curious citizens, crime aficionados, and bored teenagers to show up and explore. Of course, it's late and cold and, perhaps most importantly, the out-of-state plates tell me the driver is likely not local.

"Painters Mill Police Department!" Calling out, I approach the fence, shine the beam into the woods beyond. "Hello! Anyone there?"

Someone has repaired the fence. I'm looking for a place to climb over when movement to my left sends a burst of hot adrenaline to my gut. I spin, catch sight of a male an instant before he plows into me with so much force that I fly backward, the breath knocked from my lungs. My feet tangle. I'm reaching for my lapel mike when the ground slams into my back. My head hits hard enough to daze; then he comes down on top of me.

"Police officer!" I shout. "Get off me!"

The command has no effect. My attacker is large and strong. He's quick. No hesitation. Straddling my waist. I grapple for my radio, only to see his hand flash, and I feel the mike ripped from my collar.

"Get the fuck off!" Snarling, I reach for my .38, fumble it beneath my parka. Shit. *Shit!* A hand clamps around my throat, thumb and fingers like a steel trap cutting off the blood to my head.

I draw back, punch him hard, body blow. He grunts, deflects a second blow. I ram my fist into the bottom of his chin hard enough to jam my wrist. I twist, bring up my knee, drive it into his spine. Once. Twice. I try to shout again, but my voice box is compressed. A pitiful sound tears from my throat. I writhe, bring up my hips, try to buck him off. My survival instinct takes control. I swing again. The punch lands squarely in his face. His nose crunches beneath my knuckles.

Talon-like fingers dig deeper into my throat. Panic sizzles hot in my chest. If I lose consciousness, I'm done. I raise both fists, try to pummel his face, but he's fast and averts. I bring up my foot, try to loop it over his head, capture his upper body, take him down that way.

The first blow lands squarely against my forehead, like a two-by-four smashing against my brain. Stars fly in my peripheral vision. I raise my hands, but I'm dazed and blind. The second blow plows into my left cheekbone. Another round of stars and I feel my body go limp.

Vaguely, I'm aware of my attacker straddling me. Grabbing my wrists, he tucks my arms beneath his knees, trapping them at my sides. He reaches for my .38, yanks it from the holster. Same with my cell phone. The Gerber folding knife clipped to my waistband. I suck in a breath, blink away blurred vision. Get my first good look at him. The lower half of his face is covered with a black scarf. Heavy brows. Dark eyes. Intent. Calm. He shifts and I notice my revolver in his hand.

"I'm a cop," I rasp.

"Shhh." Leaning close, he sets the muzzle of the revolver against my mouth, forces it between my lips. I jerk my head left, then right, but he rattles it against my teeth. When I open, he shoves it into my mouth, depressing my tongue.

"Don't speak," he whispers. "And I won't make you eat a bullet."

I go still, heart raging, breaths coming fast. I taste gun oil, try not to gag, fear sliding down my throat like bile.

"I'm only going to say this once, so listen good. Do you understand?"

I stare at him, jerk my head, try to take in as many details as possible.

Caucasian.

Dark hair. Brown.

Forty years old.

Somewhere in the periphery of my consciousness, I hear my dispatcher's voice come over my radio.

"Milan Swanz was a deviant," he says. "He walked in step with the devil. He rejected God. He disrespected the Amish. He hurt people and would have done worse."

Deep voice.

Inflection I can't quite place.

I try to speak, but he jabs the gun deeper into my throat, making me choke.

"Shhh." A teacher shushing an overwrought student. "Don't speak." Tilting his head, he looks at me closely, as if I'm some apparatus whose inner workings confuse him.

Average build.

Athletic.

Plenty of muscle.

"His death is a weight on my soul," he says. "But it was my sacrifice to make." He raises his hand. "One I will take with me to hell when I go."

I flinch, expecting another blow, but he sets his palm against my cheek, runs gloved fingers gently from my temple to my chin, touching me almost with reverence.

"Your silence is your sacrifice to make, Kate Burkholder," he whispers. "Don't forget that."

Keeping his eyes on mine, he reaches for my duty belt. For an instant, I think he's going to unbuckle my trousers to assault me. Instead, he unsnaps the handcuffs compartment, studies them for a moment.

"Do not move," he whispers.

My instincts scream for me to fight. If he gets the cuffs on me, I'll be helpless. But with the muzzle of my .38 pressed against my tongue, his finger inside the trigger guard, I do as I'm told.

Using his free hand, he captures my right wrist with the cuff. "I'm going to remove the gun from your mouth," he says. "When I do, do not make a sound. Or I will kill you. Do you understand?"

I jerk my head.

The muzzle slides from my mouth. I turn my head and hawk spit.

Effortlessly, he rises. Bending to me, he uses the cuff encircling my wrist to pull me to my feet.

"Who are you?" I ask.

Eyes on mine, he puts his index finger to his mouth. "Shhh."

"I'm a cop," I tell him. "You can't—"

I lunge, but he's ready and muscles me over to the barbed-wire fence. There, he swings me around and throws me to the ground. I land on my knees.

"You can't get away with this," I snarl.

"Maybe I will." Bending, he snaps the unused cuff around the wire, trapping me. "Time will tell."

"You murdered Milan Swanz," I say.

Black jacket.

Black trousers.

Giving me only part of his attention, he snaps open the cylinder of my .38, empties the ammo into his palm, and flings all of it into the woods. He drops the .38 into the snow.

"Tell me why," I say.

He gives me a final look, his expression inscrutable, and then he turns away and walks to the sedan.

Blue BMW.

Four-door.

Gray interior.

"Stop!" I yank at the handcuff. "*Stop!*"

The wire holds. Though the fence is old and rusty, it'll take wire cutters to get me free.

Damn it.

Out of the corner of my eye, I see him slide into the sedan.

"Who are you?" I call out. "Why did you kill Swanz?"

Without looking at me, he starts the engine and pulls onto the road.

• • •

No matter how vigorously you train, or adhere to the policies and procedures set forth by your department, no matter how fervently you exercise your God-given good judgment, if you're a cop, there will come a time when you encounter a situation that goes south. Tonight is a case in point.

It's midnight. I'm handcuffed to a barbed-wire fence on a little-traveled rural road. My radio, service weapon, and cell phone are out of reach. I'm freezing my ass off. And there's not a damn thing I can do about any of it. It was over an hour ago that I informed my dispatcher I'd "arrived on scene." I didn't, however, follow up with an "assignment completed" call. My best hope is that she'll notice and dispatch my graveyard-shift officer.

The ambush replays in my mind's eye for the hundredth time as I work the handcuff against the barbed wire, back and forth, in an effort to snap it.

Milan Swanz was a deviant.

He walked in step with the devil.

My attacker spoke with an accent that wasn't Holmes County Amish, but similar. His words contained an undeniable religious element that I recognized. An old Amish saying tickles the back of my mind.

Walk in step with the devil, and you'll hear the flap of his wings.

"The son of a bitch is Amish," I whisper, my breath puffing out in front of me.

It's not a perfect fit. Far from it. For one thing, the Amish are pacifistic; violence is prohibited. They will not defend themselves or their property and view themselves as "defenseless Christians." In times of war, they are conscientious objectors. How, then, could this man who all but admitted he'd murdered Milan Swanz, and threatened to kill me, be Amish?

He's formerly Amish, a little voice adds.

I'm hunkered over the spot where handcuff meets steel, working on the wire, when I spot approaching headlights through the trees. For an instant, I wonder if my attacker has come back to kill me. But I recognize the silhouette of the police cruiser the moment it comes into view.

I get to my feet, bent slightly because the cuff won't allow me to straighten, and I wave my free hand. "Skid! I'm here!"

The cruiser rolls to a stop behind the Explorer. The spotlight comes on, the beam skimming over my vehicle, the ditch, and finally washes over me. An instant later, the red and blue overheads light up and Skid gets out.

"Chief?" His Maglite flicks on.

"I'm here. Cuffed to the fence."

"What the hell?" Keeping his eyes on me, he jogs around to the trunk, pops it, and digs into his equipment box. Then he's striding toward me, fence tool in hand. "What happened?" he says. "You okay?"

"I was ambushed," I tell him. "Male suspect at large. Skid, get the sheriff's department out here."

He reaches me, blinks once at the sight of my face, and for the umpteenth time in the last hour, I feel like a fool. "Uh, Chief, you're bleeding pretty good. You need an ambulance?"

"Just get the sheriff's department."

Without speaking, Skid goes down on one knee.

"Give me your cuff key," I say.

He digs into the compartment on his utility belt, passes me the key. As I unlock the cuff, he tilts his head to his radio mike and requests assistance from the sheriff's department.

CHAPTER 16

Two hours later, I'm sitting in the interview room at the Holmes County Sheriff's Office, ostensibly for a "debriefing." I know it's more likely to be an all-hands-on-deck ass chewing. I spotted Chambers's official vehicle parked outside. Right next to Mayor Auggie Brock's Cadillac.

I gave my initial statement at the scene to the chief deputy of the sheriff's office detective bureau. Skid recovered my radio, my .38, my knife, and my cell phone, which were dusted for prints and returned to me. An APB for the vehicle with a description of the suspect and the plate number was issued. The information was broadcast to all law enforcement agencies in the region, including the Ohio State Highway Patrol.

Now, it's after one A.M. Sheriff Mike Rasmussen sits across from me, looking as if he was roused from a nightmare and didn't get coffee before leaving his house. He's doing his utmost not to make eye contact with me, which only adds to the butterflies wreaking havoc in my gut. Next to him, Chambers thumbs something into his cell phone with the speed of a high-school student. His satisfied expression reveals he's pleased by my being back in the hot seat. Auggie Brock is sprawled in a chair next to the sheriff.

Of all the people in the room, Tomasetti is the most difficult to look at. He's standing at the wall, next to the door, his arms crossed at his chest. I can tell by his expression he's troubled, not only by the situation but by the cuts and bruises on my face. He's a master at keeping all of those gnarly emotions out of the picture. I know him well enough to read between the lines.

Auggie's staring at me. Not exactly making eye contact, but taking in my injuries. I try not to glare at him, but don't quite succeed.

"Kate, did you get yourself checked out at the hospital?" he asks.

"EMT checked me out at the scene," I tell him. "I'm fine."

"Even so." Tomasetti looks at his watch. "I'm sure the chief would appreciate it if you made this quick."

"In that case, let's get started." Chambers hits a button on his cell, drops it on the table in front of him, and takes a moment to look around the room, letting us know he's the man in charge, and we, his underlings, don't quite measure up. "APB is out. Suspect description is out. Vehicle description."

"Anything come back on the plate?" I ask.

"Fraudulent." Chambers rubs his hands together as if he's just sat down to his favorite meal, then looks at me. "Run us through what happened again."

I spend fifteen minutes taking them through the incident from beginning to end, relaying all the details I put to memory.

"So you didn't recognize him?" Chambers asked.

"No, but as I mentioned, the lower half of his face was covered with a scarf," I say.

"He recognized you, though?"

THE BURNING

"He called me by name."

"What exactly did he ask of you?" Chambers continues, not because he doesn't recall my earlier account, but because he wants the others—namely Auggie—to hear it again.

"He said something to the effect—and I'm paraphrasing—that my silence was my sacrifice to make."

"That mean anything to you?" Rasmussen asks.

"Not a thing."

"You mentioned before," Rasmussen says, "that you think he's Amish or formerly Amish?"

I nod. "The accent is Amish-like, but I don't think he's from this area."

"Any idea where he might be from?" the sheriff asks.

"With the Pennsylvania plates, maybe Lancaster County," I reply. "Hard to say."

Chambers doesn't do a very good job of hiding his smirk. "You're certain this man wasn't your brother?"

It's not only a bad joke, but a personal dig designed to spur my temper. I keep my cool, but I know where he's going to take this. I know why we're here. I know why the mayor is here. I know why I'm being asked to repeat information no one needs to hear a second time.

"As I said before, I didn't recognize him," I say.

Looking smug, Chambers glances at Rasmussen.

The sheriff scowls. "Just so you know, we're going to talk to your brother tomorrow, Kate."

"That's your prerogative." Of course, their insistence upon doing something that I've already done makes a clear statement: They don't trust me to do my job.

As if reading my thoughts, he adds, "We don't have a choice, Kate. Your brother is now a person of interest. In light of the alleged argument, he has a motive for wanting Swanz dead."

165

The urge to argue rattles its chain inside me, but I hold my tongue.

"It's late," Tomasetti says from his place at the door. "We're tired. I think we're done here."

"One more thing." Chambers clears his throat, then sends a pointed look to the mayor. "Mayor Brock?"

For the first time, I realize all of them—minus Tomasetti—have already discussed how this is going to end, and I experience a twinge of anxiety.

When Auggie only continues to stare back at him, Chambers sits up a little straighter. "Mayor Brock," he says. "I've made my recommendation to you. That's all I can do at this point. The rest is up to you. In all fairness, I think taking the actions we discussed is the most equitable way to handle this."

Looking uncomfortable, Auggie scoots his chair forward, folds his hands in front of him, and finally meets my gaze. "I'd like to preface by saying none of this is a reflection on Chief Burkholder's competence, her leadership, or her character."

"What are you talking about, Auggie?" My voice comes out surprisingly strong and crisp and I have no idea how I managed because I'm shaking inside.

The mayor looks around as if hoping for approving nods from everyone in the room. The only one he gets comes from Chambers. "We think it's best for the investigation and the township if you took a break from this case, Kate."

"Take a break?" I repeat dumbly. "What the hell does that mean?"

The mayor raises his hand, trying to look as if he's in command. He only manages to look ridiculous and weak and everyone in the room knows he doesn't have the balls to say what he's been asked to say.

"This isn't about you personally or professionally," Auggie continues. "This is about perceptions. The citizens of Painters Mill are uneasy about this murder and understandably so. Because of your brother's possible involvement and your connection to the Amish—"

"It hasn't been determined that my brother is involved," I say.

He cuts me off. "Like I said, this is about public perception. Not you or your capabilities."

"Kate's record and reputation speak for themselves," Tomasetti interjects. "She's a good cop. A damn good investigator. And she's the one person the Amish will talk to. They trust her. That makes her the most valuable resource we've got."

Chambers swivels his head around. "You're not exactly impartial yourself."

Tomasetti's face darkens. It's subtle, but I see his fingers twitch as if he's trying not to clench his hands into fists. "If this is about the case—and that's a big fucking if at this point—Chief Burkholder is the best person for the job and everyone in this room knows it."

Auggie Brock swallows hard. "We don't ask any of this lightly, Agent Tomasetti."

Arms folded across his chest, Tomasetti stares back at him, saying nothing.

Auggie clears his throat and looks at me. "This is just a temporary thing, Kate. When things settle down, I'm sure we'll need you back to help us out. But until we get a better handle on this, I'd like you to take a step back."

I fight to maintain self-control. "How big a step are you suggesting, Auggie?" I ask, my voice taut.

"All the way," Chambers cuts in.

"Limited duty," Auggie clarifies. "Of course, you'll still be paid," he adds hastily. "We just want you to sit things out for a few days. You know, handle the administrative side of things until we can figure out how or if your brother is involved. You understand, don't you?"

For several minutes, I don't move. Then I nod. "I understand perfectly," I say.

Taking my time, I make eye contact with each man in the room. I get to my feet, walk to the door, and go through, not bothering to close it in my wake.

• • •

It's three A.M. and I'm sitting at the table in my quaint farmhouse kitchen, trying not to feel sorry for myself—and failing miserably. This farm—this house—has always been the one place where I don't allow the pressures of my job to intrude. It is my refuge, my escape, and I try very hard to leave the demons of my job at the door.

I left the station without waiting for Tomasetti. As I pulled away, I saw him emerge from the building, and watch me pass. Though I know I have his support, I was too upset to talk to him. The last thing I want to do is lash out. Or, God forbid, cry.

I've just poured two fingers of bourbon into a tumbler when the back door opens. Tomasetti enters with a puff of cold air, his eyes on me, his expression impassive.

His eyes flick to the glass in front of me as he hangs his coat on the rack and he frowns. "Just one glass?"

"I thought two might be overkill," I tell him.

He doesn't quite smile as he crosses to the counter, grabs a tumbler from the shelf, and pours. It's incredibly quiet here at the farm. Tonight, that quiet is so complete I can hear the patter-patter of snowflakes against the window above the sink.

Glass in hand, Tomasetti comes to the table and takes the chair across from me. "Do you want me to pull that knife out of your back?"

"You're the only person in the world who can make me laugh when I'm completely immersed in agony."

"In case you haven't noticed, Neil Chambers is an asshole."

"I noticed." I shake my head. "The problem is, he makes a valid point."

"Yes, he does."

I lift my glass and sip. "I guess I expected more from Auggie and Rasmussen."

"Don't be too hard on Auggie," he says, and frowns. "Chambers recommended he place you on administrative leave."

"Of course he did," I mutter, not liking the bitter taste the words leave on my tongue.

"Auggie and Rasmussen were against that and held their ground."

"Some of it, anyway."

He shrugs. "So, you're not *officially* off the case."

"Just relegated to desk duty."

We fall silent, listen to the wind push against the door. The hum of the refrigerator. The hiss and ting of heated air through the HVAC vents.

Grimacing, he swirls the bourbon in his glass. "Did Milan Swanz molest your nephew?"

Just like that the conversation shifts.

I look at him, think about tossing back the bourbon and pouring another. I don't. "Jacob didn't murder Swanz."

"They're going to pick him up first light. They're going to take him to the station and they're going to question him hard."

"He won't talk to them. Not about his son," I say. "About what happened."

"That's going to be a problem. For Jacob."

"I know. Damn it." I smack my hand against the tabletop because I hate the idea of my brother being subjected to that.

"If Jacob doesn't cooperate, they'll assume he's lying."

"I know." I tell him what transpired between Swanz and my nephew. "Jacob interrupted before anything happened."

"Do you believe him?"

"Yes."

"All right." He turns thoughtful. "On the bright side, it might do Rasmussen and Chambers good to get a taste of that Amish wall of silence."

I'm not feeling quite so optimistic, so I say nothing.

Tomasetti shrugs. "Who knows what you might uncover in the interim."

I feel myself go still, look at him. "What's your point?"

"My point is, it's four o'clock in the morning and fortunately for us insomniacs, the Amish are early risers."

The exhaustion that had been pressing down on me shifts and lightens. I look at the glass of bourbon, sigh, push it aside. "I don't think we should talk to Jacob."

"I agree," he says. "Let Chambers and Rasmussen beat their heads against that brick wall for a few hours." He pauses. "Who else?"

Something that feels vaguely like hope jumps in my chest. "The bishop may be able to tell us something."

He arches a brow.

I tell him about my conversation with Bertha Swanz. "Milan Swanz and Clarence Raber drove to the Troyer farm, forced their way inside, and assaulted the bishop and his wife. When I initially made contact with the bishop, he didn't mention it."

His eyes narrow. "The bishop is well thought of among the Amish."

"Surly as he is," I say, "Bishop Troyer is revered."

"Sounds like Swanz has crossed a lot of people."

"And a lot of lines." I think about that for a moment. "If someone found out Swanz assaulted the bishop. If they found out Swanz had acted inappropriately with a young boy."

"The bishop knew about both of those things?" Tomasetti says.

I nod. "Who's to say someone didn't take it upon themselves to mete out a little justice."

"Sounds like the bishop and his wife are a good place to start."

"I don't think he'll talk to us."

"You underestimate your powers of persuasion."

My smile feels halfhearted.

"Keep your chin up, Chief. We've got a couple of things going for us."

"For the life of me I can't imagine what they might be."

He shrugs. "For one thing, you can probably count on the Amish to not tattle on you to the English police."

I can't help it; I laugh. "What else?"

He glances at the clock. "What time does an Amish bishop get up?"

"About four A.M."

Grinning, he reaches for his keys. "Anyone ever tell you you have excellent timing?"

"No one has ever told me that."

•   •   •

Half an hour later, Tomasetti and I are standing on the front porch of the farmhouse Bishop Troyer shares with his wife, Freda. This time, she doesn't keep me waiting. The hinges squeak and the door rolls open a few inches.

The Amish woman squints at me through the gap, thick-lensed glasses making her eyes look huge. "*Ach du lieva*," she says in a gravelly voice. Oh my goodness. "You again."

Her eyes travel to Tomasetti and her upper lip curls. "*Was der Schinner is letz?*" What in the world is wrong?

She may be a tiny thing, but the force of her personality more than makes up for her lack of physical stature. No one, Amish or English—maybe not even the bishop himself—speaks out of turn to Freda Troyer without risking a verbal beatdown—or a smack with the horsewhip she purportedly keeps on her kitchen counter.

"I'm sorry to bother you so early this morning, Mrs. Troyer," I say in *Deitsch*. "I need to speak with the bishop."

She doesn't open the door any wider; she doesn't give up any ground, literally or figuratively. Her stare flicks from Tomasetti and back to me. "If you think he's got anything else to say about a dead man, I reckon you have another thing coming."

"I'll take my chances," I say.

A flash of annoyance, an instant of hesitation, and the door creaks open. Without speaking, she turns and trundles toward the kitchen.

Tomasetti and I exchange looks and follow. In the kitchen, the aromas of pancakes and some kind of breakfast meat lace the air.

"*Sitz dich anne.*" Sit yourself there. "*Witt du kaffi?*" Would you like coffee?

"*Dank.*" I take one of six chairs at the rectangular table that's draped with a checkered cloth. Tomasetti takes the chair across from me. Between us, a lantern flickers next to salt and pepper shakers in the shape of cats.

Freda is pouring from an old-fashioned percolator when the back door swings open. Bishop Troyer enters with a gust of wind, a flurry of snow, and glares at me.

"I thought I saw a car come up the lane." His voice is like a dog growling through wool.

"*Guder mariye,*" I say to him. Good morning.

He looks at his wife and responds, "Never a good sign when trouble comes to your door before you've fed the cows."

"I had no say in the matter." Huffing, she brings our cups to the table and sets them down. "Now come on over here and talk to this *druvvel-machah* before she gets too comfortable." Troublemaker.

CHAPTER 17

"What's so important that you've come to our home at four o'clock in the morning?"

Bishop Troyer sits at the head of the kitchen table. Tomasetti and I are across from each other. Freda Troyer busies herself at the counter, clanging the occasional dish, listening.

"Last time I was here, I asked you specifically if you'd had any problems with Milan Swanz," I say. "You lied to me."

He takes the accusation in stride. "Milan Swanz is gone. He met a bad end. I'll not speak ill of him. Nor should you."

Impatience thumps, but I knock it back, concentrate on keeping my focus. "Tell me about the night Milan Swanz and Clarence Raber came into your home and assaulted you and your wife."

Behind me, I hear Freda's quick intake of breath.

The bishop stares at me, unruffled, rheumy eyes as sharp and cold as the night outside. "I've nothing to say about Milan Swanz."

"I know what he did to you," I tell him. "I know what he did to your wife."

The old man waves his hand dismissively. "Even as a girl, you always thought you knew more than you did."

"Bishop, this isn't about me. It isn't even really about Milan Swanz or his shortcomings. This is about finding the person responsible for his death."

"That is your path to walk, Kate Burkholder, not mine."

I bring my hand down on the tabletop hard enough to rattle the salt and pepper shakers. Out of the corner of my eye, I see Freda jump. Across from me, Tomasetti's brows go up.

"Don't give me that crap," I snap. "Stop playing games with me. A man is dead. He was killed in the most horrific way imaginable. His killer is still out there. If he does it again, if he takes another life, it's going to be on you, Bishop."

The old man doesn't react. Nothing seems to shake him. Nothing moves him. "It is in God's hands. Not yours. Not mine."

Freda comes to the table, sets a steaming cup in front of her husband, and addresses him, ignoring me and Tomasetti. "Milan Swanz was no friend of the *Amisch*."

The bishop's expression is hard to read, but he doesn't dispute her claim. Something within him seems to shift.

Grumbling beneath her breath, Freda goes back to the counter.

The silence that follows drags on for so long that I don't think he's going to respond. When he finally speaks, his voice is so low, I have to lean closer to hear.

"Milan came in the middle of the night," the bishop begins. "By the time I got downstairs, he'd already let himself into the kitchen. He'd been excommunicated for a few weeks by then, and he wanted to be reinstated. He'd been drinking, you know, crying and shouting. I told him it had been decided by the congregation and the decision was unanimous and final."

"What did he do?" I ask quietly.

The bishop looks down at his hands on the tabletop in front of him. "He took my cane. Pushed me to the floor. Took a knife out of his pocket. And he cut my beard. Some of my hair. Hacked off a big chunk of it."

"I thought Milan was going to cut his throat," Freda says from her place at the sink.

The bishop waves his hand at her.

"Was Clarence Raber with him?" I ask.

"*Ja.*"

"Did Clarence participate in the attack?" I ask.

"No."

"Didn't do anything to stop it either," Freda puts in.

I look at her. "Did Milan hurt you, too?"

"He pushed me down," she huffs. "Tore off my *kapp.* Sawed off some of my hair."

I nod, trying to absorb the scenes they are describing. An elderly Amish couple attacked in the middle of the night. I consider what that could mean in terms of Swanz's fate. If someone found out about it . . .

"Mr. and Mrs. Troyer, does anyone know what happened that night?" I ask. "Did you talk to anyone about it?"

Even as I ask, I realize the question is moot. Bertha Swanz knew about it. The women who'd told her knew. Still, I let the question stand to see where it leads.

The couple exchanges a look. "The *Diener,*" the bishop says. "I told them. I thought they should know."

The *Diener,* or "servants," are the elected officials who are the leaders of the church district. In Painters Mill, that includes the bishop, the deacon, and the minister. I think of Monroe Hershberger, the deacon whose cornfield was destroyed, and make a mental note to talk to him again.

"Can you think of anyone else who might've been wronged by Milan?" This from Tomasetti. "Someone he'd hurt? Or crossed in some way?"

"The Amish are not violent," the bishop says adamantly, then turns his iron gaze on me. "You know that."

"Why did you and the *Diener* and the congregation finally decide to excommunicate Milan?" I ask.

A moment's hesitation and then the bishop shakes his head. "There were many reasons. Too many. Milan was a fool and his own worst enemy."

It doesn't elude me that he didn't answer the question.

As if unable to maintain her silence any longer, Freda slings the kitchen towel over her shoulder and comes back to the table, sets her hands on her hips. "I was close with his *mamm* for a time. We thought Milan's misbehaving would get better once he got baptized. Got married. Had children. Responsibility, you know." She shakes her head. "But it didn't get better. And we began to hear things."

The bishop looks up at her and frowns. "A man's marriage is not the business of others."

"A child being hurt is," Freda snaps.

"What kinds of things did you hear?" I ask.

She tightens her mouth. "We saw little Aaron come to worship with his arm in a cast. I noticed the way Bertha wouldn't look at me. Saw a black eye on her, too, once or twice. Said she fell down the steps." She clucks her lips in disgust. "As if I was born yesterday. Wouldn't talk about it. But I knew. All of us knew."

"They don't need to hear all of that," the bishop grumbles in *Deitsch*.

"*Sei ruich.*" Be quiet. The Amish woman utters the words gently, then puts her hand on his shoulder and pats it. "A few days later, Bertha came to me. She was at wits' end. Needed to talk. To an elder, you know. A woman. And I got an earful."

"Freda." There's a warning in the bishop's voice.

His wife pays him no heed. "He'd been hitting her. The little ones too—and not just spanking when they needed it."

The bishop picks up his spoon and taps it hard against the tabletop. "Enough."

I look from the bishop to Freda. "Did anyone else know Bertha and her children were being abused?" I ask. "A father? Brother? Uncle? Someone who might've wanted to protect them? Someone who might've confronted Milan about it?"

"We've said our due," the bishop growls. "You'll have to ask Bertha about the rest of it."

"Mr. and Mrs. Troyer." Tomasetti's voice seems loud and deep in the silence of the old farmhouse. "Do either of you have any idea who might've done that to Swanz?"

The bishop stares at him for a long time. Wily, intelligent eyes belie the failing body, and not for the first time I'm reminded that there's nothing even remotely frail about David Troyer.

"No," he says simply.

I look at Freda, but she turns back to the counter without meeting my gaze.

I rise. "Thank you for the coffee." Without waiting for a response, I start for the door.

I hear Tomasetti behind me as I stride through the living room. The hiss of the potbellied stove in the corner. The tinkle of ice crystals against the north window.

Frustrated that we didn't glean any new information, I yank open the door, step onto the porch, take in a breath of cold air.

"That was a waste of time," I mutter.

"Old man's a hard case." Tomasetti closes the door behind us, looks out into the darkness. "Why the hell did I get the impression that they know more than they're letting on?"

"Welcome to Amish country."

We're midway down the steps when I hear the front door creak. I turn to see Freda close it behind her and come down the steps.

"I knew he wouldn't talk to you," she says.

"Nice of you to come out and tell me that." I start to turn, but she stops me.

"Katie. Wait." Her face is a mosaic of conflict, of warring emotions, and a loyalty she cannot betray.

Because I understand, because I've felt all of those things myself when I was Amish, I wait.

"There are whispers," the woman says quietly. "About a group of men. Former Amish mostly. Mennonite and Hutterite, too, maybe. Anabaptists, you know."

"What about them?"

"These men . . . Katie, I don't know if you can understand. The things they do . . . it goes against everything we know. Everything we believe. It goes against God's will." She struggles for a moment, then stiffens her spine. "These men . . . their souls are dark. They know that when they die, they will not be going to heaven. They live with that knowledge. They accept it. Somehow, they see the ungodliness of that as the freedom they need to do the things that a godly man cannot."

I stare at her, perplexed, and yet at the same time I feel a distant memory scratch at the back of my brain. A story or rumors that I'd heard in my youth but were lost over the years.

"What does this group have to do with what happened to Milan Swanz?" I ask.

"These men have given their souls to *da deivel*," she tells me. The devil. "They do bad things—very bad things—but for a greater good. If that's even possible. Things that a good *Amisch* cannot and will not do."

"Are you telling me these men, this group, had something to do with the murder?"

"I couldn't say." She shrugs. "I always thought it was a rumor. A *shtoahri*." A story. She lowers her voice. "Now, after all of this, I'm not so sure. I think there may be some truth to it."

I almost can't believe what I'm hearing. Not from the bishop's wife. The notion that such a group exists is so crazy I can't get my head around it. "Freda, how do you even know about these men?"

"I don't. But I'll tell you what I *do* know." She pauses as if searching her memory. "I have relatives in Shipshewana. I spent many a happy time there with my cousins when I was little. Spent a whole summer there once when my niece was born. Anyway, an Amish man was killed that last summer I was there. A *druvvel-machah* by the name of Marvin Lengacher." Troublemaker. "Awful thing. Hanged himself in the barn. Or so everyone believed."

"What do you mean?" I ask.

"Turned out someone did that to him. Tied him up and hung him up by his neck. I was thirteen years old that summer. Scared me and my little cousins half to death."

"Who did it?" I ask.

"Everyone was talking about the Schwertlers. Even the elders were whispering about it, saying they're the ones came for Marvin and done him like that. And it never got told to the police."

I scribble the name in my notebook. "Who are the Schwertlers?"

"I couldn't say."

"Freda, what year was that?"

"Well, I'm eighty-six this fall. My goodness, happened over seventy years ago, but I remember it like it was yesterday."

"Do you have any names?"

"No one knows their names."

"How many people in this group?"

"No one knows that, either, Katie." She makes the statement with impatience, as if I should already know the answer.

I look down at my notes. "Freda, if that happened over seventy years ago, whoever belonged to that group would be elderly now. Most would be gone."

"Unless there's new blood for every generation. There are a lot of fallen men out there, ready to step up to do what they need to do."

"Are you telling me this group of men still exists and they're in Painters Mill?"

"They're everywhere," she whispers.

"How do I find them?"

Freda glances over her shoulder, toward the door, which has remained shut. In the back of my mind, I wonder if she has any idea how crazy her story sounds. How unlikely it is that any of what she's told me is seated in reality.

"I don't know," she tells me.

"Is there someone I can talk to who knows about them?"

"I heard there's a Hutterite man." She whispers quickly now, as if the words aren't meant to be spoken aloud or heard by others. "He lives in a compound over to Dundee."

Another vague memory, something I've heard . . .

"What's his name?" Tomasetti speaks up for the first time.

"Last name is Hofer. That's all I know." She shakes her head. "I shouldn't even be speaking to you about it. Most Amish don't believe this group exists. Call it folklore. But I'm old enough to remember."

The door creaks. I glance past her, see Bishop Troyer standing in the doorway, holding open the door, looking out at us. *"Die zeit fer kumma inseid is nau."* The time to come inside is now.

"Find him," the old woman whispers, and turns away.

I call out her name.

She doesn't stop and she doesn't look back.

CHAPTER 18

"Do you have any earthly idea what the hell she was talking about?" It is the ten-thousand-dollar question and Tomasetti is the one to pose it.

We're in the Explorer, parked on the street outside the police station. We didn't talk much after leaving the Troyer farm earlier. Neither of us has a clue what to think of Freda Troyer's assertion that there's a group of Anabaptist men who do away with fellow evildoers.

"She *is* elderly," he says slowly, "is it possible—"

"This is going to sound odd, but I *think* I've heard of them."

He makes a sound of incredulity. "Are you saying you believe this group actually exists?"

"I'm saying I remember a story like that from when I was a kid. Like a ghost story that gets repeated and yet no one really believes it."

He looks dubious.

"I don't blame you for being skeptical. I'm right there with you."

I consider the scene back at the Troyer farm for a moment. "I think it's noteworthy that the bishop stayed inside while Freda talked to us. If he'd objected, you can bet he would have stopped her."

"So, she did it with his blessing."

"If I didn't know better, I might think he *wanted* us to have the information."

"If we can even refer to that as 'information' at this point."

I frown at him. "I'm going to dig around. See what I can find. Run the name. See if anything pops."

"In the meantime, if I were to plug a few signature aspects into ViCAP, what the hell would they be?"

ViCAP is a database administered by the FBI that's used to match connections between cases. I shrug. "Amish. Homicide. Suicide. Religious. Fire. Burning. Wooded area. Barn. Ritualistic." I feel my brows furrow as my memory stirs. "Tomasetti, I *do* recall reading about a Hutterite community opening a business in Tuscarawas County. They've been around a few years."

"If you don't mind my asking, what exactly *is* a Hutterite community?"

"The Hutterites are Anabaptist, as are the Amish, but the similarities end there. The Hutterites use more technology—like vehicles and electricity—and seem to have more industrial-type businesses. Probably the biggest difference is that they live in a commune-type colony."

"Haight-Ashbury meets the Amish?"

I can't help it; I smile. "Sans the peace signs and dope."

His cell hums from its place on his belt. He reaches for it, growls his name. I try not to notice when he frowns. "I'll be there in a few minutes," he tells the caller.

A short silence ensues, and then he sighs, ends the call without responding, and turns his attention to me. "Guess we knew that was coming."

"You've been summoned?"

He nods. "Chambers wants me gone."

"He say that?"

"Just reading between the lines."

We watch Glock pull into his parking space. Spotting the Explorer, he raises his hand and waves. I wave back.

I put the Explorer in gear. "I'll take you back to your vehicle so you can go get your ass kicked."

He sighs. "What are you going to do about Hofer?"

"I'm going to dig," I say. "I think that's the one thing I can still manage on my own."

•   •   •

I drop Tomasetti at the farm. It's still early. Ordinarily, I'd swing by the station to touch base with my team before beginning my day. Because I've been placed on administrative duty, I skip the station and call Dispatch on my way to Dundee. To my relief, Mona is still there after working graveyard shift.

"I need a favor," I tell her.

"Lay it on me."

"Dig up everything you can find on the last name Hofer out of Dundee in Tuscarawas County." I spell the name.

"First name?"

"No go."

"Male? Female? White? Black?"

"White male. I think."

"That'll get me started," she says. "How quick do you need it?"

"An hour ago?"

She snickers but I can hear the click of her keyboard in the background. "Firing up my time machine now." A moment of silence and then, "Chief?"

"Yeah?"

"Thought you should know . . . it's kind of weird around here."

I take a breath, brace. "How so?"

"It's almost as if the sheriff's office has, you know, taken over the investigation."

The last thing I want to do is involve her in the politics that run hand in hand with my position as chief. That said, Mona is tight lipped when she needs to be. I need her in my corner, so I give her the lowdown on the situation with my brother and my being asked to step aside.

"My inquiry into Hofer is kind of unofficial, okay?" I say.

"Unofficial is my specialty, Chief. I'll call you as soon as I know something."

Dundee is a pretty little hamlet half an hour northeast of Painters Mill. I called the Tuscarawas County Sheriff's Office on the way and spoke to one of the deputies who patrols the area. He was able to give me the address of the Hutterite community, which I plugged into my GPS. Mona came through, and to my relief, there aren't many Hofers in the county. She narrowed it down by age, race, and sex, and came up with the name Isaiah Hofer, forty-six years old. Clean record. No outstanding warrants. The address matches the one given to me by the deputy. Bingo.

I enter Dundee's main thoroughfare from the south, pass by a Methodist church, a post office, and a restaurant with a big sign out front advertising their Thursday Big Meal. I'm through town before realizing I missed my turn. I'm searching for a place to hang a U-turn when my GPS instructs me to take a left on Walnut Creek Bottom Road.

The road lives up to its name. Walnut trees and various native hardwoods tower over the narrow stretch of asphalt. There's a shallow swamp on both sides of the road with patches of winter-dead cattail reeds. Four miles in I pass over a creek and then drive past an ancient-looking German bank barn. The barely-there gravel track on my left comes up quick and I brake, make the turn, and start down a lane that's more dirt than gravel. The Explorer bumps over rough ground and deep ruts. Trees and brush scrape at my doors like fingers seeking the warmth inside. A quarter mile in and I begin to wonder if I made a wrong turn. I'm second-guessing my GPS and looking for a place to turn around when the trees part.

"Destination ahead," comes the mechanical GPS voice.

I enter a large gravel lot, its borders demarked with massive cut stones. To my right, a billboard with a stop-sign graphic warns:

SUGARCREEK COLONY
DO NOT ENTER

I roll past the sign. Farther in, a row of six identical structures, each about the size of a double-wide trailer, backs up to the woods. The façades are the same, the doors and windows in exactly the same place, along with duplicate sapling trees in each front yard. Ahead, I see a larger two-story building with a portico entrance and a dozen or so windows. To my left, a steel barn is set back a few yards from the gravel area. Behind it, I see livestock pens and a small herd of Black Angus cattle gathered at a round bale of hay, their backs dusted with snow.

I watch for movement all around, but there's not a soul in sight, and I wonder if this is what it would feel like to be the last person on earth. I park in front of the two-story building. The snow is coming down in earnest now. Thanks to a cold front that slipped through earlier, the temperature has dropped and the white stuff is beginning to stick.

A brisk wind cuffs me as I get out and start toward the building. The aromas of woodsmoke, manure, and snow lace the air. I'm not sure where to go, so I continue toward the largest building. Midway there, I spot a sign on the façade telling me the social hall is to my right. I follow the covered sidewalk to an official-looking building with paned windows and board-and-batten siding. A sign next to the door reads QUARRY OFFICE. I notice lights inside, so I go to the front door and enter.

A woman sits at the reception desk. She's wearing a navy-and-black jumper over a white blouse with a high neckline. I guess her to be about thirty years old. Dark hair parted in the middle and covered with a black-and-white polka-dot scarf. *Hutterite,* I realize, or some version thereof.

"Hi." I have my shield at the ready. "I'm the chief of police in Painters Mill," I tell her. "I'm looking for Mr. Hofer."

Her eyes widen as she inspects my badge. "Um." Tilting her head, she looks at me quizzically. "Is there a problem?"

"No, ma'am," I tell her. "I just have a few questions for him."

"Whatever she's selling, we're not buying!" comes a jovial male voice from somewhere in the back. "Unless they're Girl Scout cookies in which case I'll take two!"

The woman and I share a smile.

A man appears at the mouth of the hallway that leads to the rear of the building. He does a double take upon spotting the Painters Mill PD insignia on my parka, his stride slowing. He sets his hand against his chest as if I've startled him. According to Mona, Isaiah Hofer is forty-six years old. White male. Six feet tall. One hundred and ninety pounds. Brown. Brown. The man standing ten feet away from me fits the bill to a T.

"Isaiah Hofer?" I ask.

He takes my measure, his expression inscrutable. "At your service."

I start toward him. "Had I known you're a fan of Girl Scout cookies, I would have brought some with me."

"Thin Mints'll do just fine." He holds his ground, his gaze flicking to the police insignia on my parka. "You're a long way from Painters Mill."

He looks closer to fifty. Not because of any physical frailty, but because his persona emanates the polish of a more mature man. He's got a muscular physique, angular and lean. He's clad almost entirely in black. Jacket with no collar. Plaid shirt. Suspenders. A tidy beard that's thick and shot with gray.

"I'm working on a case in Painters Mill," I tell him. "If you have a few minutes, I'd like to ask you some questions."

He's got an interesting face. Classically handsome features, direct eyes, and a mouth that seems to smile easily. His is a poker face, too, and though I'm standing close enough to discern the pine and leather scent of his aftershave, I can't tell if my presence is welcome or if it will be rebuffed.

"Of course," he says. "Though I must admit I'm curious as to what case you're referring to."

"The Milan Swanz case in Painters Mill," I tell him.

"The murder?" His brows go up as if I've surprised him. "I read about it. Heinous to say the least, especially for a small town in Amish country. Have you made an arrest?"

"Still working on it."

"Do you mind if we walk?" For the first time I notice the coat beneath his arm. He glances down at my feet. "Unfortunately for those clean boots of yours, I was on my way out to the equipment yard."

"No problem."

Holding my gaze, he slips on the coat, and addresses the woman at the desk. "I'm going to get the VIN number off that dump truck in the back, Elisabeth. We'll be right back."

"Thank you, Mr. Hofer." Her eyes slide to me and then she goes back to her computer work.

He strides to the door, opens it for me, and we go through. "Getting cold," he says conversationally.

"Snow on the way," I tell him.

On the porch, we take a moment to slip on scarves and gloves. Now that I'm closer to him, I notice that one of his eyes is blue, the other brown.

"Have you ever been to Painters Mill?" I ask.

"I think I've been through there a couple of times. Bought some nice Amish cheese there last summer. Some eggs."

"Have you ever met Milan Swanz?"

"Never heard the name until I read that awful piece in *The Budget* this morning."

We've reached the end of the sidewalk that wraps around the building. "Ground's a little messy but we've just a short distance to go. Is that all right?"

"Sure."

We leave the sidewalk and start toward a wooded area where a well-used path cuts through the trees.

"I understand you're Hutterite," I say.

"I am. This is a Hutterite community. Sixteen people live and work here. We've been running the quarry for nearly eight years now."

He eyes me intently. "Burkholder is an Amish name."

"I was born Amish," I tell him. "Left when I was eighteen."

"Ah." He nods, thoughtful. "Some would see pacifism as being incompatible with law enforcement."

I'm not here to talk about my Amish roots, so I don't respond. "And the Hutterites?"

The hint of a smile. "We're defenseless Christians, too, of course."

The trail is wide enough for us to walk side by side now. I'm keenly aware of his proximity to me. His size and strength. The .38 in the shoulder holster beneath my coat. I hear the rise and fall of heavy equipment ahead. Through the trees I can see the silhouette of a large truck. Hofer sets an easy pace. He seems as comfortable with the cold and mud as he is with the chitchat and talk of murder.

The tremolo of a loon sounds in the distance. He stops, looks over at me, and smiles. "On his way to Canada, no doubt."

"It's unusual to hear them this far south."

"Especially so late in the year. One more reason why the beauty of the call is so appreciated by those of us who pay attention. We understand the worth of rarity."

We pass a sign that reads SUGARCREEK SAND AND GRAVEL, and the path opens to a large area of excavated ground. Dozens of trees have been felled, the trunks piled high. On the far end of the clearing, two men work in tandem, dragging branches to form a second pile. A dump truck and John Deere backhoe sit several yards from a mound of freshly excavated earth. Beyond, the scarred land sweeps down to a pit so deep I can't see the base.

"This is our main gravel pit here at Sugarcreek." He leaves the path and starts toward the dump truck. "We've a defunct quarry a quarter mile or so to the north. Unfortunately for us, this one is just about spent, too."

I follow him, trying to avoid the mud as best I can. "Seems like a good business to have in this part of Ohio."

"It was," he tells me. "But with our second quarry nearly depleted, we'll likely be closing up shop inside a year."

We reach an old Kenworth truck with a green cab and beat-up dump body. Hofer wades through mud to the driver's-side door, opens it, and bends to look at the forward doorframe. I watch as he pulls out a pad, and writes down the VIN.

"Mr. Hofer, what can you tell me about the Schwertler Anabaptists?" I ask.

He looks at me over his shoulder. "Not many people have heard of them."

"Do they exist?" I ask. "Have they ever existed?"

He pulls reading glasses from his pocket, slips them onto his nose, and goes back to the VIN. "Depends on who you ask. Where you look."

"Is it possible there's some connection between this group and what happened to Milan Swanz?"

Taking his time, he double-checks the number, straightens, and drops the notebook into his coat pocket. "Is it true what the newspapers said, Chief Burkholder? That Milan Swanz was burned at the stake?"

"I believe that's what happened to him."

"I'm sure you're aware that during the Reformation, the Anabaptists were persecuted, and many of them were burned at the stake." For a split second the kindly persona vanishes and I see the flash of something feral beneath the carefully tended surface.

"*Martyrs Mirror,*" I say.

Approval whispers across his features. "Is that the kind of connection you're looking for?"

"No."

"Let me ask you this, Chief Burkholder. What kind of man was Milan Swanz?"

"I didn't know him personally," I hedge, purposefully keeping it vague. "According to some, he was troubled."

"He was Amish?"

"Excommunicated."

"Any idea why?"

"I suspect he broke the rules one too many times."

His eyes have a piercing countenance despite the crinkles on the outer corners. And while this man may look like some kindly father figure at first glance, the energy coming off him doesn't jibe.

"Was he violent?" he asks.

"On occasion."

"Did he ever hurt anyone?" he asks. "The people around him? Loved ones?"

"Mr. Hofer, why do you ask?"

He shrugs. "Troubled people do troubled things. Sometimes they do unsavory things. They make mistakes. They make enemies. No?"

When I don't respond, he studies my face for a moment. "Do you believe in fairy tales, Chief Burkholder? Legends? Folklore?"

The change of subjects annoys me, but I'm just curious enough to let him continue. "No, I don't."

"How well do you *know* your fairy tales?"

"Well enough to know they have absolutely nothing to do with my case or this conversation. No offense."

"None taken." He smiles, a parent amused by a precocious child.

"Mr. Hofer, do you know anything about the Schwertler Anabaptists? Do they exist? If so, are they still around?"

"If you'll indulge me?"

I stare at him, taking in the intensity in his eyes, the weird energy coming off him, and I realize he's going somewhere with this.

"Go ahead," I say, hoping it has something to do with the case.

"I'm sure you're aware that most fairy tales were originally very dark. Monstrous, even. Tales of cannibalism. Torture. Rape. Mutilation. Murder. Some of those fairy tales, or legends if you will, hold a thread of truth that has been lost over the years. We humans have become quite weak, you see. We've developed a fondness for euphemisms."

"Are you referring to a specific legend or fairy tale?" I ask.

The question elicits the shadow of a smile. "When I was a boy, my grandfather regaled me with tales of the Schwertler Anabaptists."

"Who are they?" I ask.

Another smile, this one darker, a cruel child exulting in tearing the wings off an insect, poking a needle into its center. "My *mamm* scolded him, of course. She assured me they didn't exist. And she forbade my grandfather from speaking of them."

"So the Schwertler Anabaptists are nothing more than a fairy tale," I say.

The kindly-father persona returns and he smiles at me, crow's-feet deepening, eyes sparkling. "You have remained Anabaptist, no?"

"For the most part," I say, aware that we've edged into an area that's too personal. "A Mennonite minister officiated my wedding."

He nods in approval. "I like you, Chief Burkholder. Yours is a face that has seen hardship. And despair, I think. You have courage and a lion's heart. When you trust, you trust deeply. You're smart, and yet here you are, out here in the snow and mud and cold, all alone with a man you don't know and probably shouldn't trust."

I think about telling him I have a .38 revolver beneath my coat, but I don't. "Tell me about the Schwertler Anabaptists."

"I'm afraid I've told you all I can." Stepping away, he closes the door of the dump truck. "If there's more to be learned, you'll have to do it on your own."

"How do I do that?" I ask.

He starts to turn away, ostensibly to return to the social hall, but I reach out and touch his arm. "Mr. Hofer, is there someone I can get in touch with who might—"

Touching his sleeve is an innocent gesture, not overly assertive, but he swivels to me. There is a fierceness to his expression. His eyes flash. Out of the corner of my eye I see his left hand clench. His right comes at me as if to reach for my throat. He stops short of touching me.

"Beware the monsters that are familiar to you, Kate Burkholder."

I blink at him, taken back. "I don't know what you mean."

"I've said my piece."

"Give me a name," I say. "Someone I can talk to."

Eyes blazing, he leans closer. So close I smell tobacco and menthol on his breath, the unpleasant redolence of coffee, and I resist the urge to step back. "You think you're tough. Strong. You trust your instincts implicitly. Perhaps this is the time for you to rethink all of that and go home."

"This isn't about me," I say, grasping for calm. "I have a job to do and I intend to do it with or without your help."

"Good luck with that."

"Mr. Hofer, I'm trying to find out who murdered Milan Swanz," I tell him. "I was told the Schwertler Anabaptists may have been involved and that you might be able to help me."

"All I can tell you about the Schwertlers, Chief Burkholder, is that if you draw their attention, you won't like the results. And you won't see them coming."

"Who are you talking about?" I snap.

He speaks over me. "If you cross them, they will come for you. They will find you. They will devour you. And they will spit out the residue. The pieces of you will never be found. There will be no resolution. No closure. Consider that the next time you look into the eyes of the people who love you."

At that, he turns away and slogs through the mud and snow to the mouth of the path. I listen to the snow pellets strike the dump truck, the shoulders of my coat, and I watch him go.

CHAPTER 19

I've experienced my share of the bizarre and I'm no shrinking violet when it comes to dealing with hostile individuals. But I'm shaking when I reach the Explorer and slide behind the wheel, partly from anger, partly from the sheer disconcerting nature of the encounter. I sit there for a moment, trying to regain a sense of calm. What the hell am I supposed to make of Isaiah Hofer and the ominous if vague threats he's made to me?

I learned nothing substantive about the Schwertler Anabaptists, but I'm exponentially more curious. I rack my brain, trying to think of someone who might be able to fill in the blanks. It's a short list. Freda Troyer gave me just enough for me to find Hofer. Hofer left me with the uneasy impression that the group is, at the very least, worth looking into. I can't think of a soul I can turn to for information.

That's the thing about the Amish. Sure, they're good neighbors. They're hardworking. Family oriented. Generally speaking, they're quiet and cooperative and will go out of their way to help you if you need a roof on your house or a chicken coop or a new barn because yours burned to the ground. The Amish are a lot of good things, but they are not always forthcoming. There are certain subjects that are taboo, particularly when it concerns their brethren, and they will not speak of it, especially to the English and even if it means lying to the police.

Cursing the Amish aversion to cell phones, I jam the Explorer into gear and start for Painters Mill.

•   •   •

It's late afternoon when I pull into the lane of my brother's farm. I'm midway to the house when the back door opens. I look up to see Jacob trotting down the porch steps.

He stiffens upon spotting me, slows his stride. I can practically see the protective shield activate.

"I need your help," I say without preamble.

"About Milan Swanz?" His mouth turns down as if he's bitten into something sour. "I've told you everything I know."

"This is about . . . something else," I say.

"I won't talk to you about James, Katie. I mean it."

"This isn't about James."

We meet in the gravel next to my Explorer, two contenders about to face off, uncertain which of us will throw the first punch. We stand there, willing our defenses to relax, snow tapping the shoulders of our coats.

"All right." He looks out at the barn. "I need to feed the cows."

"I'll help you."

A quick look of surprise, and then he starts toward the barn. "You always were one for a lot of talk." But his expression softens. "Mamm used to call you her little *shvetzah*." Her little talker.

"She might've been onto something." I fall into step beside him. "Not quite like old times, is it?"

"Let's just say the career you chose suits you." He gives me the side-eye. "Always asking too many questions."

In the barn, he strides directly to the raised wooden floor at the rear, which is directly above the livestock pens. There, he bends to a half-full burlap bag, picks it up, and hands it to me. I take it, my muscles recalling the weight, the routine of it, my olfactory nerves remembering the smell of the feed, even though I haven't fed cattle in years.

He hefts a fifty-pound bag onto his shoulder, and we carry the bags to the feeding cutouts in the floor. He removes the wood cover and I dump the contents of my bag into the trough below. I'm aware of the cattle coming in from outside, pushing and shoving, vying for position. Jacob goes to the second cutout, removes the cover, and dumps feed into the other end of the trough.

When he's finished, I fold the burlap bag in half and we walk back to where a dozen more bags are stored. "I spoke to Bishop Troyer and his wife this morning. Freda mentioned a group called the Schwertler Anabaptists. Have you heard of them? Do you know anything about them?"

Before he turns to stow the empty bags, I see a flicker of something I can't quite identify in his expression. "I don't know anything about them," he says.

"You've heard of them?"

He concentrates on the bags, not looking at me. "That group, Katie . . . it's nothing but a *shtoahri*." Story. "The kind parents tell their teenagers when they've reached their *rumspringa* years. To keep them from doing things they shouldn't do. Keep them out of trouble."

"Tell me what you know," I say.

He gives me an annoyed look over his shoulder and then starts toward the stairs to the loft. "I told you; I don't know anything about them."

Only then does it strike me that my brother is lying. For whatever reason, he doesn't want to answer my question. It's an interesting development because Jacob is one of the most straightforward people I know, sometimes to a fault. If he doesn't want to talk about something, he says so. This time . . . . he chose to lie.

I follow him to the stairs and then up the steps. "To your credit, you're not a very good liar."

"I'm just telling you I don't know much about them. What little I've heard is probably wrong. By all accounts, I doubt they even exist. That's all."

"Some Amish are very much under the impression that they do exist."

"Then you should talk to them and leave me to my work."

My temper stirs, but I push it back. "I'm asking you."

He bends to pick up a bale of hay, glares at me over the top of it. "Why are you so interested in this group?"

"Jacob, I think they may somehow be involved with what happened to Milan Swanz."

"You've always had an active imagination." Without looking at me, he grabs another bale and carries it to the door that looks out over the cattle pens below. "The Schwertler Anabaptists are a tall tale, Katie. Folklore. They don't exist. You should leave it at that and move on to something else."

"You've never lied to me, Jacob. But you are now, and that tells me your reluctance to talk about this group is more important than any morals you have about lying."

He makes a sound that's part laugh, part annoyance. "Think what you will."

I reach for a bale of hay, heft it onto my hip, carry it to the door, and set it on the floor next to the door. "At least tell me what you *think* you know. Or what you've heard. I need a starting point. Something to work with."

He drops the bale of hay he'd lifted and gives me a deadpan look. "If you want to know about the Anabaptists, do what the English tourists do and go to the Heritage Center. Talk to the man who runs it. I've had enough of your questions."

He's referring to the Amish and Mennonite Heritage Center in Berlin. "Damn it, why won't you help me?"

"I've got to feed the hogs now." He lifts the bale, sets it atop the others near the loft door. "We're finished here."

I finally lose my temper. "What happened to you, Jacob? What happened to your honor? Your integrity? Your courage?"

He swings to face me, sets his hands on his hips. "I could ask you the same questions. I'm not the only one who thinks so."

"I'm doing my job."

"You always are." Turning away, he starts toward the stairs.

I call out his name. The only sound that greets me is the slamming of the door.

• • •

The Amish and Mennonite Heritage Center is located on a quiet county road, a short distance from Painters Mill. The museum is a Holmes County fixture that appeals to tourists as well as locals, and informs all visitors of the Amish, Mennonite, and Hutterite cultures. Though I've lived in the area most of my life, I've only visited once. It was a few years ago, and I found it pleasant and surprisingly enlightening.

Unfortunately for me, the center closes at four thirty in the wintertime, and I make it by the skin of my teeth. I enter to the smells of lemon oil and old paper. An Amish woman stands behind the counter, in front of a large display of devotional head coverings mounted on the wall, a set of keys in her hand.

"Can I help you?" she asks.

I remove my shield as I cross to the counter and identify myself. "Is the curator around?"

Her eyes flick to the wall clock. "We're getting ready to close. We open at nine thirty tomorrow morning—"

"This is actually an official visit." I soften the statement with a smile. "I'd appreciate it if I could speak to someone now. This won't take long."

"Let me call him for you."

I peruse the gift shop while she speaks in low tones into her phone. A minute later, a man dressed in dark trousers, a white button-down shirt, and an elbow-patch blazer appears in the doorway of the next room and looks at me quizzically. "Can I help you?"

I go to him and identify myself. "You're the curator?"

"Director and all-around jack-of-all-trades mainly." He offers a smile and his hand. "Daniel Neufeld. Call me Dan. What can I do for you?"

He wears a nattily cut beard, no mustache, and suspenders beneath the jacket. I suspect he's Mennonite or one of the more liberal factions of Amish. "I understand you're an expert on the Anabaptist culture," I say.

"My wife will tell you I'm not an expert on anything." He grins. "I am, however, a lover of history, especially when it comes to the Anabaptists."

"I'm looking for information on the Schwertler Anabaptists."

His brows shoot up. "Wow. Now there's an interesting topic for you, not to mention unusual." He looks at me a little more carefully.

"And here I thought this was about that parking ticket I didn't pay last time I was in Painters Mill."

I smile. "I'm working on a case, actually. Any information you can offer would be greatly appreciated."

He glances past me at the woman, who's standing behind the counter, looking at us, her hands on her hips. "Anna, you can go ahead and take off if you'd like," he says. "Lock the door behind you if you don't mind."

"G'night," she says.

"Night." Turning his attention back to me, he motions toward the doorway from which he'd emerged. "If you don't mind a little dust, we can sit in my office. I'll tell you everything I know, which isn't much."

I follow him through a museum-like chamber with half a dozen lighted display cases lining the wall to my right. He notices me looking at the ancient-looking tomes inside—Bibles and a leather-bound edition of *Martyrs Mirror.*

"Awe-inspiring, aren't they, Chief Burkholder?"

"Very much so." I nod. "They look old."

"Some of those Bibles date back hundreds of years. People died to keep them hidden and safe."

The persecution of the Anabaptists is a somber topic for the Amish, and not for the first time, I'm reminded of the hundreds who were hunted down, tortured, and killed for their beliefs during the Reformation in Europe.

We reach a small, cozily cramped office more befitting a college professor. An antique-looking desk holds an old-fashioned banker's lamp. Dozens of manila folders are stacked not so neatly on the corner. A Y2K-era computer rests on the adjacent credenza. An intricate Amish quilt hangs on the wall. Outside the window, the sun has set and I see a light snow falling. The whistle of wind through the eaves.

"Make yourself at home." Dan motions me into one of two visitor chairs adjacent to a desk piled with indistinguishable documents, forms, and books. "I have to tell you, Chief Burkholder, we receive thousands of visitors every year and I don't believe I've ever fielded a question about the Schwertler Anabaptists," he says.

"Who are they?" I ask.

"It's an obscure group that existed hundreds of years ago; not many people—the Amish included—are even aware of its existence. Do you mind if I ask why you're inquiring about them?"

"All I can tell you is that it may or may not be related to a case I'm working on."

"The mystery deepens." He studies me intently. "You must be referring to the Milan Swanz case."

I smile. "Are you *assuming* it's about the Swanz case or do you know something I don't?"

"Well, it was such an unusual crime. Painters Mill is a small town. And Milan Swanz was Amish." He shrugs. "I must admit I was intrigued."

"So you're aware of how he was killed."

"Of course. Dreadful to say the least, but I was captivated." Folding his hands in front of him, he leans back in the chair. "There's a certain symbolism, if you will, involved with burning a man at the stake."

I get the impression this charming man could talk about Anabaptist history all day, so I guide him back to the topic at hand. "What can you tell me about the Schwertler Anabaptists?"

"My knowledge is limited, I'm afraid. That said, I have a lot of resources here at the center." He shrugs. "I do know that the Schwertlers came to be during the Reformation, and they were a very unusual group for the time." His brows knit. "Let's see what we can find." He swivels to the bookcase behind him, plucks a massive tome from the shelf, and blows off the dust. "Sorry. My housekeeping skills are almost as bad as my weakness for straying off topic." Setting the book in front of him, he pulls wire-rimmed spectacles from his breast pocket, opens the book, and flips several pages. "Ah, here we go.

"Balthasar Hubmaier played a role in the Anabaptist movement during the Reformation." He turns the page. "He was born in Bavaria, Germany, around 1480. Graduated from the University of Ingolstadt with a doctorate. He was a priest for a time." He flips another page. "In 1524, Hubmaier married his wife, Elizabeth. Shortly thereafter, they moved to Zurich and he became acquainted with Heinrich Glarean. It was there that Hubmaier had a change of heart, if you will, and rebuffed the Catholic doctrine of infant baptism. Such a belief was extremely radical at the time—and risky business, of course. During that period, Hubmaier became a respected Anabaptist theologian. But it was a violent era and men were hardened. Later, he helped orchestrate a violent pogrom against Regensburg's Jews."

"That doesn't sound very pacifistic," I say dryly.

He looks at me over the top of his glasses. "Just so you know, *'schwertler'* translates loosely to 'of the sword.' In fact, during that time, Hubmaier wrote a manuscript called *On the Sword*, challenging the nonresistant views of the Anabaptists. As I'm sure you're aware, the Reformation was a dangerous time for religious dissent. Because of his beliefs, he fell out of favor with Ferdinand, who was the Holy Roman Emperor. Ferdinand was a powerful man and a ferocious persecutor of heretics. Twice Hubmaier was imprisoned and tortured on the rack. He did not recant and in 1528, in Vienna, Austria, he was executed—burned at the stake."

He raises his gaze to mine and for the span of a few seconds, the words echo between us.

Burned at the stake.

"Three days later," the curator tells me, "his wife, Elizabeth, had a rock tied to her neck and was thrown from a bridge into the Danube River and drowned."

Having grown up Amish, I'm no stranger to the savagery inflicted upon the early European Anabaptists for their religious beliefs; I read much of *Martyrs Mirror* as a kid and the accounts of torture and murder made an indelible impression on my young mind. Even now, as an adult—a cop—hearing the brutal details of those stories sends a chill up my spine.

"What exactly does 'of the sword' mean?" I ask.

"My interpretation?" Dan considers the question, thoughtful, weighing his words carefully. "Hubmaier believed that violence could be used for good. He defended the government's use of force to protect innocent Christians. He did not, however, believe in the use of force by an individual to defend one's self, family, other defenseless Christians, or their property. He also very much believed in a benevolent government."

"Evidently, the government wasn't as benevolent as he believed," I say.

"Ironic, isn't it?"

"And ruthless."

For a moment, neither of us speaks. It's as if we're caught up in those troubling times nearly five hundred years ago. I think about Milan Swanz and I struggle to find some cogent link between the murder and the Schwertler Anabaptists, but there's nothing there.

"I'm a curious man, Chief Burkholder." The director smiles despite the grim subject matter. "How interesting that an Amish man is found dead, having been burned at the stake, and a few days later, you're in my office asking about the Schwertler Anabaptists. I'm incredibly intrigued."

It's bad form for an investigator to divulge too much about an ongoing case to a civilian outside of law enforcement. People talk, and the last thing any cop wants is some sensational headline based on an exchange that never should have taken place. This conversation—namely the prospect of relevant information—is worth the risk as long as I don't reveal anything sensitive.

"Mr. Neufeld, would it be possible for you to keep this conversation private?" Even if he agrees, I know he may not keep his word. Still, it's good policy to ask so that he understands the nature of our discussion.

"Of course."

"Thank you." I take a moment to get my words in order. "I interviewed an Amish person with regard to this case and they mentioned the Schwertler Anabaptists. I don't know if there's a connection, but I thought it was worth looking into."

He nods. "The burning of a man at the stake is, indeed, symbolic in terms of the persecution of the Anabaptists," he says. "It is not, however, symbolic in terms of the Schwertler Anabaptists."

"Because the Schwertlers believed in the 'of the sword' philosophy only when it was in the hands of a benign government."

"Exactly."

As I work to process the information, my cop's mind considers all the dark corners of the homicidal mentality. "Is it possible we could be dealing with some bastardized version of the group?"

For the first time, he looks troubled, as if we've ventured into an area in which he's not quite comfortable. He covers his discomfiture with a chuckle. "That's a little out of my bailiwick."

"In the course of your Anabaptist studies, have you ever come across any information on ritual or symbolic murder?" I ask. "Modern day or historic?"

He sighs. "I'm a religious man, Chief Burkholder. A student of history. As brutal as some of that history is, I'm a wimp when it comes to true crime." He laughs. "That stuff's too dark for me. That said, there are times when history and crime overlap and my curiosity gets the best of me." He looks down at his desktop. "I recall reading about a murder in an Amish settlement in Canada. Milverton in Ontario, I believe."

I write it down. "What happened?"

"It was back in the 1950s, I think. An Amish man was accused of killing two of his children. I don't recollect the details of the case, but the police were involved. And at some point during the investigation, the man disappeared."

"How does a case like that relate in any way to the Schwertler Anabaptists?" I ask.

"Everyone assumed this man had run away to avoid capture and stay out of jail. But that spring, his body was recovered from a lake a few miles from his farm. There was a rock secured to his neck."

"Foul play?" I ask. "Or suicide?"

"If memory serves me, his death occurred in the dead of winter. The lake was frozen and authorities surmised a hole had been chopped in the ice. Most of the Amish believed it was suicide."

"Seems like an odd way to commit suicide."

"Indeed." His eyes meet mine. "I don't believe the police ever figured it out. I'm sure you see the correlation."

"Elizabeth Hubmaier."

He nods.

"So, in your opinion, the Schwertler Anabaptists existed."

"For a time."

"How long?"

He smiles tiredly at the open-ended question. "I'm afraid that's beyond my area of expertise, Chief Burkholder. The history we know is based on events that were documented and verified."

"Is it possible the Schwertler Anabaptists still exist?"

Linda Castillo

"I don't see how. As you well know, violence is renounced by all Anabaptists, particularly the Amish. Even in times of war, they are conscientious objectors." He shrugs. "I think it's safe for us to assume the Schwertler Anabaptists are nothing more than a dark chapter of our history—and rightfully so."

CHAPTER 20

It's fully dark by the time I leave the center and start toward the Explorer. I'm lost in thought as I walk down the steps and start across the parking lot. Everything the director told me swirls in my head like some morose, Middle Ages–set movie as I open the driver's-side door and slide behind the wheel.

"Schwertler" translates loosely to "of the sword."

. . . wrote a manuscript called On the Sword *. . .*

. . . helped orchestrate a violent pogrom against Regensburg's Jews.

I think about the murder of Milan Swanz and struggle to find some parallel or connection, but it's like trying to fit a square peg into a round hole. In the backwaters of my mind, my exchanges with Bertha Swanz float untethered.

Did he break your son's arm?

She closes her eyes, nods.

. . . had a knife on him and hacked off a piece of the bishop's beard . . .

209

"Swanz was violent," I mutter, my voice sounding like that of a stranger in the silence of the cab. "But he was also the victim."

You're blaming the victim, Kate, whispers the voice of reason.

"And now you're arguing with yourself." Sighing, I buckle up and pull out of the lot. A quick glance at the dash reminds me I should have been home by now. Tomasetti and I were supposed to have dinner together. A bottle of wine. Some conversation. I'm forty minutes late and half an hour from the farm. If I rush, I can still spend some time with him.

Driving slightly above the speed limit, I take Highway 77 north. Around me, the night is quiet. Not much traffic. The snow has stopped, but there's a rise of mist in the air. I think back to my conversation with Neufeld as I fly past Heini's Cheese Chalet and then the 77 Housewares home-goods store. I've just made the turn onto County Highway 207 when I hear something shift in the back seat. At first, I think my laptop case has slipped off the seat and onto the floor. I glance over my shoulder, sense movement directly behind me. Alarm jolts me.

"What—"

I'm reaching for my .38 when something loops over my head and is yanked against my throat. I raise my hand to protect my neck, but I'm not fast enough. The bind is drawn impossibly tight. I put one hand on the wheel. I grapple for my .38 with the other. My hand on the butt. Out of the holster. Finger inside the guard. I twist, try to put eyes on my attacker. A dark figure in the periphery of my vision. I try to speak, but I can't make a sound.

I fire blind. The explosion deafens, the concussion of it puffs against my face as it tears a hole in the roof. My attacker grasps my wrist, jerks it back. I get off another shot before he tears the gun from my grasp. I stomp the accelerator. The engine roars. I yank the wheel right. The front end drops. The headlights play crazily over tree trunks. The undercarriage scrapes the ground. The Explorer lurches forward, bounces violently. I see night sky. Headlights on the treetops. Blood hammering inside my head.

I see the massive trunk an instant before the Explorer slams into it. The seat belt digs into my pelvis. The airbag explodes, a giant boxing glove punching my face and chest. The figure is catapulted between the front seatbacks, hitting my right shoulder. I jab him with my elbow. Once. Twice. I draw back my left hand and punch blind. No good because my neck is bound to the headrest.

He hits my right cheek, but I can tell he's shaken from the impact. He scrambles from between the seats. Growling like a beast, he crawls across the passenger seat. I try to get a look, but I can barely turn my head and it's too dark to see. The passenger door flies open and he's out.

I fight away the deflated airbag and jam the fingertips of both hands between the bind and my throat. It's too tight.

Shit. *Shit.*

Blood pounds in my face. My mouth is open wide. My tongue sticking out. No air in my lungs. Brain going fuzzy.

"Last warning," comes a raspy male voice.

I glance left, see a figure standing outside. Somehow, the door is open. His torso visible, not his face. I don't know where my weapon is and for a terrifying instant, I envision it in his hand, a bullet slamming into my temple. I claw at the bind. Why isn't it loosening? My vision swims. Blood pounding in my head. Panic knocks hard at the door and involuntarily I try to raise my hips. Locked in by the seat belt, I kick mindlessly.

I reach for the Gerber folding knife. Fingers of my left hand digging deep into the skin of my throat.

Don't pass out. Don't pass out.

I unclip the knife. Thumb off the safety switch. Hit the release button with my thumb. The knife fires. My hand shakes as I bring it up. Set the blade against the bind. A belt, I think. Leather. And in that instant I'm damn glad I keep my tools sharp, because the bind falls away.

I collapse against the steering wheel, choking, and I let the blood come back to my head. For the span of several seconds I can't move. I sit there with my forehead against the wheel, drooling and wheezing and thanking God the son of a bitch didn't kill me.

When I'm able, I unbuckle my seat belt. I stumble out, go to my knees, spit what tastes like blood in the snow. Vaguely, I'm aware that the Explorer is nose down in the ditch. Trees on either side of the road.

I reach for my radio. "Ten-thirty-three." Officer in trouble. I rasp out my location. "Suspect at large."

• • •

Six minutes pass before I see the flash of emergency lights coming down the road. My vehicle is basically a crime scene now, so I touch as little as possible. Because my attacker is still at large, I do reach in and pull out my Maglite. A quick search reveals my .38 on the floor of the back seat area. I slip on my duty gloves and keep my weapon at my side while I wait.

Relief slips through me when Glock's cruiser slides to a stop behind my Explorer. His door swings open and he jogs to me, sidearm and Maglite at the ready, eyes on the woods all around.

"Chief!"

"I'm okay," I tell him.

"Suspect?"

"He's on foot."

"Armed?"

"I don't know."

His eyes widen as he takes in my appearance, but he doesn't say anything. Instead, he speaks into his radio, letting the dispatcher know that he's arrived on scene. That the suspect is at large and possibly armed. And that an ambulance is needed.

"Get the sheriff's department out here, too," he tells her.

For several minutes, we walk the scene, our Maglites illuminating the ground, flicking occasionally to the woods on either side of the road.

"Looks like he may have come this way."

I glance across the road to see Glock kneel, and I start toward him. Sure enough, midway between the Explorer and the woods, there's a print of a man's shoe in the snow.

"Nice impression," I say.

"Plaster guy's going to like it."

We look at each other and, despite the fact that I'm still shaken, we smile.

"What the hell happened?" he asks.

I lay out an abbreviated version. "There's no way I left the Explorer door unlocked."

Holding my gaze, he pulls out his cell, puts it on speaker. "Mona?"

"'Sup, dude."

"Cruise over to the Amish and Mennonite Heritage Center. Rope off the parking lot. No one in or out."

"You got it." A heavy pause and then, "The chief okay?"

"I'm fine," I cut in.

"Glad to hear it, Chief. On my way over there now."

• • •

213

Pomerene Hospital ER is quiet this evening. I'm a regular here, either for one of my officers who was injured on the job, for my own follies, or for some incident in which a citizen was hurt and I need to talk to them. I'm acquainted with most of the ER staff and have a friendly relationship with the staff and doctors. It's those little things that bolster you when your shirt is covered in an alarming amount of blood, you're good and shaken up and trying not to show it, and you have a professional image to uphold.

"Were you unconscious at any time during the incident, Chief Burkholder?"

I'm sitting on a gurney in a curtained area of the ER. The young medical practitioner is grilling me while pecking information into a handheld electronic device. I guess him to be just south of thirty, wearing his usual Peanuts scrubs, and not a facial wrinkle in sight.

"No," I tell him.

He looks at me over the tops of his glasses as if to make sure I'm telling the truth. "Well, the X-rays are all good," he says. "Looks like your nosebleed has stopped." His eyes flick down to my neck. "You've sustained a new contusion there on your throat. Bruises on top of the bruises from last night. All of it's going to bloom come morning."

"I've been wanting to wear that new turtleneck I bought a couple weeks ago," I say dryly.

Grinning, he shakes his head. "Tylenol this evening for pain, use an ice pack if you need it, and you're good to go."

I stick out my hand for a shake. "Thanks."

As he prepares to walk out the door, he turns and points at me, his expression turning serious. "Nothing personal, but I don't want to see you back here for a while."

"I'll do my best."

And then he's gone.

I'm trying to decide if I should put my coat on over the gown I'm wearing or slip back into my blood-spattered uniform shirt when the curtain is yanked open. I look up to see Tomasetti enter. He slows as his eyes sweep over me. I try not to squirm beneath the weight of his stare, and I resist the urge to raise my hand to cover my throat. I can tell by his expression that he's already seen the damage.

"Did they get him?" I ask.

"Dogs lost him in the woods," he tells me. "There were tracks. Looks like someone picked him up."

"So, there were two people involved." It's not a question.

"Evidently."

"Tomasetti, there's no way he had time to call someone. There's no way someone could have gotten there so fast. It had to have been planned."

Tomasetti's not listening. Shaking his head, he crosses to me, eyes on mine. Not quite angry, but unhappy with me nonetheless. "Kate, what the hell . . ."

"I'm okay."

"I can see that," he says dryly. His anger shows as he gets a better look at the bruises and the bloodstains on my trousers.

I hate it that I'm finding it difficult to hold his gaze. That I feel as if this were somehow my fault.

I try to steady my hands. I can't help thinking about how this scenario might've played out if I hadn't had that knife. Or if the son of a bitch who ambushed me had decided to use the .38 instead of running. That Tomasetti might have been making a trip to the basement instead of the ER.

"I'm sorry," I finally manage.

"I know you are." He practically snarls the words.

"I didn't—"

215

He cuts me off. "How many times am I going to walk into this ER and find you bloodied and beaten and cracking jokes like some twenty-year-old fucking rookie?"

Angry, I snap at him, "Cut it out."

I know he loves me and doesn't want to lose me to violence, the way he lost his family years before. But I feel the need to remind him that I had no choice in the matter. I was doing my job and sometimes that's the way it goes.

The silence that follows seems to cool the temperature a bit.

"Did you recognize him?" he asks.

"He was in the back seat, waiting for me. Once I realized he was there, things happened fast." I'm not sure what it means that both of us are more comfortable dealing with this in terms of our jobs rather than our roles as husband and wife. I think there might be a lesson in there.

"Any chance you got him when you fired your weapon?"

"He didn't react," I say. "I don't think so."

"Same guy from before?" he asks.

"I don't know," I say. "One thing I do know is that I did not leave the Explorer unlocked when I was inside the Heritage Center."

"I know you didn't."

It's not the response I expected. "You do?"

He nods. "Mona found what's called an 'air wedge' in the parking lot."

"I have no clue what that is."

"An air wedge is a tool used by burglars to gain access to vehicles. It's basically a flat, heavy-duty balloon they stuff into the opening between the door and the frame. They pump up the balloon, which gives them enough space to use a reach tool to either unlock the door or roll down the window."

"Odd tool for your everyday average Joe to have in his back pocket."

"Either he's a thief or this was premeditated." He frowns at me. "Take me through it."

As I recount to him the moments in the Explorer, I can still feel the tremendous pressure of the belt at my throat, the blood to my head cut off. "When I hit the tree, the impact threw him between the seats and into the front."

I almost reach for my throat, think better of it, look down at my hands instead. "That's it."

"Did he say anything?"

"He said something like: 'This is your last warning.'"

"Original." His expression is like ice. "He left you to asphyxiate."

I shudder. "I was able to get to my Gerber and I cut the damn belt."

"We found the belt," he says. "He'd buckled it. If you hadn't had that knife on you, you'd be dead."

He says the words with brutal honesty.

"Anything else?" he asks.

"I hit that tree pretty hard," I tell him. "He may be injured."

"Definitely did some damage to the Explorer." Eyes holding mine, he slides his cell phone from his pocket, thumbs something into it. "We'll check area hospitals and clinics just in case."

I look over at the tiny closet next to the bed where my coat and uniform shirt hang. I see Tomasetti looking, too, taking in the blood, and he shakes his head. "What the hell am I going to do with you?"

"You can start by taking me to the station. I can at least write up an incident report. Get myself a rental car—"

"Said the woman who doesn't know when to quit." He strides to the closet, pulls out my shirt and coat, and thrusts them at me. "The only place you're going is home."

CHAPTER 21

People were a predictable lot. They were sheep, really, ruled by their emotions and petty needs, their actions based on a lack of courage or some fanatical conviction that was negotiable for the right price. Unfortunately for everyone involved, Kate Burkholder didn't fit the mold; she'd become an unexpected problem. And he was quickly running out of options.

"What are we going to do about the woman cop?" asked the man in the passenger seat.

He glanced over, took a moment to consider the question and all of its gnarly implications. "I haven't decided yet. We've still some time."

They'd cruised past the farm south of Wooster three times in the last hour. It was past one A.M. now, and the lights inside had gone dark. Ordinarily, this would have been the ideal time to see things through, to finish it cleanly and permanently. Unfortunately for them, it wasn't going to be that easy this time.

He'd underestimated Burkholder. A serious oversight he knew was probably going to cost him. She was going to force his hand, a move he should have anticipated and countered long before now.

"She's not going to stop," said the man in the passenger seat.

On the road in front of the farmhouse, he stopped the vehicle and cut the headlights. For the span of several minutes, they took in the scene, entrances and exits, cover, lights, and the quickest ways in and out of the property.

"I know," he said. "The problem is, she's outside the realm of our obligation."

"And yet you know what has to be done."

"I do." He looked away from the house and eyed the man sitting next to him. "Still a risk."

"Riskier if we do nothing. There's no other way."

"I'll think about it."

"Don't take too much time. People like her don't stop. She's close as it is and getting closer."

Nodding in acquiescence, he pulled away from the farm. Killing Burkholder was a last resort. The one thing he didn't want to do. Not only would it draw a large amount of unwanted attention, but it went against what few ethics he had left. He wasn't a fool, after all; she was going to back them into a corner. Soon, they would have no recourse.

Blind, stupid woman still believed in the fundamental goodness of mankind. What a fool.

Thanks to this formerly Amish woman turned cop, the situation was out of their hands—hands that would soon be covered with innocent blood.

CHAPTER 22

There's nothing like a near-death experience to give you a fresh perspective on life. When you're a cop and the person you're investigating wants to do away with you, it's a pretty good sign that you're on the right track.

I wake to full daylight outside the window. Rolling, I grab my phone, check the time, and I'm annoyed when I see that the digital display indicates it's 8:01 A.M. I'd set my alarm for seven. Tomasetti must have turned it off while I was sleeping. I'm not quite sure how I feel about that, but at least his motives were good.

I sit up, set my feet on the floor. Every muscle in my body aches as I rise and snatch my sweatpants off the rocking chair. It's cold in the house this morning, so I slip my old cardigan over my T-shirt. As I step into slippers, I vaguely recall Tomasetti rising before daylight. He'd kissed me lightly on the cheek, lingered for a minute or two, and left.

All of this serves as a reminder that my life isn't just about me anymore; we're married and I have to take that into consideration, especially when it comes to the dangers inherent to my job. It's particularly difficult for him given his past. I think we made things right last night. We made love, which is always good, but our emotions remain raw.

What are your priorities, Kate?

Am I a wife first and foremost? A cop first? A woman? Where does Tomasetti fall into the mix? That's not even to mention the prospect of motherhood and a family. I'd always thought it would happen. I would know when it was time. And yet here I am, thirty-six years old and hearing the tick of my biological clock more loudly with each year that passes. This morning, I feel as if I'm caught in the shuffle of all those things.

In the kitchen, I plug a pod of dark roast into the coffeemaker, slap down the lid. Outside the window above the sink, rain pours down from a slate sky. It's melted most of the snow, giving the farm a cold and bleak resonance. I shift my focus from the untidy pieces of my life to the investigation. Right or wrong or somewhere in between, and despite the fact that I've been virtually barred from the case, I'm compelled to find and stop this killer.

In the office, I snatch my laptop off the desk, the file I've amassed so far, a legal pad and pen, and I carry everything to the kitchen. Armed with coffee, I pull up a chair at the table and set to work.

I'm swept into a history that spans nearly five hundred years and stretches from Austria and Switzerland to Germany and the current-day Czech Republic. I learn about the secret police force called "the Anabaptist Hunters" who were charged with finding and arresting heretics. As I read, I struggle to find a parallel between the Schwertlers and the case.

Nothing stands out.

The early Anabaptists who were killed and became martyrs were

221

not guilty of crimes. They were murdered because of their faith. Milan Swanz was not killed because of his faith.

"What the hell is the connection?" I say aloud.

My pen hovers above the paper and then I write: *Violence. Murder. Schwertler = "of the sword."*

Is it possible the only link is the acceptance of violence? Are we dealing with some bastardized version of the original Schwertler Anabaptists? Did someone take that small parcel of history and twist it to justify murder? Someone who saw Milan Swanz as a heretic?

Frustrated, I toss the pen aside. "Shit."

I'm reading through notes on my interview with the bishop when pounding on the door startles me.

On impulse, I reach for the .38 on the table next to my laptop. My hand is on the butt, my fingers itching, when I glance up and see my brother at the back door. I rise, my mind whirling. I don't remember the last time my brother came to see me.

I unlock the door, open it. Jacob stands on the small back porch, looking at me. Not happy about something. Dressed mostly in black, soaking wet, water dripping from the brim of his hat.

"*Kumma inseid,*" I say.

"I can't stay."

I frown at him. "Is everything all right?"

His eyes hold mine as he enters, brushes past me. "I heard what happened last night," he says. "You are hurt?"

"I'm fine." I wave off his concern, but I have to resist the urge to cover the bruises at my throat. "How did you hear?"

"Guy at the feedstore."

I shake my head, wondering about the speed of the small-town grapevine. Then again, it's big news when someone tries to murder the chief of police, small town or not.

"He said you were hurt," he says. "And that you've passed the case to the sheriff."

My temper stirs, but I tamp it down before it can take root. "That's not quite the way it happened."

He raises his brows.

"My counterparts," I begin. "The mayor. They don't want me on the case."

"Why not?"

I tell him. "They think I'm protecting the Amish. That I'm protecting you."

"I'm sorry." His eyes flick to my laptop and the papers spread out on the table, then back to me. "They don't know you very well, do they?"

I laugh despite my dark mood. "Evidently not."

Leaving the kitchen, I pass through the living room and on to the linen closet for a towel. Back in the kitchen, I hand him the towel, and go to the coffeemaker. As I pop in a pod, I'm aware of him drying off, draping the towel over the back of a chair.

"You're the one person I wasn't expecting this morning," I say as I hand him a cup.

"*Dank.*" He takes it and sips. "I didn't like the way we left things."

"Is this about Milan Swanz?"

"You know it is."

I sip coffee. Wait. When he only continues to stare at the floor, I go to the table, pull out a chair. "Sit down."

Sighing, he does. I take the chair across from him. "I'm going to find the person who murdered Swanz with or without your help. If you know something that will help me do that, please tell me."

Neither of us speaks for a time. The only sound comes from the tick of the clock on the wall. The hum of my laptop. The creaks of the farmhouse settling.

Staring down at the mug in his hand, Jacob breaks the silence. "I didn't tell you the truth about what happened with Swanz. Not all of it. Katie, there are things that should never happen in this life. Some things that are so bad, they shouldn't even be talked about."

"I know that."

He turns thoughtful, his lips twisting as if his mouth is suddenly full of bile. "The day I caught Swanz in the barn with James . . ." Jacob tells me what happened.

As I'd suspected, Swanz was clearly intending to have sex with James. The coffee in my stomach turns sour. "I'm sorry."

"I went to James. Checked him over. Sent him to the house." Jaw clenched, Jacob shakes his head. "I was so angry I couldn't see. It was as if God had blinded me because I was close to doing something that would have . . . changed me. Anyway, Swanz ran out of the barn. I went after him. Caught up with him over by the neighbor's fence. I don't remember what I said to him. It was as if the words weren't coming from me." He gives another head shake. "Swanz left."

"Did it get physical?" I ask.

"I pushed him. Twice."

I nod. "Jacob, did you have anything to do with his death?" The words drop off my tongue like poison.

"No."

"What did you do next?"

"I harnessed up and went to see Bishop Troyer. Drove straight there. I told him everything. The bishop . . . he's an old man. I've talked to him many times over the years. That day, I saw something in his face I've never seen before."

"Like what?"

"I'm not sure. It wasn't . . . hate or anger. It was more like . . . resolve. As if he'd made a difficult choice that he hadn't wanted to make."

"Any idea what that was?"

"No."

I choose my next words carefully. "Do you think the bishop had anything to do with the death of Milan Swanz?"

"No." He says the word adamantly. "*Of course not.*"

Another uncomfortable silence ensues. Both of us stare into our cups. Listen to the din of rain outside. I try in vain to settle my thoughts, but they roil, troubled and tossed.

"I'm glad James is okay," I say.

"God was looking over him. I think He was looking over all of us that day, including me."

"Jacob, why did you come here this morning?"

He raises his gaze to mine. "That Sunday, after worship, Irene came to me. She told me she'd talked to Bertha Swanz a while back. The subject of Milan came up and Bertha told her she thought something bad was going to happen to him."

"What?" I sit up straighter. "Like what? Why would she say that?"

"She didn't say, but Irene thought it was strange."

"Did Bertha say what kind of bad thing?"

He shakes his head. "Irene didn't ask. She thought Bertha was just talking, you know. Making gossip about a no-good ex-husband. Then Milan was killed and she came to me and told me what she'd heard."

"Jacob, why didn't you tell me this sooner?"

"With everything that's happened, Katie, I wish I had. I'm sorry I didn't."

•   •   •

I sit at the kitchen table for a long time after my brother leaves, troubled, thinking, trying to make sense of everything he'd said.

"The subject of Milan came up and Bertha told her she thought something bad was going to happen to him."

Did Bertha Swanz know her ex-husband was going to be murdered? Did she have something to do with it? Did she plan it? Persuade her lover to kill him? The questions pound my brain like a fist.

I've questioned Bertha three times so far; each time I asked her specifically about her ex-husband's life and death. Did she lie to me? She did, after all, have motive to want him gone. He abused her. Cheated on her. He broke their son's arm. Not to mention her affair with her neighbor, Lester Yoder. All are compelling motives for murder.

I glance at the wall clock. Almost ten A.M. I look down at my sweatpants and ratty cardigan. I wonder where my counterparts are in terms of the investigation. Have they made any progress? Had any breakthroughs? Have they drawn any of the same conclusions that I have?

It doesn't elude me that they haven't kept me updated. Of course, I'm not *officially* off the case. But for all intents and purposes, I've been blacklisted.

. . . until we get a better handle on this, I'd like you to take a step back. "Like hell," I mutter.

I consider calling Tomasetti, but think better of it. Bertha Swanz will be much more likely to speak openly to me if I'm alone. If any new information emerges from the conversation, I can share it with the rest of the team then.

Holding that thought, I rise and make a beeline for the shower.

• • •

The only positive aspect of driving our old farm truck is that no one will recognize it. That's particularly beneficial when I'm being stonewalled and about to approach an individual who doesn't want to speak with me.

It's a little after eleven A.M. when I park in the driveway of the Swanz house and take the flagstone path to the front porch. I hear the whine of an approaching train as I knock. The door opens and Bertha Swanz looks at me as if I'm the last person she expected to find. She saw the truck, I realize, and thought it was safe to answer the door.

Surprise.

"Do you have a few minutes to talk?" I begin.

Her mouth opens and then closes. "I've got to be at work in a bit," she finally spits out. "Tomorrow would be better."

"This won't take long."

When she doesn't step aside, I offer her a polite smile and brush past her. As I enter the living room, I sense the irritation coming off her. A fire blazes in the fireplace and I feel the heat from ten feet away. The aromas of coffee and this morning's breakfast float on the warm air. Light slants toward me from the kitchen, and through the doorway I see the table, upon which two steaming cups sit.

Interesting.

"I heard you're a forward woman," she mutters as she closes the door. "I don't think you can just force your way in here like that."

I stop before reaching the kitchen and turn to her. "I didn't realize you have company," I say. "I didn't see a buggy outside."

I have a pretty good idea who she's sharing a cup of coffee with this morning. Judging from her expression, she knows it. Glaring at me, she grasps the open front sides of the cardigan she's wearing and yanks them together, folds her arms over her bosom. "I heard you're a rude one, too. Guess I can vouch for that."

"My manners aside," I say slowly, watching her, "how is it that you knew something bad was going to happen to Milan before he was killed?"

"I don't know what you're talking about," she huffs.

227

"Did you know someone was going to kill him?"

"I knew no such thing."

"Do not lie to me," I say. "I have a witness."

She has the audacity to assume an offended countenance. "I have never lied to you. Not once!"

"You lied by omission," I return evenly. "Same thing. Frankly, I'm starting to wonder what else you're hiding."

"I've nothing to hide."

I glance toward the kitchen doorway, which is behind me. "Who's in the kitchen?"

"No one. The kids are at school."

Giving her a tight smile, I turn away and start toward the kitchen. An instant before I pass through the doorway, I hear the shuffle of feet, but when I enter, the room is empty.

Bertha follows me, looking uncertain and increasingly angry. "I heard they fired you down to the police station. I suspect you deserved it. You can't just barge in here like this. Maybe I'll run down to the pay phone and call the sheriff."

I take in the two cups on the table. Still steaming. Barely touched. I turn to Bertha. "Cozy."

She hits me with a withering look. "I don't like you much, Kate Burkholder."

"How did you know something bad was going to happen to Milan?" I ask.

"I want you to leave," she snaps. "Right now. Get out of here. Go on."

I'm keenly aware that there is a line I cannot cross and that I'm very close to crossing it. Every citizen has God-given rights that may not be infringed. That's especially true since I'm here without a warrant—not to mention without the backing of my peers. That said, I'm not above using any tool I have in my arsenal to impel her to talk to me.

"All right, Bertha. I'll leave." I say the words quietly, maintaining a serene expression as I hold her gaze, keep her engaged. "But you should know that if you had prior knowledge that your ex-husband was going to be harmed, that makes you an accessory to murder. If that's the case, you can bet the farm someone will be back with a warrant."

Without warning, the Amish woman charges. A sound that's part whimper, part sob pours from her throat. The next thing I know her hands slam into my chest and I'm reeling backward. I stumble over my own feet and nearly go down. But my butt hits the counter, stopping my backward momentum, and I quickly regain my balance.

"Stop it!" I shout. "Bertha! I'm a police officer!"

But she's reached the limit of her emotional tolerance. I see her lips pull back, her teeth clench, and she charges again. I'm ready this time and grasp her arms at the biceps, swing her around fast, and lower her to the floor. She's heavy, but not in very good physical condition, which makes her easier to handle.

I kneel, roll her onto her stomach, set my knee on her back. "You need to calm down."

A scream that's part rage, part panic rends the air. "Don't tell me to calm down!"

Out of the corner of my eye I see someone emerge from the mud-room. My hand flies to my sidearm. I look up, see Lester Yoder come through the door. I nearly pull my .38, but one look at his face and I know he's not a threat.

"Bertha!" he cries. "*Was der schinner is kshicht?*" What in the world is happening?

I point at him. "Do not move!"

The Amish man stops, raises his hands as if I'm holding him at gunpoint.

Beneath me, Bertha lowers her cheek to the floor and begins to cry.

"You're a cruel one, Kate Burkholder. No wonder you left. None of us would have you. *Fagunna!*" It's the *Deitsch* word for "to desire another's misfortune."

Keeping an eye on Yoder, I pull the handcuffs from the compartment on my belt. "Mrs. Swanz, I do not want to handcuff you, and I do not want to arrest you. Do you understand?"

"I don't understand any of this!" she cries. "I didn't do anything wrong."

I look at Yoder. Wide-eyed, his gaze flicks from me to Bertha and back to me. As if at a complete loss, he shrugs.

"Bertha, will you stay calm if I sit you up?" I ask the Amish woman.

"Please," she sobs. "I wish you would just go away!"

"I'm afraid I can't do that." Shoving the cuffs back into their compartment, I rise and offer my hand to her.

A few feet away, Yoder stares at us, his hands still raised, his mouth hanging open.

The Amish woman takes my hand and maneuvers into a sitting position, her legs splayed in front of her.

"Are you okay?" I ask

Tears streaming, she shakes her head.

I give Yoder a nod and together we help her to her feet. "Mrs. Swanz, I'm going to give you the benefit of the doubt and assume you stumbled," I say. "The reason I'm giving you that kind of leeway is because you have four school-age children to care for. If you lie to me, even by omission, I will come down on you like a ton of bricks. Do you understand?"

Eyes shimmering with tears, she looks away, and concentrates on brushing nonexistent dust from the front of her dress. "I understand."

I look at Yoder, then point at one of the chairs. "Put your hands down and sit."

Without speaking, he obeys.

The Amish woman pulls a wadded-up tissue from her pocket and uses it to blot tears from her cheeks.

"I think it's time the three of us had a heart-to-heart chat about Milan Swanz," I say to them.

Looking miserable, the Amish woman goes to the counter, pulls a mug from the cabinet. "Have yourself a seat there," she says in *Deitsch*. "And I'll tell you everything I know."

CHAPTER 23

"Milan was never quite right in the head. Had a hard time telling the difference between right and wrong. Seemed like he always chose wrong over right."

Bertha Swanz, Lester Yoder, and I are seated at the kitchen table. It's so quiet I can hear the pop and crackle of the woodstove in the living room. The hiss of the gas lamp overhead. The tick of the stovetop behind me as it cools.

"All he knew was what he wanted and he didn't care who he hurt to get it." Bertha's brows knit as if she's struggling to piece together a difficult puzzle. "You put all of that together and trouble just seemed to follow him wherever he went."

Her mouth curves into a melancholy smile. "When he was younger, it didn't seem so bad. He was funny and charming and all those mistakes seemed harmless. Datt liked him; Milan was a decent cabinetmaker, after all. Handsome, too, and a lot of the girls noticed."

She sighs. "I was a silly thing and didn't know my head from a hole in the ground. Once we got married, the babies came quick. And so did the problems."

Yoder picks up his cup, sips, his eyes downcast.

A dozen questions arise, but I hold them at bay and let her talk.

"Everything he did," she continues, "everyone he dealt with, there were problems. He got into arguments with people for no good reason. Had trouble with everyone. The older he got, the worse it got." She shrugs. "That's not to mention the children. I'm not against discipline, mind you, but Milan had a temper. Overdid the whipping. Seemed like everything he did was an overreaction."

She heaves a sigh, goes on as if she's just warming up. "It wasn't long before he started hitting me. Not too bad at first. A slap or two here and there. But I knew it wasn't okay. It wasn't right and it got to be a bad situation. Next, he started having problems at work. Got fired. Boy, that made him mad. He couldn't let things go, and he wanted to get even for every little slight, even when it was his own fault.

"Bishop Troyer put him under the *bann* half a dozen times over the years. Milan always made it right. Confessed to the congregation, asked for forgiveness, and they let him come back. But how many times does it take?" She shakes her head. "By then, most everyone—the Amish—knew there was something wrong with him. Everyone knew he was a bad egg. No one talked about it. No one did anything, least of all me. And it got worse."

"How so?" I ask.

She quiets, looks down at the tabletop. "One afternoon Milan came home. Had Clarence Raber with him. They'd been boozing it up. He broke my boy's arm. Said it was an accident. But I saw it happen; I saw his face." She raises anguished eyes to mine. "That hurt me something awful. I went to Bishop Troyer the next day. I told him everything. That's when the bishop got with the *Diener* and, later, the whole congregation, and Milan was excommunicated for good."

The Amish woman looks down at her hands. "I filed for divorce. Told everyone he was the one done it." Her mouth twists. "Milan didn't like it one bit. Shortly after he got the final papers, Milan went after the bishop and his wife."

"Had I known about that," I tell her, "I would have arrested Milan."

"For goodness' sakes, you know how the Amish are." She waves off the statement. "Last thing anyone wanted was for the English police to get involved."

She shakes her head. "After the divorce was done, I didn't hear from Milan for a time. I thought everything was going to be okay."

She closes her eyes; the energy of the room shifts. Lester lowers his head, his chin against his chest, and he stares down at the tabletop.

"Milan came here to the house," the Amish woman says. "Middle of the night. Kids were sleeping. He woke me up, pulled me out of bed, dragged me down the stairs by my hair. He had some bad things in his head that night. Talking like a madman. Blamed me for all his problems. Said I'd betrayed him. Betrayed our vows." Her mouth draws tight. "He took me right there on the kitchen floor like we were a couple of farm animals."

I feel myself sit up straighter, horrified by what she is telling me. "He raped you?"

"Oh, he said it wasn't that. He said I was still his wife and in the eyes of God he had a right." She shrugs. "I was so shook up. I remember being on the floor." She motions to a place behind my chair. "His hands around my neck."

Her breaths quicken, as if she can't get enough air into her lungs. "Don't know how long that went on. I think I must have blacked out once or twice. The next thing I know there were two strangers in my kitchen. Men. Dressed all in black. Big, strong men with the kind of eyes that mean business. It was the craziest thing. One of them helped me up. Put me in a chair here at the table. Didn't say a word. But he was . . . kind. Gentle, you know. Then they took Milan . . ."

"Where did they take him?"

"I don't know."

"Did you recognize the men?" I ask.

"No, ma'am. Never seen them before in my life."

"Were they Amish?"

Her brows crease. "Not Holmes County Amish. Their beards were trimmed up. Neat-like, you know, the way some of those Beachys do. To tell you the truth, they didn't look like any Amish I've ever seen."

The Beachy Amish are a progressive subgroup, some of whom have been known to use electronics, gas-powered tractors, even a motorized vehicle for transportation.

"Was Milan ever Beachy?" I ask.

"No."

"Did he know the men?"

"I don't think so." She mulls that a moment. "I got the impression he was as surprised to see them as I was."

"Do you know what they wanted?"

"No idea."

"When did this happen?" I ask.

She makes a face as if to search her memory. "A week or two before Milan was killed."

I puzzle over the incident as I write it down. "These men," I say, "did they drive a vehicle?"

"I'm not sure. I mean, I was in the kitchen and didn't look out the window." Her brows furrow. "But I do recall seeing lights." She looks at me. "Headlights, maybe. Bright, you know, as if from a car or truck."

I note it. "What happened next?"

"They took Milan outside and he went with them."

"Willingly?"

"Seemed that way."

"Did they argue?" I ask. "Or fight?"

"Didn't say anything." Her brows knit. "But there was something about those men, Chief Burkholder. The way Milan acted, he might've thought he didn't have a choice."

"Can you give me a physical description of the men?"

She considers a moment. "Well, they were wearing black jackets. Kind of Amish-like. You know. Plain. White shirts. Suspenders."

"Height? Weight?"

"Taller than me. Average build."

"What about eye color?" I ask. "Hair?"

She shakes her head. "I don't remember. I was so upset that night."

"Did the men speak at all?" I ask.

"They spoke to each other. Low voices, you know, so I didn't hear most of what they said."

"*Deitsch* or English?"

"English."

"When's the last time you saw Milan?" I ask.

She tightens her mouth. "Day or two before he died. Came over to pick up some tools, but he was nervous as a cat. All sweaty. Said he'd been working out to your brother's place."

"Did he say anything else?" I ask.

Across from me, Lester shifts, clears his throat, casts a longing look at the back door as if wishing he could get up and leave. He doesn't.

Bertha nods. "Told me he'd had an argument with Jacob Burkholder over some pay. Called Jacob a cheat." Her brows furrow. "He claimed Jacob had accused him of some things he didn't do."

"Did he say what?"

"I didn't ask and he didn't say. To tell you the truth, Chief Burkholder, I didn't want to know."

I think about the timing of the men's appearance and the murder of Milan Swanz and I realize with a keen sense of discomfort that the timeline doesn't jibe.

I look from Bertha to Lester and then back at her. "Did Milan know about the two of you?"

Pressing her hand to her bosom, Bertha chokes out a nervous laugh. "We never told anyone. We were . . . careful, you see. Didn't say a word to anyone or let ourselves be seen in public until after the divorce."

"Where were the two of you the night Milan was killed?" I ask.

Shifting uncomfortably in his chair, Lester looks at Bertha. "I was home. Next door. Alone."

I look at Bertha. "I was here with the kids. Like always."

•   •   •

When you're a cop and working on a case, particularly a homicide, urgency is your worst enemy—and your best friend. My personal philosophy goes something like this: Everything must be done yesterday and it had damn well better be done right or you will screw up your case and risk the guilty party getting away with murder. The stakes are high, the stress is astronomical, and there is zero room for fucking up.

I'm unpacking the mountain of information given to me by Bertha Swanz as I pull out of her driveway and head toward town. A good portion of what I learned qualifies as motive. Domestic violence. Rape. An illicit affair. Neither Lester nor Bertha have verifiable alibis. The most obvious question is: Did they want Milan Swanz gone so they could be together? So that Bertha and her children could escape the cycle of violence?

I think about her claim of two strange men showing up the night she was assaulted. Was she telling the truth? Or was she fabricating some mysterious villain in the hope I'll direct my suspicions elsewhere?

Even as I entertain the notion, I recall her description of the men:

Dressed all in black.

. . . eyes that mean business.

Kind of Amish-like.

Mentally, I superimpose that information atop the description of the mysterious man Britney Gainer had seen with Swanz the night he was killed.

. . . he was wearing black . . .

. . . kind of looked Amish . . .

The man who attacked me wore a black jacket and trousers.

Are the similarities purely coincidental?

The answer to that is a resounding no.

Filing the information away for later, I hit the speed dial for Auggie Brock. Six rings. Seven. Avoiding me, I think. I'm about to disconnect when he picks up, feigning breathlessness.

"I was just going to call you to make sure you're being kept up to date on the case," he begins.

I know Auggie pretty well. I understand him. He's a good mayor, and I actually *like* him as a person. But I know he's a politician first and my friend second. He may be fond of me in a superficial way, but he sure as hell doesn't want to talk to me, or, God forbid, deal with the politics of my being forced into a limited-duty situation. I suspect he knows me well enough to grasp that I'm not going to stand for it.

"I'm on my way to the station," I tell him.

"What? Why? I thought—"

"I'm calling a meeting."

"But, Kate, you're on limited duty. Are you sure that's wise?"

"I want one thing from you this morning, Auggie. You're my boss and I need to know you trust my judgment. I need to know you have my back."

"Well . . . um, of course I have your back. I mean, come on, Kate. We're friends. You're still the chief of police. You're not on adminis- trative leave—"

"Good," I cut in. "I have some new information on the case and I'd like to bring everyone up to speed."

A sound that's part groan, part gasp hisses over the line. "Kate, Chambers has pretty much convinced everyone you're too personally involved. That you'll protect your brother and—"

"You're the mayor and you know better, though, don't you?"

For the span of several seconds, the only sound comes from the hiss of the airwaves between us. Then he clears his throat, coughs quietly, and says exactly what I knew he would. "Of course I do."

"I'll be there in ten minutes."

Another beat of silence and then, "Kate, can I ask one thing of you?"

"Lay it on me."

Even his laugh sounds tense. "Don't rough Chambers up too bad."

"I'll do my best." Without hanging up, I hit the speed dial for Mona.

"Chief, I'm so glad to hear from you. Everyone's saying you stepped aside because your brother—"

"He didn't," I cut in. "And I didn't step aside. In fact, I'm on my way in. I need everyone there for a briefing." I glance at the clock on the dash. "Twenty minutes. War room. Tell them to drop everything and come. Call Rasmussen last."

A minuscule pause, and then, "What about Chambers?"

"Call him *after* you call Rasmussen."

"My pleasure." I can practically hear her smiling. "Anything else?"

"You might want to wear your flak jacket."

"Hell yeah." She lets out a *whoop!* as I disconnect.

CHAPTER 24

Mike Rasmussen calls twice on the short drive to the station. I let both go to voicemail. Evidently, he wants to know what I'm up to. I wish I had a definitive answer. Best-case scenario, this briefing will give me the opportunity to pass along everything I've learned about the Schwertler Anabaptists and add Isaiah Hofer's name to our persons-of-interest list. With me still relegated to limited duty, the rest is up to them.

As I pull into my parking slot, I send a silent thank-you to Mona; the majority of my officers are already here. No sign of the sheriff's SUV or Tomasetti's Tahoe. Trepidation churns in my gut as I enter the building. I've barely set foot inside when someone calls out to me.

"Chief!"

I glance toward dispatch to see Margaret standing, the headset clamped over her ears, mouthpiece shoved to one side. She's waving a tome-size stack of message slips. Her expression tells me the aforementioned messages are secondary to whatever else she has to say.

"Thank God you're back," she mutters.

I stride to her. "I appreciate you and Mona getting everyone here so quickly," I say as I pluck the slips from her hand.

"Tomasetti helped."

Inwardly, I smile. Margaret wasn't born yesterday. "Glad to hear it," I say.

"Your officers have their heads on straight, Chief. Just about everyone else around here has their head up their ass." Her mouth twitches. "No offense."

"None taken."

Eyes flicking toward the door, she lowers her voice. "Rasmussen, Chambers, and Tomasetti are five minutes out."

"Auggie?"

"Just talked to him. He's parking." She grimaces, lowers her voice. "I hear Chambers is on the warpath. There's something going on."

"Any idea what?" I ask.

"No clue, but I don't like it."

"You and me both." I start toward my office. "Call that meeting to order."

She grins.

A few feet away, Glock's head pops up over the top of his cubicle. "Want me to round everyone up, Chief?"

"I'm glad your hearing is good," I say over my shoulder as I unlock the door and snatch the file and notes from my desk. Then I'm back in the hall in time to see Skid and Pickles come around the corner.

"Just talked to Mona," T.J. tells me. "She's a minute out."

"Evidently, Tomasetti picked up Chambers earlier," Skid says beneath his breath.

Pickles's mouth twitches. "Last I heard, Tomasetti was going to swing by Mocha Joe's for coffee."

"Always a line at Mocha Joe's." Glock comes up behind us. "That'll slow them down."

"Coffee's worth the wait." T.J. feigns sympathy. "But I bet Chambers wasn't too happy about the holdup."

"Son of a bitch'll be good and primed by the time Tomasetti gets finished with him," Pickles grumbles.

I enter the meeting room and stride directly to the half podium set up at the head of the table. The men shuffle into chairs. I glance down at my notes, aware that my pulse is up. That I'm nervous and running hot and neither of those things is going to serve me well in the coming minutes.

The door swings open. My pulse jumps. Not Chambers, but a breathless Mona. "Sorry. Cows out over on Hogpath Road. Mr. Cline gave me an earful." She slides into the nearest chair.

I jump in headfirst. "Milan Swanz may have been Amish," I say, "but he was a violent man. A troubled man. He abused his wife. His children. Broke his son's arm, in fact. Behaved inappropriately with a minor child. Those are the things we know about him and I believe that kind of conduct is a pattern of behavior that may be related to and led up to his death."

Glock sits up straighter, listening intently.

I continue. "He burned his neighbor's cornfield, destroyed the deacon's corn crop and garden. After Swanz had some problems with his boss, the cabinet shop burned to the ground. I also found out Swanz assaulted the Amish bishop and his wife. All of this is a pattern of behavior."

Skid whistles. "Busy sumbitch."

"One of the things we don't do in the course of any investigation is blame the victim," I tell them. "We do, however, look at the victim's

243

life. His lifestyle. The people he was close to. If he had any ongoing disputes. If anyone was angry enough to want him gone."

"Sounds like there was plenty of motive to go around," Glock says.

"To say the least. And that's exactly where this behavior pattern comes into play." I find a dry-erase marker and turn to the whiteboard behind me. "Persons of interest," I say, speaking as I write. "His ex-wife, Bertha Swanz. He abused her. Sexually assaulted her. Seriously injured her young son." I hit the highlights of my interview with her. "Lester Yoder. He and Bertha Swanz were involved in a relationship before the divorce was final. Both had reason to want Swanz out of the picture. Neither of them has an alibi for the night Swanz was murdered."

The door opens. Tomasetti enters the room as if he owns the place. As cool as a tomcat slinking out the door at midnight. His gaze sweeps from me to my officers and back to me. Something akin to satisfaction flashes in his eyes as he takes the chair next to Mona. Chambers isn't as subtle. Giving me a withering look, he takes his place against the wall and leans, like a truculent teenager forced to sit through a boring dinner. Auggie Brock enters last, his reluctance obvious to everyone.

"Glad you could make the briefing, gentlemen." I turn back to the whiteboard and give them a quick recap of the points I've laid out so far. "Noah Stutzman and his father own the cabinet shop that burned. They lost everything in the fire. No insurance. They believe Swanz was responsible—particularly Noah—but Swanz was never formally charged."

I go to the next name. "Jacob Burkholder."

"Here we go," Chambers mutters beneath his breath.

I ignore him, but I can feel my heart tapping hard against my breastbone. "Jacob Burkholder said Swanz acted inappropriately with his young son, who is eleven years old—"

"We interviewed Jacob Burkholder," Chambers cuts in. "He didn't mention any sort of inappropriate behavior by Swanz."

"Sounds like she got more out of him than you did," Pickles says.

Chambers frowns. "Let me get this straight, Chief Burkholder, you were placed on limited duty and yet you went to see your brother, who happens to be a person of interest—"

I cut him off. "He came to me," I say. "I listened to what he had to say and I'm updating you now." I look around the room. "Because I am related to Jacob, I think it would be more appropriate if all future dealings with him—interviews, phone calls, warrants, whatever—are handled by either the sheriff's office or BCI. I hope you guys can work it out."

Calmer now, feeling as if I've found my feet, I go back to the board and write: *Mystery man at McNarie's bar.* I face my team. "According to three patrons who were at the bar the night Swanz was killed, the victim sat down and talked with a middle-aged man for some time. An unidentified man that may or may not have been Amish."

"If he was local, seems like someone would have recognized him," Glock says.

"No one recognized him," I say.

"You get a physical description?" Pickles asks.

"A vague one." I glance down at my notes. "Caucasian. Early middle age. Black clothing, including a hat. Possibly Amish or formerly Amish."

Anabaptist, a little voice whispers in my ear, and I put the thought to memory.

"That covers half the males in Holmes County," T.J. mutters.

"Maybe it was your brother," Chambers mumbles.

I ignore him, keep moving forward, winging it. I know my material, but I'm not sure how all of it fits together. "During my interview with the Troyers, in the course of a conversation about the phenomenon of burning someone at the stake and how it relates to Anabaptist history, Freda Troyer mentioned an individual by the name of Isaiah Hofer." I add the name to the list and recap my conversation with Hofer. "He's Hutterite and operates a quarry in Dundee."

"He got a sheet?" Skid asks.

"Clean."

Chambers all but rolls his eyes.

"Could he be the mystery man who was at the bar the night Swanz was murdered?" Glock asks.

"Hofer claims he was home that night." I shrug. "Alone. But his physical description and the dress I observed fits the bill in a general way."

"Any connection to Swanz?" T.J. asks.

"I'm still looking." I pause. "Interestingly, the two strangers who allegedly showed up at Bertha Swanz's place the night she was assaulted may have been wearing similar clothing to the man at McNarie's bar."

"One of them may have been the same dude?" Glock asks.

"I don't know," I say honestly. "I thought it was worth noting."

Pickles slants a look at Chambers and Rasmussen. "Until now, we didn't know most of this."

Chambers tosses Tomasetti a this-is-bullshit look, but Tomasetti hands it right back to him.

Having had enough, Chambers clears his throat. "Chief Burkholder, with all due respect, ma'am, I'm sure you're aware that we've developed an updated persons-of-interest list. We're in the process of interviewing them now. In fact, we were on our way to interview Troyer when we got the call that you were here, holding this so-called meeting."

I give him my attention. "You didn't know about Hofer."

"Evidently, we would have after speaking with Troyer instead of wasting our time here, listening to you."

"Neither Freda nor the bishop will speak openly to you," I point out.

"That remains to be seen," he says.

"For the record," Tomasetti says, "Chief Burkholder makes a valid point. She has a good relationship with the Amish. They trust her. And they respect her."

"Duly noted." Chambers mutters the words beneath his breath, then looks around, a king being forced to reprimand an unruly court. "With all due respect to everyone in this room, it has been established that Chief Burkholder's personal ties to this case—as now made clear by the unfortunate incident involving her brother and minor nephew—have rendered her too personally involved to remain lead in this investigation."

He looks at me. "At this point, I think it would be prudent for you to recuse yourself from the case."

I've never clashed with another law enforcement officer or agency over jurisdiction. It's counterproductive and bad form. My department works closely with the sheriff's department; sometimes our responsibilities overlap. Most often, I'm the first to ask for assistance and I appreciate any manpower I can get. While Chambers's argument is sound, it is not the be-all and end-all of the investigation. If I'm going to maintain the respect of my team, I can't let it stand.

I point at him, relieved that my finger is steady. "This is my briefing. I have some additional information I'd like to share. Sit down and be quiet."

Out of the corner of my eye, I see Auggie's mouth open and hang, but I don't look at him. Rasmussen squirms in his chair as if his breakfast doesn't agree with him. Tomasetti meets my gaze and I'm bolstered by the approval I see in his eyes.

Chambers has the audacity to look amused and raises his hands in surrender. "Hey, the floor is yours."

Shaking inside, I look down at my notes. "I don't have to point out that burning a man at the stake is an extremely unusual method of murder. It's risky and messy with a lot of variables that could backfire and get the killer caught. Yet this individual was willing to take the risk. I believe that is key. I believe this murder was somehow symbolic. And I believe once we understand the why, we'll be in a better position to find the who."

This is my entry into uncharted territory. I'm keenly aware that this is exactly the kind of situation that could go south and make me look like a fool. The theory I'm about to put forth stretches believability—mine included—and not everyone sitting in this room supports my even being on the case.

"During my interview with Freda Troyer," I begin, "I learned of an obscure group that was a small part of Anabaptist history. In a nutshell, during the Reformation, a sect of Anabaptists known as the Schwertlers came to be. As most of you know, one of the hallmarks of the Amish, and the vast majority of all Anabaptists, is the tenet of pacifism. The Schwertler Anabaptists differ in that they were—and I quote—'of the sword.'"

"Are you saying this group condoned violence?" Mona asks.

The room falls so quiet I can hear the switchboard chiming and Margaret speaking to a caller from the reception area. Even Chambers is watching, his eyes sharp with interest. I look down at my notes, take a moment to organize my thoughts.

"The Schwertler Anabaptists believed the government was a Godly institution and felt that government had a responsibility to defend helpless Christians. That included taking up arms."

Sheriff Rasmussen speaks up for the first time and asks the obvious question. "What's the connection between the murder of Milan Swanz and this mysterious group?"

"I'm not certain there is a connection. What I do know is that both Freda Troyer and Isaiah Hofer mentioned the Schwertler Anabaptists when I spoke with them about the Swanz case."

"In what context?" Rasmussen asks.

"This group is folklore mostly. But in the course of my search for parallels, I learned one of the early leaders of the Anabaptist movement was burned at the stake. I learned that this group not only condones but engages in violence. I think it's worth taking a look at."

"Kate, with all due respect," says Rasmussen, "seems like a precarious link."

Seeing a couple of uncertain expressions, I press on. "Take into consideration everything we know about Milan Swanz, his pattern of behavior—hurting people, abusing children, engaging in amoral behavior." I say the words with emphasis. "What if some bastardized version of the Schwertler Anabaptists is still around? What if this group took it upon themselves to protect the Amish community?"

Texting, Chambers looks up from his cell and hefts an incredulous laugh. "You mean like the Amish Mafia?"

I'm thankful when no one laughs.

"Kate, just to clarify," the sheriff says. "Are you saying these Schwertler Anabaptist people may be living in or around Holmes County? That they planned and executed the murder of Swanz because he was a threat to the Amish community?"

"I'm putting forth a loose theory that warrants a closer look," I tell him. "Anyone can call themselves a Schwertler Anabaptist. What we're talking about here is motive."

"One person?" This from Skid. "Or a group?"

"I don't know, but I'm leaning toward the possibility that we're looking for at least two individuals."

Glock jumps in with the next question. "So you believe that the perpetrator or perpetrators are likely Amish."

"Or formerly Amish or some denomination of Anabaptist," I tell him. "Remember, the Anabaptists are comprised of three core groups: the Amish, the Mennonites, and the Hutterites."

T.J. poses the next question. "How does this group find their victims?"

It's a difficult question I've considered and not been able to answer. "It has to be word of mouth," I tell him. "The Amish community is tight-knit. Everyone knows everyone. Word gets out. And this group catches wind of it."

"So you don't believe someone here in Painters Mill made contact with this group?" says Tomasetti. "The bishop? An elder?"

I think about the bishop and his wife, of the Amish community as a whole, and my own years growing up as one of them, and I shake my head. "I can't see that."

Chambers sighs as if he's heard enough. "Chief Burkholder, with all due respect, how in the hell does burning a guy in a pile of pallets tie into some mysterious vigilante group and Amish history?"

"That method of execution was used to do away with Anabaptists during the Reformation. There are many cases documented in *Martyrs Mirror*."

"'Martyrs mirror'?"

"It's an old book," I explain. "Written in the seventeenth century. It depicts stories of persecution of the early Anabaptists. A lot of Amish keep this book in their homes."

Smiling, he scratches his head, his expression a mix of skepticism and amusement. "Chief Burkholder, with all due respect to you and the Amish, that's one hell of a stretch."

A cacophony of ringing cell phones breaks the tension. Chambers glances down at his and rises. "Just a second," he says, and leaves the room.

Next to him Rasmussen frowns at the display of his own cell and then swipes up without answering. Auggie Brock gives his iPhone the side-eye then quickly silences it.

"Shit," Tomasetti mutters.

I look at him, puzzled, inexplicably alarmed, keenly aware that neither my cell nor Tomasetti's rang.

The door swings open. Chambers strides in, cell phone in hand, and addresses Rasmussen without looking at me. "We got the warrant."

Muttering a curse beneath his breath, Rasmussen gets to his feet. I watch him from where I stand, but he doesn't make eye contact with me.

"Warrant for who?" I direct the question to the sheriff.

Chambers finally looks at me. "Jacob Burkholder for the murder of Milan Swanz."

CHAPTER 25

It's two P.M. and I'm sitting in my office, trying—and failing—not to feel betrayed. I want to believe I'm angry about the secrecy surrounding the warrant for my brother's arrest. That I'm pissed because my counterparts didn't trust me enough to even give me a heads-up, and then they sprang the news on me in front of my team. But, I'm not just angry. I'm hurt—and I'm worried as hell for my brother.

A mountain of foreboding threatens to overwhelm me when I think of what will happen to Jacob in the coming hours and days. I don't believe he murdered Milan Swanz. I know him—his heart, his mind. The circumstantial evidence against him looks bad, but I know he isn't a killer.

Miserable, I look out the window at the intermittent snow and I wonder if the sheriff's department deputies have made the arrest. I wonder if Jacob blames me. If he thinks I betrayed his confidence. The wrongness of that is almost too much to bear.

"Kate."

I swivel to see Tomasetti stride through the door. His expression is one of commiseration and also remorse for the way we left things earlier. I'm not quite ready to talk to him. But I need him, I realize, in a way that has nothing to do with my job or the case.

"Did they arrest him?" I ask.

Frowning, he sinks into the visitor chair across from me. "They're at his farm now."

I groan, set my elbows on the desk. "I hate this."

"Me, too."

"Did you know?"

"They didn't tell me shit." He snaps the words, and then I see him regain control. "I wouldn't have allowed that shitshow."

He's talking about Rasmussen and Chambers sitting in on the briefing while they were waiting for the warrant without giving me some kind of warning.

"So how did it go down?" I ask.

"Evidently, Chambers wrote the affidavit this morning and took it to a judge up in Millersburg."

"The son of a bitch."

"I was going to go with fucking bastard, but son of a bitch'll do."

I try to smile, but it feels phony on my face. "What do they have on Jacob?" I ask. "I mean, aside from what happened with my nephew? I don't see how that's enough for an arrest warrant."

"An anonymous tip came in this morning. Someone claiming they saw Jacob in his buggy on Dogleg Road shortly before the murder."

"He wasn't there," I say. "He would have told me." Even as I say the words, I know there's more bad news coming.

"Jacob purchased two dozen pallets a week before the murder."

I stare at him, surprised, trying not to show it. "You know that's not such an unusual purchase on a farm. A lot of farmers use pallets to store hay or—"

"He bought six gallons of diesel fuel the morning of the murder."

"That's another typical farm item, especially for the Amish."

"Well, his timing sucks," he returns. "Combine those purchases with the tip and what happened between Swanz and your brother—and your nephew—and it's damning. Chambers has motive, means, and opportunity."

I smack my palm down on the tabletop. Because I'm angry. Frustrated. And scared because I can't deny the sliver of doubt I feel. I know better than most that when it comes to the power of love and the instinct to protect our children, all of us are vulnerable to our human frailties and that includes rage.

"What about an alibi?" I ask.

"Says he was with his wife."

"Jacob is not a killer," I tell him.

"I know."

The reassurance brings tears to my eyes, but I blink them away, go back to the window, grapple for control.

Hearing the crinkle of paper, I turn back to him, see him pull several folded sheets from an inside pocket. "I got a couple of interesting hits on my ViCAP query."

I'd nearly forgotten. My heart does a quick leap as I take the papers. "How interesting?"

"There are four cases," he says. "Homicides. Three involving the Amish. One Mennonite."

I skim the particulars, making note of the dates. "Cases are pretty cold," I murmur.

"Not to mention a long shot in terms of a connection."

I give him a pointed look. "If you have a better idea, I'm all ears."

"I don't."

Sighing, I turn my attention back to the papers and take in the preliminaries of a case out of Pennsylvania. "Which signatures did you query?"

"Amish." He shrugs. "Rural. Farm. Field. Wooded. Homicide by fire. Ritual."

I nod. "Thank you."

"Keep your chin up, Chief. We'll get through." Smiling tightly, he rises. "I need to get out to your brother's farm."

I stand, too. "Make sure they treat him right."

"You know it." He comes around my desk. "You?"

"I'll take a quick look at these cases, then head home." I try for a smile, but don't pull it off. "Maybe break the seal on something strong."

"Do me a favor?" he says as he bends to me.

"Well, since you came through with that ViCAP report . . ."

"Wait for me."

He brushes his mouth against mine.

And then he's gone.

• • •

The first case included in the ViCAP summary is from July of 2012 out of Lancaster County, Pennsylvania. The victim, twenty-six-year-old Amish female, Lena Stoltzfus, was found facedown in a farm pond. Initially, her death was ruled a suicide. But after a second autopsy, the manner of death was revised to homicide. There aren't many details included, and I need more information before I can proceed, so I highlight the particulars and move on to the next.

The second case is out of Cashton, Wisconsin, from 2005. A forty-two-year-old Amish male, Daniel Miller, perished in a barn fire.

Initially, the fire was thought to be accidental, but the presence of an accelerant proved it to be an arson and a homicide investigation was opened. No further details available.

I've moved on to the third case, from all the way back in 1999, when I hear a tap at my door. I glance up to see my dispatcher Margaret standing in the doorway, a cup of coffee in her hand. "Coffee, Chief?" she asks. "Just made it."

We both know that when it comes to coffee here at the station, the freshness point is moot. But her effort makes me smile. "I'd love some."

She enters, sets the cup on my desk. "Agency delivered your rental car earlier."

"Thank you."

Stepping back, she puts her hands on her hips. "Tomasetti told me they put you on administrative duty."

"I have a personal connection to the case, so that is the protocol." I do my best to keep my explanation vague and professional. It's not easy.

"Excuse me if I'm overstepping, Chief, but everyone here thinks it's bullshit," she says. "Tomasetti's word, not mine."

I feel my brows go up. "Well . . ."

She motions to the ViCAP report on my desk. "He asked me to print that for you earlier. He said you might be on administrative duty, so you can damn well still administer. I thought that was a good call."

"Tomasetti said that?"

She nods. "You did good," she tells me. "Marrying him, I mean. I like him."

"I do, too." It's a dumb response, but my brain is focused on other things.

"Do you need some help with that?" She sends a pointed look at the ViCAP reports. "I'm still learning the ropes, but I'm pretty good at figuring things out."

Temptation sparks, but I tamp it down. I know better than to involve her in something I shouldn't be involved in myself. A smarter woman would call it a day. Drive back to the farm. Break the seal on that nice bottle of WhistlePig. . . .

I hand her the reports. "Make yourself copies of these. Get me contact info for the sheriff's departments and state police on each of these cases. See if you can find the name of the lead investigator."

"You got it."

"For administrative purposes only," I add.

"That's what I thought." She grins as she plucks the papers from my hand.

• • •

Margaret isn't as adroit as Mona when it comes to mining the internet for data, but she's a fast learner. Once she's supplied me with contact info for the pertinent law enforcement agencies, I hit the phone. While I burn up the line, she expands her searches and continues digging for anything else she can find on the cases: news stories, social media posts, and updates on the crimes.

After nine calls and nine assurances that someone would get back to me, not a single investigator has responded. One is on vacation. Two have retired. Four have left for the day. I've left messages for the rest.

All the while, worry for Jacob presses down on me. No one has updated me, so I can only assume he's been arrested. I wonder if Irene and the children were there, if they witnessed him being handcuffed and placed in the back seat of a sheriff's cruiser.

"Here's another newspaper story on the Lena Stoltzfus case."

I look up to see Margaret charge through the door, a sheet of paper in hand.

"Thanks." I take the sheet and pass her my notes on the Wisconsin case. "The detective retired two years ago. See if you can find his home number. Public information officer at the sheriff's office said he moved to Florida six months ago."

"I'll find him."

I force my concentration to the newspaper story Margaret just delivered. It's out of Lancaster, Pennsylvania, about the Amish woman found dead in a farm pond. Margaret has highlighted the name of the investigator that handled the case. I shuffle through the papers on my desk and punch in the number for the Pennsylvania State Police.

"Let me transfer you to the public information officer," comes a high-speed female voice.

"Wait—"

Too late. Three clicks and another voice picks up. Quickly, I identify myself. "I need to speak with Lieutenant Gersch."

"Let me transfer you to the Criminal Investigation Section."

I'm on hold for nearly four minutes and hoping I haven't been relegated to phone hell when a curt male voice comes on the line. "Shulte."

I introduce myself. "I'm looking for Lieutenant Gersch."

"Actually, Chief Burkholder, Lieutenant Gersch passed away two years ago," he tells me. "You're stuck with me."

I give him a brief explanation for my call. "I got a ViCAP hit on the Stoltzfus case in relation to a homicide we're working on here in Painters Mill."

"Let me pull up what I've got." I hear the finger-peck of computer keys. "The Lancaster County coroner initially ruled the death a suicide. Amish woman found in a pond. The woman's husband recalled seeing bruises on her neck. At that point, Lieutenant Gersch requested a second autopsy, which revealed the victim did, indeed, have ligature marks on her neck."

"So the cause of death was strangulation?" I ask.

"Cause of death was drowning," he corrects. "No one could explain the ligature marks until the sheriff's department sent a diver into the water. They found a concrete block and a rope. The rope matched the ligature marks. Lieutenant Gersch theorized the killer had tied the rope around the victim's neck, secured it to the block, and forced the woman into the pond, where she drowned."

"How is it that the rope and block were no longer secured to the victim when she was found?"

"Presumably, the killer went into the water and cut the rope off her. We can only assume he thought law enforcement would draw the conclusion that she'd committed suicide."

None of those details had made it into any of the reports I'd read. "Was an arrest made?"

"No, ma'am."

"Persons of interest?"

"Initially, the husband. You know how it goes. But the guy had a solid alibi. He was at a neighbor's all day, helping with some sick livestock."

"Suspect?"

"Not a one. Case is still open. Gets looked at every year. Unfortunately, we've not made any progress."

"What about physical evidence?" I ask. "At the scene? Were there footwear impressions? On the bank of the pond? Did you guys look at the concrete block? The rope?"

"By the time we realized we were dealing with a homicide, Chief Burkholder, any footwear impressions were either trampled by first responders or washed away by the rain that came that night," he replies. "We looked at the rope and block. Both were relatively new. We checked with area retailers, looked at hundreds of hours of CCTV, and we came up with nothing."

Silence ensues and I sense his curiosity about my inquiry. "Chief Burkholder, if you don't mind my asking, how is this cold case related to your investigation in Painters Mill?"

I outline fundamentals of the Swanz homicide. "The ViCAP signature match is likely the Amish angle and that the crime occurred in a rural area."

"I guess we're in the same boat. No suspect."

"Yet," I add.

"Gotta love an optimist cop." I hear the smile in his voice. "If you come up with a connection or lead, I'd appreciate a heads-up."

"Bet on it," I tell him.

And we end the call.

•　•　•

I spend twenty minutes scouring the internet for information on the Stoltzfus case, looking for a link to Painters Mill or *Martyrs Mirror* or any of the names connected to the case, but my efforts net zero. I'm about to mark it off my list when I spot the underscored hyperlink on one of the pages Margaret brought in earlier. *Suicide in Amish Country—or Was It?* It's a teaser headline written by a popular Amish-centric citizen journalist out of Lancaster County who also produces a successful podcast. This one was published in July 2012.

Was the death of Lena Stoltzfus a suicide, as the police initially believed? Or was this young Amish woman's death something much darker? Find out by tuning in to my latest podcast.

My interest surges. Snatching up the paper, I spin to my computer and pull up the podcaster's YouTube channel.

"Hi, everyone! I'm Dan with AmishWorldUSA. Welcome to my

show! Crime is the last thing on your mind when you think of the Amish here in peaceful Lancaster County, but that's exactly what we have today. This one's got some dark undertones, folks, and probably isn't appropriate for kids, so consider yourselves forewarned."

The young host chose the ideal spot for an on-location report. He's standing in front of a pretty Amish farm with a white farmhouse, mature trees, a red bank barn, and a silo in the background. The house sits relatively close to the road, so he's close enough for his viewers to feel as if they have a front-row seat to the action. The bucolic setting is perfectly juxtaposed with the flashing lights of a sheriff's department cruiser, a string of yellow crime scene tape, and uniformed deputies and khaki-clad detectives milling about in the background.

"Behind me is the farm where twenty-six-year-old Lena Stoltzfus was found dead a few hours ago," the podcaster begins. "The Amish woman lived here with her husband of six years, John."

He assumes a solemn countenance. "According to police, Mr. Stoltzfus discovered his wife's body when he arrived home after helping his neighbor with a sick cow. Like most Amish, the Stoltzfuses don't have a phone, and John ran half a mile down the road to an English neighbor's house where he called 911.

"I spoke to one of the neighbors earlier—who wished to remain anonymous—and they informed me that Lena had been troubled as of late. Her husband knew she sometimes found solace walking the fields of this pastoral farm. So, today, when Mr. Stoltzfus came home to an empty house, he went looking for her—and found her facedown in the pond, dead." The narrator motions to the property behind him. "Just two hundred yards away, behind that barn."

Over the next minutes, the podcaster interviews several Amish standers-by. Some are neighbors. Friends. One of the interviewees was driving by in his buggy and stopped by to find out why all the police cars were there. Most of the Amish who are interviewed don't show their faces on camera, but a couple do.

"Lena was a troubled thing," says a middle-aged Amish woman, her back to the camera. "I talked to her just a week ago at worship. She wanted a family so badly. When she lost those three sweet babies, the sadness just crushed the life out of her."

The podcaster watches her walk away and turns back to the camera. "Not everyone, however, believed Lena Stoltzfus was without fault." He thrusts the microphone toward a young Amish woman, who tosses him an annoyed look, and quickly turns her back. "Ma'am, I understand you have a differing take on what might've happened to Lena Stoltzfus."

She starts to walk away, but the podcaster keeps pace with her. "When we spoke earlier, you mentioned rumors," he prods. "Can you tell us about that?"

She doesn't slow down. "All's I'm going to say is I heard some things that weren't so nice."

"Like what?"

"Like maybe those babies didn't die from SIDS like everyone was saying."

"That's a bold statement," he says. "Can you clarify that for us? Do you have anything to back up that claim?"

"I think I said enough." Waving her hand at the camera, the woman turns and walks away.

The camera pans back to the podcaster, his expression puzzled and curious as he approaches another Amish woman. "Ma'am, did you know the victim?"

The camera pans so that only her back and the podcaster's face are showing. Evidently, a second person is operating the camera.

"Lena was the sweetest thing. . . ." The fiftysomething woman tells him that the Stoltzfus family is upstanding, hardworking, and Godly.

As I watch, I'm trying to figure out how the signature of this case relates to my case here in Painters Mill when a man crosses behind the podcaster, who's facing the camera. The figure is little more than background, only on screen for a second or two, but the image stops me cold.

"What the hell . . ."

Grabbing the mouse, I rewind the clip and watch again. This time, I freeze the clip so that the man's face is visible. It's not a quality still. The details are blurred and his face is angled away from the camera. He appears to be Amish. Wearing dark trousers and suspenders. Black felt flat-brimmed hat.

"He's wearing a plaid shirt," I whisper.

The rules of the *Ordnung* vary from church district to church district. But the one thing you can count on is that Amish males do not wear plaid. This man is too mature to be on *rumspringa*. As unlikely as it seems, there's something familiar about him. But how can that be? Lancaster County is over three hundred miles away.

A memory bubbles, not quite reaching the surface. I've seen similar clothing recently. I took notice because it was odd. This person wasn't Amish. Where the hell did I see it and what does it have to do with this man who is hundreds of miles away?

The memory hits me like a truck. "Isaiah Hofer. Shit!"

Spinning, I grab my reading glasses off the desk, go back to the monitor. A click of the mouse enlarges the still. The image becomes grainy and I lose detail, but I can see the shirt clearly. Rust and red plaid. Suspenders. A not-quite-Amish hat. I click again, put the video into motion. I watch him walk. Take in the swing of his arms. The long legs. Long stride. The slight hunch of broad shoulders.

"What the hell were you doing in Pennsylvania the same day that an Amish woman was killed?"

Linda Castillo

The only answer is the tap of snow against the window and the foreboding knowledge that while I may have found the missing link connecting the two homicides, I'm in no position to do a damn thing about it.

CHAPTER 26

Milan Swanz was burned at the stake, executed in the same manner that Balthasar Hubmaier was during the Reformation five hundred years ago. Lena Stoltzfus drowned in a farm pond with a concrete block secured to her neck. Elizabeth Hubmaier had a rock tied around her neck and was thrown into the Danube River. Both methods of execution were commonplace during the Reformation, especially against the Anabaptists. There's no cut-and-dried connection between the historic and modern-day crimes, but the parallels are unequivocal.

I've watched the video six times, enlarged it, played around with the brightness, contrast, and resolution—and I'm almost *certain* the individual in the video is Hofer.

Almost . . .

"Why was Milan Swanz burned at the stake?" I whisper.

I answer my own question. "He was a danger to the Amish community."

Next I say, "Why was Lena Stoltzfus drowned?"

265

I glance down at the notes I jotted on the interviews conducted by the podcaster on the Lena Stoltzfus murder.

. . . you mentioned rumors . . .

All's I'm going to say is I heard some things that weren't so nice.

Like maybe those babies didn't die from SIDS like everyone was saying.

A chill scrapes down between my shoulder blades. "Someone thinks she murdered her children?" I murmur.

The words hang like a toxic cloud.

I go back to the case file, pull out my notes, my fingers pausing on my exchange with Freda Troyer.

There is a rumor. . . . a group of men.

. . . their souls are dark.

. . . they see the ungodliness of that as the freedom they need to do things that a godly man cannot.

. . . for a greater good.

I recall the story about her summer in Shipshewana when she was thirteen years old.

Druvvel-machah . . .

Hanged himself in the barn.

. . . someone did that to him.

Tied him up and hung him up by his neck.

Everyone was talking about the Schwertlers.

And it never got told to the police.

When I'd pressed her on the number of years that had passed since the summer of 1951, she'd responded with:

New blood for every generation.

And then she'd given me Hofer's name.

I flip the page, stop at the notes I jotted after my interview with Hofer.

. . . you won't see them coming. If you cross them, they will come for you. They will find you. They will devour you. And they will spit out the residue. The pieces of you will never be found. There will be no resolution. No closure. Consider that the next time you look into the eyes of the people who love you.

It was a threat. Even now, the words chill me. Is it possible some modern-day version of the Schwertler Anabaptists does, indeed, exist? That the only attribute the two groups share is an endorsement of violence? Was Milan Swanz murdered because this group had identified him as a modern-day heretic?

The last thing I should be considering is driving to Dundee to talk to Isaiah Hofer. The notion has BAD IDEA written all over it in flashing red neon. Chances are, the guy in the video *looks* like Hofer. On the outside chance that it *is* him, he may have been there for something as benign as a wedding or funeral. That's not to mention the small inconvenience of my having been removed from the investigation. Interference by me at this juncture could jeopardize the case, especially if it goes to trial.

The problem is, my brother is in jail for a crime he didn't commit.

Chambers doesn't necessarily care if Jacob is guilty or innocent as long as he scores a win for himself. My cop's sensibilities won't allow me to sit this out. The question now is, what the hell am I going to do about it?

"Not a damn thing," I mutter.

Even as I say the words, I know I'm not going to follow my own good advice. Not giving myself time to debate, I snatch up my keys and head for the door.

I call Tomasetti as I back out of my parking spot. He picks up quickly. "Where are you?" I ask without preamble.

"I'm still at the sheriff's office. Jacob was processed an hour ago. They're interviewing him now."

"They cut you, too." It's not a question.

"I'm his brother-in-law, so it wasn't exactly unexpected."

I think of my brother alone in a room with Chambers and Rasmussen. I know Jacob won't talk about what happened between Swanz and my nephew. I also know his silence will be considered a lack of cooperation at best. An outright lie at worst.

"Does Jacob have a lawyer?" I ask.

"I don't think so."

"Tomasetti, he probably doesn't know enough about the way the law works to understand that he has a right to one."

I hear muffled voices on the other end and he lowers his voice. "Look, I know a good criminal defense lawyer in Wooster. Went to college with him a couple hundred years ago. I'll give him a call."

I close my eyes against an unwelcome rush of emotion. "Thank you."

"You at the farm?" he asks.

"Not exactly." I tell him about recognizing Hofer on the video and lay out my suspicions. "Tomasetti, I don't think it's a coincidence."

"What are you going to do about it?"

"I'm going to talk to him."

He mutters a curse. "Kate, you know that's not a good idea for too many reasons to count."

"I'll do it . . . unofficially. Ask a few questions. Feel him out."

"I think we both know that's bullshit, right?"

"I know I'm right about this. Everything fits."

He curses beneath his breath. "Give me Hofer's address," he growls. "I'll meet you there."

I recite the address from memory. "I owe you one."

"If we're going to screw up our careers, we may as well do it with some fucking panache."

"We're not—"

He hangs up on me without letting me finish.

•   •   •

It's nearly dusk by the time I enter the corporation limits of Dundee. The drizzle that had been falling most of the day has transformed to snow. The thermometer on my dash hovers at the thirty-two-degree mark when I make the turn into the gravel lane of the Sugarcreek Sand and Gravel Company. I'm thinking about my pending conversation with Isaiah Hofer as I pass by a yellow backhoe, exhaust spewing, as the blade shoves a cut rock the size of a Volkswagen to demark the edge of the lot. I don't expect him to admit any wrongdoing; he's too smart for that. The best I can hope for is some scrap of information that will set me on track to either prove or disprove my premise—and his involvement.

I park in the same spot as the last time I was here. Cold seeps underneath the collar of my coat as I take the sidewalk to the office. I notice the sign on the door a few yards before I reach the building.

SUGARCREEK SAND AND GRAVEL HAS CLOSED. I recall Hofer telling me the quarry was spent, but the timing of it ruffles the edges of my cop's suspicions.

I knock, but no one answers. The blinds are open just enough for me to see inside. The desk is bare, but the light is on. I go back to the door, turn the knob, and it rolls open.

As I step inside, I remind myself that this is a business, not a private residence. I'm not trespassing, simply walking inside in search of help.

"Hello?" I call out. "Mr. Hofer? It's Kate Burkholder."

The reception desk where the woman had been sitting last time I was here is vacant. The chair is gone. There are no papers or clutter or folders lying about. The computer and keyboard are gone, too. I'm thinking about taking a peek in the rear office when I notice the old-fashioned telephone on the credenza behind the desk, a single light telling me that either someone is using it or there's a line off the hook.

"Mr. Hofer?"

I'm aware of the rise and fall of the backhoe's engine outside as I start down the hall. I pass by a partially closed door marked RESTROOM and continue on to the office. The lights are on. There's a chair and desk with a smattering of papers on the desktop. A SUGARCREEK SAND AND GRAVEL mug sits on the blotter. I go to it, set the backs of my fingers against the side, find it warm.

"Mr. Hofer?"

My phone vibrates against my hip. I glance down, see Tomasetti's name on the display, and pluck it off my belt. "Where are you?"

"Pulling in now." I can tell by his tone he's not happy with me. "You?"

"Main building. Once you enter the parking lot, you'll see it. Blue SUV parked in front is my rental."

"Meet you there."

I'm clipping the phone back onto my belt when a thunderous *clang!* sounds from outside. Alarmed, I jog down the hall and through the reception area. Somewhere in the back of my mind, I'm aware of the backhoe's engine revving. I'm nearly to the door when through the window, I catch a glimpse of the backhoe. The fill bucket is against the passenger side of the Tahoe, pushing it sideways at a high rate of speed.

"What the hell?"

I yank open the door, take in a hundred things at once. The backhoe moving fast, the fill bucket shoving Tomasetti's Tahoe sideways across the lot. The Chevy's tires plow through gravel and mud, the engine whining. Not an accident.

"Tomasetti!"

I drop my hand to my .38 as I fly down the steps and then I'm running full out. Laser focus on the vehicles. I thumb off the holster break strap, yank it out. Finger inside the guard. And I level it at the cab of the backhoe.

"Stop!" I scream. "Police! Stop!"

The driver's side of the Tahoe slams into the solid wall of rock. The *pop! pop! pop!* of gunfire sounds. I see a puff of smoke as a bullet tears through the Tahoe's window. Tomasetti, I realize, firing through the passenger window, defending himself.

"Stop! *Stop!*"

I fire two shots at the backhoe cab. I'm midway across the lot, sprinting, my .38 trained on the operator. A flash of light to my right. I glance over, see headlights bearing down. The scream of an engine. Too close and coming fast. I twist, get off a shot at the driver.

The vehicle rams me. A knife-stab of pain in my hip. My feet leave the ground, and then I'm airborne. Engine roaring. The world a blur around me. My left shoulder and hip slam against the ground. My head bounces. Stars scatter and my vision goes dark. Vaguely, I'm aware of my body skidding on gravel. I roll, my arms and legs flopping.

The next thing I know I'm lying still. Cold and wet against my face. The same cold seeps into my clothes. Pain courses through me, but I can't quite isolate where. The knowledge that I'm in dire straits dances in the periphery of my consciousness. I bring up my right arm, but my .38 is gone.

I blink to clear my vision. Spit grit from my mouth. Two seconds and the world comes back into focus. I see a black-clad figure approach. Leather boots crunching. I raise my head, look around, shake off another round of dizziness.

Where the hell is my gun?

"Be still," comes a deep voice.

I hear the rise and fall of the backhoe engine. In my mind's eye, I see Tomasetti's Tahoe being crushed. Adrenaline rushes through me and I roll onto my stomach, try to get my arms and knees beneath me so I can get up. My muscles betray me. A wave of nausea hits me. I raise my head, spit, see blood. My head swims, so I lie back down, focus on pulling myself together.

Hands grasp my left shoulder and turn me onto my back. Pain streaks up my spine, and I groan. My head lolls and I find myself looking up at the gray sky. Snow coming down. Cold and wet soaking into my back.

"You made a very foolish decision, Kate Burkholder." Isaiah Hofer kneels next to me. He's wearing a black coat, the wool damp with melting snow. Black leather gloves. His expression is strangely sympathetic as he tucks my .38 into his waistband. "But then I expected no less from you."

He leans over me, his hands moving over my shirt and trousers, being especially diligent with my pockets. While he searches me, I take inventory of my injuries. Headache. Fuzzy brain. Pain in my right hip. My back. I glance left. The vehicle that struck me is ten feet away, wipers and headlights on, engine purring. Hofer slides my radio from my belt, plucks the mike from my shoulder. Impersonally, he unbuckles my duty belt, slides it off me, and drapes it over his arm.

I blink, try to clear my head and assess the situation. Even dazed, I know things couldn't be much worse.

"Where's Tomasetti?" The words come out as little more than a croak.

"Apparently, he made the same miscalculation as you." He looks right, toward the backhoe.

I follow his gaze and the ground seems to break away beneath me. The rock bucket rests atop the crushed roof of the Tahoe. The windshield and windows are buckled. There's no movement. No sign of Tomasetti. No sign of life.

Horror overtakes me and I sit up, snatch Hofer by the throat, my hand squeezing with every ounce of strength I possess. "You son of a bitch."

I don't recognize my own voice. It's primal, suffused with panic and terror and rage.

Twisting, I get my elbow beneath me, try to get a better grip on him, my heels digging for purchase. "Where is he?" I shout.

I don't see the blow coming. The impact is like a stick of dynamite going off in my head. My hand falls away from his throat. I fall back to the ground. When I'm flat, he leans close, both hands going around my neck. I grasp his wrists with my hands, my fingers digging and scratching. I twist, raise my legs to kick, but it's no use. He's stronger and I'm in no condition to fight.

Tomasetti.

Shadows crowd my vision. Sound fades. The only thing I hear is the pounding of my heart. Darkness overtakes the light and it's as if I'm seeing the world through a tiny hole. I'm aware of movement and voices. The sensation of being jostled and my body being dragged.

And then I feel nothing at all.

CHAPTER 27

I wake to the sensation of being inside a moving vehicle. Bumping over rough terrain. Engine purring. I feel heat blowing down from an overhead vent. I open my eyes, see rain on the window. I'm in the rear of my rented SUV. My hands are bound behind my back. I look toward the driver's seat, see the back of Hofer's head.

Raising my head, I look around, try to get my bearings. I see trees outside the window, but recognize nothing. We're off-road. Woods all around. My equipment box from my Explorer, where I keep my tactical gear, is next to me. Inside, I keep extra ammo. My Kevlar vest. A first aid kit. Water. Next to the box, I see a coil of rope that I don't recognize. None of it will help me with my hands bound. I look forward, spot my shotgun in its case between the seats. If I can get to it, I might be able to stop Hofer.

I test the binds on my wrists. It feels like rope, but my hands are numb; I can't be sure. My .38 and radio are nowhere in sight. I glance down at my clothes, but I can't tell if the knife I keep clipped to the inside of my waistband is still there or if Hofer took it.

Shit. Shit. Shit.

The image of Tomasetti's Tahoe flies at me. I don't know if he's alive or dead or injured. The need to go to him runs like a freight train through my chest. Panic threatens, but I beat it back, knowing if I succumb I won't survive.

I look toward Hofer. Find him looking at me in the rearview mirror. His eyes are level on me, his expression inscrutable and cold.

"You're back," he says.

I suppress a nasty response.

"Where's Tomasetti?" I ask.

He turns his attention back to the road and doesn't answer.

Closing my eyes, I bite down so hard my teeth hurt and I shove back another wave of panic. "Where the hell is he?" I snarl.

He ignores the question.

"Ah. Here we are." He jams the shifter into park and kills the engine. I look out the window, see nothing but treetops, gray sky, and lightly falling snow.

Hofer gets out, comes around to the back and opens the door. "Let's get you out of there."

"What are you doing?" I ask.

Leaning in, he picks up the coil of rope and loops it over his head and shoulder, like a crossbody bag. When I don't move, he grasps my arm and hauls me from the SUV. Pain shoots up my hip, but when my feet hit the ground, my legs hold and I'm able to stand.

I take note of my surroundings. Gravel road. Wooded area. The sight of the quarry a few yards away elicits a wave of fear. The body of water is about an acre in size, with sheer rock walls that sweep down to water as smooth as black glass.

"Let's walk," he says.

"Where are you taking me?" I don't move, meet his gaze, hold it. His eyes show no emotion, but his expression is intent. I can feel my legs shaking, hear my breaths coming shallow and fast. As I look at him, I test the binds. Definitely rope. Not too tight, but secure; some of the feeling coming back into my hands.

Taking my arm, he urges me forward. "I knew the day I met you that you were going to be a problem, Chief Burkholder. I know it's little comfort at this moment. I know you're frightened and worried for your husband. All I can tell you is that I did not want things to end like this."

. . . *end like this.*

We're walking side by side. The quarry is to my right, a ten-foot drop to the water. I struggle to remain calm. To come up with a plan to talk him down. Outsmart him. Outmaneuver him.

Kill the son of a bitch.

I glance back toward the SUV. If I can break free and get to my shotgun . . . If Tomasetti is able, he'll come. Dispatch knows where I am. Of course, no one knows I'm in trouble.

"End like what?" I ask.

He looks at me as if I'm a recalcitrant child that must be chastened. He doesn't answer.

"I'm not part of the investigation," I tell him.

"They fired you?" He raises his brows. "How's that for loyalty? Reward for a job well done?"

"They arrested my brother."

"Ah, I see." He nods, thoughtful. "Jacob."

His right hand is wrapped firmly around my biceps, urging me forward.

"You know his name," I say.

"I know many things. Sometimes knowing so much is not a gift."
He says the words with regret. "I know things I wish I didn't. Things
I wish I could change, but can't."

"Where are we going?" I ask.

No response.

"You don't have to do this," I say.

We're ascending a hill, the surface of the quarry below us falling
away. It's an easy hike, but I'm aware of his quickening breaths from
the exertion.

"No one has proof of anything," I say, leaving the statement purposefully vague. "You're not wanted. You're not even a person of
interest."

He ignores me, keeps walking.

"It's not too late to stop this," I say. "You can still get away. With
my brother in jail, no one will come after you."

I glance over at him, find his eyes on me, cold and skeptical and
mildly amused.

"No one?" he asks. "Even you?"

"They fired me, remember?" I try for flippant, but I don't manage.
"It's not easy to be loyal to someone who's stabbed you in the back."

"You are, however, loyal to yourself, no?"

I don't respond.

He hefts the coil rope more solidly onto his shoulder. "I understand
you because in some ways you and I are alike."

"I'm nothing like you."

"People like us . . . we don't give up. We don't know how to give
up. We are driven. Sometimes by demons. Sometimes that's a strength.
Sometimes it's a weakness."

Keep him talking. Engage him.

"I do what I have to do to survive," I tell him.

A smile whispers across his mouth. "That's why you're here, Chief Burkholder. That's why you're a problem. That's why both of us find ourselves in this situation."

"Let me go," I tell him. "I won't come after you. You have my word."

He scoffs. "You insult my intelligence."

My mind zigs and zags as we continue up the trail. I'm aware of the quarry below. The binds at my wrists cutting into my skin. That we're getting farther away from the SUV—and the shotgun. I glance down at my waistband, but I can't discern if my folding knife is there.

We ascend a dozen rock steps. I glance right to see that the water's surface is twenty feet down now. The trail widens and we enter a clearing. It's the kind of place that's probably pretty in the summertime, rife with wild raspberry and goldenrod. A perfect spot for a picnic or photos. This evening, it feels like a deathtrap.

"I know about the Schwertler Anabaptists," I tell him.

He stops, turns to me, studies my face, and I realize I've surprised him. "You did your homework."

"I know why you do what you do," I say.

No response.

Get him talking. Sympathize with him. Gain his trust. Make him think you're an ally.

"Milan Swanz hurt people," I say. "He hurt them physically. Emotionally. He destroyed the lives of a lot of people, especially the ones who cared for him."

He nods as if reluctantly impressed, saying nothing.

"I know you were in Lancaster County in July of 2012," I say.

No response.

"Lena Stoltzfus murdered her babies. She smothered them. Three innocent infants. She got away with it by saying it was SIDS. She

Linda Castillo

would have done it again. You stepped in because it was the only way to stop her."

He raises his hand as if to silence me.

I speak faster, my mind spinning through everything I've learned in the past days, and all of it comes pouring out.

"How many of you are there?" I motion with my eyes in the direction we came from. "The backhoe operator? The woman at the desk? How many?"

"That's enough." He makes the statement with patience, but I can tell his tolerance is wearing thin, my time running out.

"How did you find out about Swanz?" I whisper. "Did someone get in touch with you? An elder? The bishop?"

"Word of mouth," he says simply. "It's the one thing the Amish are good at, no? All that gossip. Such an active rumor mill."

"And yet you know you won't be going to heaven," I say. "You accept the reality of that because the work you do is too important."

"And what work is that?" he asks.

"You martyr those who would otherwise spend eternity in hell. Evidently, it's a sacrifice you're willing to make."

"I must admit, Chief Burkholder, I'm impressed."

For the span of several heartbeats, we stand looking at each other. I hold his gaze, keenly feel the intensity coming off him, the fear crawling over me, the knowledge that I'm in grave danger and if I want to live, I have to act.

"Let me go," I say. "I won't come after you."

He offers a sympathetic smile. "You're a very charming woman. You are courageous. You know your mind. And you've no patience for fools. Under different circumstances . . ."

Keep him talking.

Buy some time.

Someone will come.

"How many have you martyred?" I ask.

His laugh chills me, but he sobers quickly. He looks around as if searching for something. I watch as he walks to a rock the size of a basketball and picks it up. He unloops the coil of rope from around his neck and drops it to the ground at his feet. Kneeling, he uncoils the rope and begins trussing it around the rock.

"If you know the history of the Schwertler Anabaptists," he says, "then you must know the fate of Elizabeth Hubmaier."

I watch, frozen, as he ties an expert knot, tests it, and then rises to his full height.

"Balthasar Hubmaier was executed by fire on March 10, 1528," he tells me. "Three days later his wife, Elizabeth, was executed by having a rock secured to her neck and being thrown into the Danube River."

"Neither Hubmaier nor his wife were guilty of crimes," I say.

"Their deaths were unjust." Fanaticism flickers in his eyes. "But they were martyred by their executioners, their passage into heaven guaranteed."

"You martyred Milan Swanz," I say. "You guaranteed his passage into heaven."

"The irony of that sears the heart, doesn't it?"

"Killing a cop in the state of Ohio is a capital offense," I hear myself say. "They will never stop looking for you."

"Shhh." Raising his hand to silence me, he strides toward me. "The Amish you care so deeply for are certain you will not make it to heaven because you left the fold. I am assuring you, right here and now, that you will. I hope you find some comfort in that."

He reaches for my arm, but I jerk away, stumble back. His hand snakes out, reaching, his fingertips scraping my arm. I spin, launch myself into a run in the direction we came from. It's not easy with my hands bound. I take the rock steps three at a time. I hear him behind me. Breaths rushing. Boots pounding the ground. Gravel crunching.

At the base of the steps I stumble, recover just in time to avoid a fall. Push myself into an all-out sprint. I try to come up with a plan as I run. I know the rented SUV is ahead. Did he lock it? Can I get to the shotgun? Can I use it with my hands bound? Is he armed? Is my Gerber in my waistband?

I'm hyperaware of the sound of his feet against the ground. The whoosh of his clothing. The hiss-hiss of his breaths. He's close. Getting closer. Closing in.

I take a curve at breakneck speed. Glance right. See him scant feet behind me. *Run, Kate! Run!*

The air seems to shift. I catch movement out of the corner of my eye. He reaches out and I feel his fingers brush the back of my arm.

The SUV looms into view ahead. No time to open the door or try to get inside. Instead, I turn on a burst of speed, throw my body against the driver's-side window. Hope ignites at the screech of the alarm.

The impact spins me around, but I maintain my balance, keep going. In the periphery of my vision, I see him slow, reach for the keys. Vaguely, I'm aware of the alarm going silent. The jet-engine roar of blood in my veins as I pant for air. I don't know how far I have to go to reach help.

I'm thinking about cutting through the woods, hoping the trees will provide cover. I hear a rustle behind me, glance left. An instant before I can cut right, Hofer plows into me. His arms wrap around my hips. His shoulder rams my lower back, throwing me forward. I slam to the ground on my stomach, snow and mud in my mouth.

He tries to climb on top of me. I twist, bring up my knee, roll onto my back.

"Be still," he hisses.

I look up as he draws back his fist. No way to defend myself. I twist again, roll left. The blow glances off my temple, his fist hits the ground inches from my face. I roll again. Use the strength of my quads to propel me. I buck against him. Twist my body left. Arm bracing for balance. I roll again and his weight leaves me.

I glance over to see him come at me. I roll down a small hill. Off-trail now. He bends to me, his hands slam down on my shoulders. Fingers digging into muscle and bone.

"Get off me, you son of a bitch!" I scream.

The ground gives way beneath me. The quarry, I realize. We're too close to the edge. I see Hofer's boot slide in mud. His arms flail. Then I find myself cartwheeling into space.

CHAPTER 28

I plunge into the water headfirst. Cold shocks my brain and paralyzes my body. I try to move my arms, can't, and panic bursts inside me.

I'm cognizant of my boots and coat dragging me down. The water sucking at me like an icy mouth. Mindlessly I fight the binds at my wrists. All the while I'm sinking. I suck in water and choke, feel my body convulse. Instinct takes over and I kick my feet with every ounce of strength I possess.

My face breaks the surface. I gulp air and cough violently, treading water as best I can. Fighting to keep my head above water, I look around. There's no sign of Hofer. I don't know if he fell with me or if he's standing on the ledge above, a pistol trained on the back of my head.

The cliff from which I fell is a wall of rock rising out of the water, fifteen feet away. I don't know if there's a foothold. I'm managing to stay afloat, but the cold is sapping my strength fast. My hands, feet, and face are already numb, my extremities starting to ache. Kicking, I twist my body, try to bring my hands around to my front. Water laps over my face as I begin to sink, but I redouble my kicking. Jamming my fingertips into my waistband, I feel around for the knife.

Please be there. Please, God . . .

A sob escapes me when my fingers brush the pivot handle. Praying my grip is strong enough, I unclip it. My thumb seeks the safety toggle, but I fumble it. Choking back sobs, I try again, hit the release button, and the knife snicks open. Struggling to keep my face above water, scissoring my legs back and forth, I saw at the rope. My angle is bad and I nearly drop the knife twice. Lucky for me, the blade is sharp and my hands spring free.

Quickly, I fold the knife and clip it back on my waistband. Keeping an eye on the cliff above, I dog-paddle to the nearest shore, drag myself onto a rock shelf. My arms collapse and I lie there in water and mud, the only sound coming from my labored breaths. For several seconds, I can't move. Shivers rack my body. Only when thoughts of Tomasetti overtake me do I lift my head and look around. Dusk has fallen. Hofer took my flashlight. I've no sidearm or radio. No way to call for help or protect myself if he ambushes me. God knows, I'm in no condition for another confrontation.

It takes every ounce of strength I possess to get to my hands and knees. Somehow, I make it to my feet. My entire body shakes uncontrollably. I put one foot in front of the other until I reach the steep bank. Using my hands and feet, I claw my way over mud and rock and tangled roots.

I reach the top, my eyes searching for Hofer. There's no sign of him. I can feel the cold and wet stealing my body heat. My teeth chatter with so much force that my jaws hurt. On unsteady legs, I take the trail Hofer and I did earlier, push myself into a wobbly jog.

Relief washes over me when I spot the SUV. I reach it, try the doors, find it locked. I want to shed these wet clothes, but I'm familiar enough with hypothermia to know I'll retain more body heat if I keep them on. I've no idea where Hofer is or how far I am from the gravel pit office. I don't know if it's safe to go back. The only thing I'm certain of at this moment is I've got to reach Tomasetti.

I'm shivering violently as I start down the trail. First at a walk, then back to a jog. Arms pumping. Breaths steaming out in front of me. I'm aware of the deepening dusk as I run. I push on and pray to God I have the strength to make it back.

Fear for Tomasetti tracks me as I make my way down the path. I know that if he'd been able, he would have followed Hofer and me. I don't let myself think about why he didn't. Instead, I concentrate on putting one foot in front of the other.

I've only run a hundred yards when I spot the figure ahead. A dark silhouette in the fading light. At first glance I think it's Tomasetti and my heart nearly bursts. But it's not Tomasetti. I slow my pace. The figure continues toward me. Male. Dark coat. The distance between us narrowing. Something familiar in the way he moves . . .

"Chief Burkholder? Oh, my God! What in the hell happened?"

I recognize the voice immediately. Clarence Raber. He's close enough for me to make out his features now. I see shock and concern on his face. Relief floods me with such power that my legs go weak. What the hell is he doing out here at the quarry?

I stop walking, my mind trying to make sense of it. "Call 911."

"Of course." He reaches into his coat pocket and pulls out his cell. "What on earth happened?" Putting his cell to his ear, he continues walking toward me. His eyes tracking my every move. Something in his expression, the way he's looking at me.

"Are you hurt?" he asks.

My brain is not so diminished by the hypothermia that I don't comprehend the danger. Raber has no reason to be here.

Other than the unthinkable.

"Stop." I raise my hand. "Don't come any closer."

He blinks as if I've confused him. He slows his pace, but keeps coming. A Good Samaritan set on helping an overwrought patient.

"My God, you're bleeding." He turns his attention to his phone. "Hello? I'd like to report an emergency. I think there's been an accident." He looks at me. "Chief Burkholder, do you need an ambulance?"

I'm trying to make sense of the scenario when he charges. I stumble backward, try to keep some distance between us, but he's fast. I catch a glimpse of his face an instant before his shoulder slams into my abdomen. My feet leave the ground. My back slams to the earth. I feel the air rush from my lungs. Out of the corner of my eye I see him draw back to strike me. I jam my hand between us, yank the Gerber from its nest. I turn my head barely in time to avoid his fist.

"Where the fuck is Hofer?" he roars.

I hit the blade release. Hear the snick of steel against steel. Using every ounce of strength I possess, I jab the blade into his side.

Raber stiffens. A scream tears from his throat. "You crazy bitch!"

I yank out the knife, bring it down a second time, feel the blade hit his rib. Gasping, he twists, reaches for the knife. I draw back again, slam the blade into his thigh. He screams, "Bitch!"

Clutching his side, Raber falls sideways. I scrabble from beneath him. I see blood on his coat. A copious amount pouring onto the mud. He's injured, but I don't know how badly; I don't know if it will stop him. For an instant, I consider taking his phone. But I don't want to get any closer to him or take the chance of him overpowering me. I don't have handcuffs, so I've no choice but to leave him.

I jab my finger at him. "Don't get up or I'll fucking kill you."

Face contorted, he lashes out with a booted foot, but I step back, easily evading the kick.

A look around, eyes digging into the shadows for any sign or Hofer. Then, turning, I walk to the trail and push myself into a run. I set a steady pace. Breaths hissing like a machine. One stride at a time. All the while I pray that the business office isn't too far.

A couple of hundred yards and the trees thin. I pick up the pace, round a curve. Relief courses through me at the sight of the building where the quarry office is located. I've approached from the rear. There's a narrow parking area. A small patio. A garbage can. A dark sedan sits alone on the far side of the lot, covered with a layer of snow. The windows are dark. No one in sight.

I glance over my shoulder. No sign of Raber. I think about Hofer, and can't help but wonder if he somehow got ahead of me and is already here, waiting.

I reach the lot, cross it, keeping my eyes on the building's windows, the door, the sedan. Wishing for my sidearm, I round the side of the building, head toward the front where I last saw Tomasetti. The first thing I see is the backhoe, silent and motionless twenty yards away. The rock bucket hovers above the crushed Tahoe. The roof is flattened so that it's nearly flush with the hood.

The rest of the world falls away as I run toward the vehicle. The amount of damage is staggering. The hood is buckled and partly open. The windshield peeled down. The passenger-side window has been shattered. If Tomasetti wasn't able to hunker down fast enough, he would have been crushed.

"Tomasetti!"

I barely recognize my voice. I reach the vehicle, set my hands against the passenger-side door. I try to open it, but it's jammed tight. Bending, I peer inside. The seatback is crunched. Busted dash. Fabric from the roof interior hanging down, blocking my view.

"Tomasetti!"

"I'm here!"

Relief pours over me with such force that I choke out a sob. I dart around the front end, approach the driver's-side door. The window opening is only about twelve inches. Bending, I peer inside. The air-bag has deployed, so I reach in, shove it aside, catch my first glimpse of him. He's jammed against the seat, his head and shoulders visible, trapped.

"Are you hurt?" I say.

One look at his face and I know he is. Sweat beads on his forehead. Mouth drawn tight. Jaws clenched. "My arm is pinned. I think it's broken."

Reaching, I tear at the airbag until I can see his left arm. Sure enough, it's wedged between the steering wheel and roof. There's blood on his shirt. More on the vinyl.

I glance toward the backhoe. "Where's the driver?"

"I think I got the son of a bitch."

"Hang on." I step away and approach the backhoe. I spot the driver immediately. Male. Duck coveralls. He's slumped over, still strapped in his seat. Blood has dripped down the side of the cushion, puddled on the floor, run down the step-up and onto the ground. It's shocking and red against the yellow paint and there's enough of it for me to know he's no longer a threat.

My cop's mind spins into overdrive as I stride back to Tomasetti. I reach the door, bend to look at him.

"He's down." I try the handle, but the door is jammed. "I need to get you out of there. Tomasetti, I don't know where Hofer is. Clarence Raber is part of this, too."

"You armed?"

"No."

He curses, his face contorting in pain as he shifts. I catch sight of his right arm, the Kimber in his hand, realize he's trying to pass it to me. He forces his arm and weapon past the tangle of metal.

"Four rounds left," he tells me. "Make them count if you need it."

I take the pistol, tuck it into my waistband. "Do you have your cell?"

"Console," he says. "Can't get to it."

"Are you injured anywhere else?"

"No."

I look at the destroyed dash. The bowed steering wheel. The buckled steel of the roof pressing down on him. There's zero space for him to maneuver or crawl out, and I have no idea how I'm going to extricate him.

"Kate, there's a pry bar in my gear box in the back. See if you can get to it."

I scan the woods behind the building as I go to the back of the Tahoe. No sign of either man, but the hairs prickle at my nape. The rear of the vehicle isn't as damaged as the front, but the door pillar post and rear window pillars are folded like accordions. The door has come unlatched, but when I try to open it, steel grinds against steel.

"Shit." Spreading my feet, I bend my knees and powerlift it. To my relief, it screeches upward enough for me to reach inside and pull out the equipment box. Bending, I set it on the ground, flip open the lid, rummage until I find the pry bar. Back at the driver's-side door, I bend to make eye contact with Tomasetti. "You're going to have to crawl out this driver's-side window," I tell him. "There's not much room."

"Free up my arm and I'll get it done."

The last thing I want to do is risk further injury to his arm, but with Hofer and Raber unaccounted for and no help on the way, I've no choice. Carefully, I insert the long end of the bar so that the tip is between the steering wheel and roof.

"Not enough leverage," I tell him.

"Don't need much."

Grasping the pry bar tightly, I force it downward, using both hands, putting my weight into it. The steering wheel creaks. The roof groans like bending iron. Face contorted in pain, Tomasetti withdraws his arm.

"See if you can get the door open," he growls.

"Yep." I step back, jam the pry bar between the door and frame. Steel grinds as I pry it open. I get my first glimpse of his predicament. Tomasetti's body is contorted into an agonizing position. I watch as he maneuvers his arms toward the door. Using his uninjured arm to push his body along, he forces his head and shoulders through the impossibly small space. He growls out a curse when his injured arm flops. When his shoulders are free, I set my hands beneath his arms and pull. Using his legs, he pushes off, forcing the rest of his body through.

I try to lower him to the ground, but he's too heavy and lands awkwardly. Groaning, he uses his uninjured arm to support the injured one. My stomach roils when I get my first up-close look at it. His forearm is clearly bowed. There's fresh blood soaking through his shirt. *Compound fracture,* I think, and I go to my knees beside him.

"I'll fashion a sling—" I begin, but he cuts me off.

"Hofer." Face screwed up and wet with sweat, he lies still, shaking; then he looks up at me. "Raber. Where the hell are they?"

"No sign of them. No movement."

He glances toward the Tahoe's destroyed interior. "My cell's in the console. Get it."

I go back to the opening and bend, reach inside. I can't see the console, so I feel around the seat. Safety belt, torn vinyl from the seatback, and the remnants of the airbag are in the way, so I dig past all of it.

Finally, my fingertips brush the console. I force my shoulders through, go deeper, find the cell phone, and I back out.

Tomasetti has gotten to his feet and is leaning against the rear fender, cradling his injured arm, his eyes on the building and wooded area beyond. His face is shockingly pale, and despite the cold, his forehead is beaded with sweat.

"That was one hell of a rescue, Chief," he says.

"You can thank me later."

Never taking my eyes from his, I call 911. Relief flares when the dispatcher informs me the nearest sheriff's deputy is six minutes away. I ask her to send an ambulance and disconnect.

Aware that the Kimber is tucked into my waistband, I go to Tomasetti, set my hands on either side of his face. "Don't ever do that to me again," I whisper.

"If I've any say in the matter, you can bet your ass I won't."

Blinking back tears, I lean into him, set my head against his chest. "Tomasetti, I thought you were—"

"I'm not." He puts his uninjured arm around me and pulls me close. "I'm right here. With you. And I'm not going anywhere for a long time."

"Promise me, damn it."

"Promise." Mustering a smile, he raises his hand, sets the backs of his fingers against my cheek. "You can take that to the bank, Chief."

"Deal," I say.

And he presses a kiss to my forehead.

CHAPTER 29

My relationship with God is complicated. That's not to say it isn't good; it is. I've had thousands of conversations with Him. Times when I've been angry or hurt or hopeless or some combination thereof; other times when I was overcome with joy and thankful for His blessings. But I've also cursed Him. I've begged Him. And I've questioned my faith. I've asked Him for help more times that I can count. Times when I probably didn't deserve it. I've asked Him to watch over my loved ones. I've asked Him to keep me safe when I found myself in a dicey situation. In all the years I've been talking to God, I've never been as desperate as those harrowing minutes when I didn't know if Tomasetti was alive or dead.

Under normal circumstances, John Tomasetti would have refused an ambulance ride to the hospital. By the time Emergency Services rolled into the Sugarcreek Sand and Gravel parking lot, I was in the early stages of hypothermia and in no condition to drive. Suffering with a compound fracture of his forearm, Tomasetti was in no condition to argue.

The deputy who arrived on scene first took statements from both of us and then loaded us into the wagon and sent us on our way.

Upon our arrival at Pomerene Hospital, Tomasetti was immediately placed on a gurney and taken to the ER. I was given hot tea, dry clothing—a set of scrubs—and a thermal blanket, and I made my way to the restroom to change. I placed my sopped uniform and underthings in the plastic bag I was given, and put my muddy boots back on. When I was dressed, I lowered my face into my hands and I sobbed. At some point, a kind-eyed woman in a pink sweatshirt came in and murmured a few words of comfort. That small kindness was all I needed to pull myself together.

I find Tomasetti in the ER, encircled by a privacy curtain, and lying on a gurney. He's changed into a gown. A blanket has been placed over his hips. The lopsided smile tells me they gave him something for pain.

I go to him, set my hand on his shoulder. "You look nice in that gown."

"That's what the doc said." He shrugs. "I wanted to go commando, but she nixed the idea right off the bat."

"Uh-huh." I nod. "What did they give you?"

"Morphine."

His injured arm is elevated on a pillow, loosely wrapped, and supported with a temporary splint. "What's the verdict?"

"I told her I was a happily married man. She wasn't happy about it, but there you have it."

I can't help it; I laugh, and I feel another layer of stress fall away. I pretend-flick his arm. "I mean, about your arm."

"Oh. That." He indicates the splint with his uninjured hand. "X-ray shows the ulna is broken. Clean break, but it was a compound fracture. Ortho doc is talking about putting in a pin."

"So you need surgery?"

"Probably going to need another morphine, too. Hurts like a son of a bitch."

Taking in the heavy lids, I'm thinking he may not be the best source of information at this moment and I make a mental note to double-check with the doc.

"Chief?"

I glance toward the curtain to see Glock peek in. "Everyone decent?" he asks.

"Sure," I say. "Come on in."

He enters, nods at Tomasetti. "Heard what happened." He whistles. "Sounds like things got pretty gnarly. Glad you two are okay."

"Thanks," I say.

When Tomasetti and I left the scene a couple of hours ago, the Tuscarawas County sheriff's deputies hadn't been there long. The situation was hectic and fluid. Both Tomasetti and I answered questions and gave reports on what had transpired. There will be more questions to answer in the coming days.

"What's going on at the scene?" I ask.

"Skid and I went as soon as we heard it come over the radio," Glock tells us. "Heavy-equipment driver is deceased. Coroner had just arrived. A lot of law enforcement on scene. BCI crime scene van is there now."

"Did they find Hofer?" I ask. "Clarence Raber?"

He nods. "Deputy found Raber trying to break into your rental vehicle at the rear of the property. Probably after your shotgun. Evidently, he was wounded. They made the arrest and they took him out on a stretcher.

"As far as Hofer . . . it's not official, but one of the deputies I talked to said they found a body in the quarry. Male. Fully clothed. Dark hair. They got him out of the water. They're working on getting him IDed now."

"Any idea how he died?" Tomasetti asks.

"Deputy said it looked like he may have struck his head when he fell and died either from trauma or drowning."

I think about the chaotic turn of events at the quarry—and the implications of Hofer's death in terms of the case. "That leaves us with a lot of unanswered questions," I say.

"Would have been nice to talk to him," Tomasetti says. "Maybe punch him a couple of times."

"Raber might be able to fill in some of the blanks." I look at Glock. "Was there anyone else at the business?"

"Don't know." Glock's brows draw together. "Cops on scene are being kind of tight-lipped about it."

"Those BCI people are assholes," Tomasetti mutters.

Glock laughs outright.

"Chief?" comes a familiar voice from outside the curtain. "Anyone home?"

Sheriff Mike Rasmussen peers in through the gap and looks at us. "Now there's a sight to warm your heart."

"Thought there was a limit on the number of riffraff they allow back here," Tomasetti mutters.

"Shield got me in." Looking genuinely pleased to see us, Rasmussen strides to the gurney and extends his hand to Tomasetti. "Heard you had a close encounter with a backhoe."

"Tahoe got the short end of the stick." Tomasetti gives another wonky smile.

"Literally and figuratively," I add.

"Going to be fun explaining that one to the insurance company," Glock puts in.

"At least the Explorer wasn't involved," Tomasetti puts in.

Sobering, Rasmussen extends his hand to me. "I'm glad neither of you were seriously hurt. The deputy I talked to said it was one hell of a scene."

"Anything new?" I ask.

"BCI crime scene guys are processing the scene and will be for some time. Raber is being transported to the hospital. Needless to say, we've still got a lot to figure out." He looks at me and sighs. "Kate, I'd like to be the first to offer you an apology. You were right about everything. We got it wrong, and we treated you like shit. I'm sorry."

He offers his hand. I take it and we shake again. "Accepted," I say simply.

"Not bad for a politician." Tomasetti looks at me and raises his brows. "I especially liked the 'we treated you like shit' line."

Glock clears his throat.

Rasmussen jabs a thumb at Tomasetti. "What the hell did they give him?"

Everyone laughs and some of the tension leaches from the room. All of us know that as bad as the situation was at the quarry, it could have been much worse and two of us in this room are lucky to be alive.

Out of the corner of my eye, I see Glock raise his hand. "See you tomorrow, Chief." Then to Tomasetti, "Good luck with that arm."

"Keep me posted on any news," I tell him.

"You got it."

He's slipping out when the curtain jiggles. My blood pressure rises at the sight of Neil Chambers. In the back of my mind, I wonder how he's going to twist things around to justify his overzealous attempts to keep me off the case.

"What were you saying about an apology?" Tomasetti says, but he's looking at Chambers.

Chambers offers a self-deprecating smile, making eye contact with each of us, and then raises his hands as if in supplication. "Go ahead. Get it off your chest. Have your fun. I deserve it."

"Did you release my brother from jail?" I ask.

"I put the paperwork through half an hour ago. Mr. Burkholder should be out within the hour."

"Was there an apology in there?" Feigning puzzlement, Tomasetti looks from Rasmussen to me to Chambers. "I didn't hear any groveling."

Chambers strides to me and, holding my gaze, he extends his hand, holds it out. "I screwed up, Chief Burkholder. I got carried away and I got this one wrong. That's not easy for an egotistical son of a bitch like me to admit, but there you have it. I hope you'll accept my sincere apology."

I wait an instant too long before taking his hand. "Apology accepted."

"I'll be making a formal apology to the mayor, too," he says. "And your team. I'll make sure all of them know how things went down."

"I appreciate that," I say.

Rasmussen clears his throat. "Evidently, we need a lot of questions answered before we can even begin to unravel this case."

"Has Clarence Raber been able to talk?" I ask.

Chambers shakes his head. "They flew him up to Mercy Hospital in Canton. He's in surgery now."

"He expected to make it?" Tomasetti asks.

He nods. "Doctor says we'll be able to talk to him in the morning."

The sheriff looks at me. "Kate, how much do you know about this Isaiah Hofer character?"

The final minutes I spent with Hofer flash in my mind's eye. The march to the quarry. The struggle to escape. The fall into the water. All the while not knowing if Tomasetti was dead or alive . . .

Though I'm plenty warm now, a chill passes through me. "Not much. I suspect he may be formerly Amish. He may have spent some time in Lancaster County, Pennsylvania."

"There was no ID on the body," Rasmussen tells me. "We're running his prints now."

"Agents are searching the sand and gravel office," Chambers adds. "Hofer's residence is on the property. We got the warrant so we'll be searching the entire compound in the coming hours. We also secured a warrant for Raber's apartment."

"How does Raber play into this?" Tomasetti asks.

"Milan Swanz is the common denominator." I remind them of my theory about the Schwertler Anabaptists and relay to them the exchange between Hofer and me during our walk to the quarry. "As far as Raber, maybe this group targeted him. Drafted him. Groomed him. Used him to get to Swanz."

Rasmussen shakes his head. "Almost like a cult."

I nod. "I don't have proof—yet—but I believe there's a small, underground community of religious zealots who use history as an excuse to murder."

"Are we talking Holmes County?" the sheriff asks.

"I think it's bigger than that." I tell them about the Lena Stoltzfus case in Lancaster County. "I don't believe Swanz and Stoltzfus are their only victims. And I don't believe Hofer acted alone."

The sheriff narrows his eyes on mine. "We're talking to several individuals who are living in the community," he says. "As soon as we locate the female who was working in the office, we'll haul her in for questioning."

"It sounds like this group has been operating for a long time," Tomasetti says.

I nod. "One thing that the Anabaptists are very good at, the Amish in particular, is the passing down of tradition to the next generation. In this case, even if that tradition is some bastardized version of their belief system."

Chambers nods, taking it all in. "We retrieved Hofer's cell, by the way," he says. "It's wet, but the data on the SIM card is likely recoverable. It's on the way to the BCI lab now."

"Speaking of his cell phone," I say, "I think Hofer is the one who called in the anonymous tip about seeing Jacob on Dogleg Road the night of the murder."

"We'll check it out." Rasmussen nods, looks from me to Tomasetti and back to me. "For now, I've got to get back to the scene. I'm glad you two are all right." He motions toward Tomasetti's injured arm. "Get yourself patched up, Agent Tomasetti, and we'll get the rest of this figured out in the coming days."

"I'd appreciate it if you'd keep me posted on any new developments," I tell them.

Chambers looks at me over his shoulder. "You got it, Chief Burkholder," he says.

And then they're gone.

EPILOGUE

It's the little things we sometimes don't notice that add that extra layer of richness to our lives. As the years make their indelible mark, those small gifts become even more meaningful. Time can take a toll if you let it. If you're wise, you'll embrace the good, forgive yourself for yesterday's mistakes, and keep your heart open for all those delicious little extras that come your way.

It's six P.M. and already fully dark when I close the back door against the gale and a flurry of snow. Outside, the blizzard is just getting started and I'm unduly glad to be out of the maelstrom. I hang my parka in the mudroom and take in the aromas of yeast bread and woodsmoke as I enter my big farmhouse kitchen. Tomasetti stands at the counter with his back to me, one-handedly slicing the bread I took out of the oven an hour earlier. On the counter, I see he's arranged grapes and thin-sliced beef around a wedge of the Stilton blue cheese we picked up at the Amish shop in town earlier. Next to the board, the bottle of tempranillo is breathing, two wineglasses waiting to be filled.

I can hear the fire crackling from the hearth in the living room. Norah Jones warms the air with the whiskey magic of her voice.

The little things, I think, even though I'm all too aware that there's nothing small about this particular moment and I count my blessings.

"Anyone ever tell you you look good in my apron?" I say, coming up behind him.

"I get that a lot." He glances at me over his shoulder and winks. "Goats and chickens secure for the night?"

"The babies weren't too happy about being penned up, but they'll be thanking me in a few hours when the drifts are two feet high."

Frowning, he concentrates on the bread. Holding it in place with the elbow of his arm sling, he saws off a slice. "Caught the weather a few minutes ago," he says.

"I'm afraid to ask."

"The bad news is we're going to get six inches of snow and forty-mile-per-hour winds."

"And the good news?" I ask.

"We're going to get six inches of snow and forty-mile-per-hour winds." He looks at me at grins. "That's not to mention the lights have been blinking."

"I noticed." I snatch up a grape and pop it in my mouth. "Good thing we've got plenty of candles."

"Not to mention a roaring fire and an extra bottle of tempranillo."

"Might be a two-glass night."

I reach around him to hold the loaf in place so he can more easily slice. "Norah Jones is a nice touch, Tomasetti."

"I thought so," he says. "Not that I have an ulterior motive."

"Good thing because I'm not sure you can handle it with that cast and sling."

"I'm game to put it to the test if you are."

"Those are big words for a one-armed man."

Setting down the knife, he turns to me, wraps his uninjured arm around me, and gazes into my eyes, his expression turning thoughtful. "You had a nightmare last night."

"I didn't mean to wake you." I try to divert our attention back to the food, but he doesn't let me.

Tomasetti isn't one to dwell on or rehash a traumatic event. We're alike that way. We've seen more than our share, and we know life's too short to spend it being afraid. And so we deal with it, we put it to bed, and we move on.

"Despite what others might say," he says, "I'm a pretty good listener if you want to talk about it."

Needing a moment, I ease away from him, go to the bottle of wine and pour. Tomasetti picks up the charcuterie board and we carry everything to the table. He's already lit a candle.

He raises his glass. "Here's to six inches of snow and forty-mile-per-hour winds."

We clink our glasses together and sip. The wine is an exquisite blend of plum and dark cherry and it dances on my tongue like an exotic fruit.

I can tell by the way he's looking at me that he's waiting for me to talk. Somehow, he knows I need to.

"It wasn't the time I spent with Hofer that terrified me," I tell him. "It wasn't Clarence Raber or the water or the cold. It wasn't even the possibility that I might not make it."

He holds my gaze, nods.

"It was the not knowing if you were dead or alive." To my embarrassment, my voice quavers. "Tomasetti, I've never been that scared. Ever. And I've never felt such despair or desperation. It was huge and that scared me, too."

"I'm sorry you had to go through that," he says. "You going to be okay?"

"I think so."

"If it gets to be a problem, you'll let me know?"

"That's the thing," I say. "I don't think there's a cure for this crazy love thing we have going on."

I can tell by the way he's looking at me that there's more on his mind. That he's got something to say and he isn't sure he's going to get it right and it's important that he does.

"You got something else on your mind, Tomasetti?"

"You mean besides this tempranillo and Stilton?" He asks the question lightly, but I don't miss the dance of nerves just beneath the surface. I feel those same nerves tingle inside me.

He reaches across the table with the hand of his uninjured arm and takes mine in his. "We've got a lot of love to go around," he says quietly. "Some to spare, maybe."

Something flutters in my chest and for a second, I can't quite catch my breath. For months, we've danced around the topic of starting a family. The idea titillates the part of me that has always wanted children. The idea terrifies the part of me that is a cop and knows too much about the dark side of a world that can be cruel to the innocent.

"We do," I say. "I think about it every day. It's a big step."

"Especially for us," he says. "Our backgrounds. The fact that we're cops. At the same time, I think both of us know that just about every step worth taking in this life is usually pretty damn big."

"That's a true statement." That flutter again. Only softer and warmer and centered in my chest.

"Something to think about." He looks down at the board. "In the interim, what do you say we dig into this Stilton and that Amish bread?"

"And maybe take a little time to mull everything else?"

"Mulling is good," he says. "Let's do that and see what happens."

I raise my glass to his. "To big steps."

"Big steps," he echoes.

And we sip.

ACKNOWLEDGMENTS

Over the course of a career, a writer owes gratitude to countless individuals who are kind and generous enough to share their time, their expertise, their love, and support. There are too many to name in this small space, but I will mention a few. I'd like to send a special thank-you to Denise Campbell-Johnson for the years of friendship and all the wonderful adventures. Thank you to Sergeant Brandon Warman with the Strasburg Police Department for the fun ride-along. Sending out a huge thank-you to Bob Scanlon for always making time to participate in my book events at our beloved Dover Public Library. Many thanks to Kimberly Jarvis, the board of directors, and all the volunteers who make the Buckeye Book Fair a highlight every year. I hope all of you know how much you are appreciated!

I'd also like to thank every single member of my publishing family at Minotaur Books. First and foremost, I wish to thank my editor extraordinaire, Charles Spicer, who always makes time to chat or brainstorm, and whose keen eye always makes the book better. A thousand thank-yous to

Acknowledgments

my brilliant agent, Nancy Yost—for sharing your wisdom, experience, and friendship. A big shout-out to everyone at Minotaur Books: Jennifer Enderlin. Andrew Martin. Sally Richardson. Sarah Melnyk. Hannah Pierdolla. Kerry Nordling. Paul Hochman. Allison Ziegler. Alisa Trager. Laurie Henderson. Omar Chapa. Kelley Ragland. David Baldeosingh Rotstein. Marta Fleming. Martin Quinn. Joseph Brosnan. Lisa Davis. My sincerest thanks to all.

ABOUT THE AUTHOR

© Pam Lary

Linda Castillo is the author of the *New York Times* and *USA Today* bestselling Kate Burkholder series, set in the world of the Amish. The first book, *Sworn to Silence,* was adapted into a Lifetime original movie titled *An Amish Murder* starring Neve Campbell as Kate Burkholder. Castillo is the recipient of numerous industry awards. In addition to writing, Castillo's other passion is horses. She lives in Texas with her husband and is currently at work on her next book.